MW00461563

What Reviewers Are Saying about Dana Roberts Stories

"There's a new occult detective in town. She's tougher than Buffy, smarter than John Constantine, and more resourceful than Repairman Jack. She's Dana Roberts, and the supernatural fears her with good reason." – Brian Keene, Bram Stoker Award® winning author of *The Rising*.

"*Terror is Our Business* is an immersive, rewarding and highly entertaining read, it's got bags of style and wonderfully rich characters. Highly recommended." – SFBook Reviews

"Pure pulp pleasure" – MysteryPeople

"When Dana and Joe join forces with Jana and Kasey, great stories become supergreat tales that provide a whole new level of entertainment for the reader." – Sandra Ruttan, author of *The Spying Moon* (fall 2018) and *Harvest of Ruins*.

"Solid characters, interesting story lines, and the perfect amount of suspense." – SciFiMoviePage

What Reviewers Are Saying about the Authors

"[Joe R. Lansdale has] a folklorist's eye for telling detail and a front-porch raconteur's sense of pace." – New York Times Book Review

"Kasey Lansdale's voice and prose are on point... [Her] future is bright in the horror genre." – Cedar Hollow Horror Reviews

TERROR IS OUR BUSINESS:
DANA ROBERTS' CASEBOOK OF HORRORS

JOE R. LANSDALE

&

KASEY LANSDALE

TERROR IS OUR BUSINESS:
DANA ROBERTS' CASEBOOK OF HORRORS

Cutting Block Books
an imprint of Farolight Publishing,
a division of Farolight Entertainment, LLC
PO Box 1521
Winchester, VA 22604
www.cuttingblockbooks.com

Terror is Our Business: Dana Roberts' Casebook of Horrors contains works of fiction.
Names, characters, places and incidents
are products of the authors' imaginations, or are used fictitiously.
Any resemblance to actual persons, living
or dead, or to events or locales, is entirely coincidental.

First Cutting Block Books trade paperback edition: May 2018

Inset Layout and Design by Bailey Hunter
www.facebook.com/BaileyHunterDesign

Cover art by Luke Spooner
www.carrionhouse.com

Published in the United States of America
1 3 5 7 9 10 8 6 4 2

Library of Congress Control Number: 2018938967

ISBN 978-1-7320090-0-4

For Karen.

For Mom: You were right about everything.

Table of Contents

Introduction:
Dana Roberts, Her Kith and Kin

by Joe R. Lansdale

When I was growing up I read all kinds of fiction. I was especially drawn to horror and the fantastic, science fiction, the odd and the weird. One branch of horror and weird fiction I particularly enjoyed was the psychic investigator.

There were a number of investigators I liked. John Silence, for one, created by Algernon Blackwood; Carnacki, the ghost finder, the creation of William Hope Hodgson; and later I discovered Seabury Quinn's Jules De Grandin adventures. The *Night Stalker* TV show was cut of the same cloth, and I loved it, especially the pilot that led to the series, scripted by Richard Matheson, based on the work of Jeff Rice. Lord Dunsany's Jorkens tales also deserve a nod. There were others, of course, but these pop to mind, and are therefore most likely the greater influences.

I also liked non-series stories where someone would go into a bar, or into a club, always a men's club back then, and they would be sitting around talking, and then someone would tell a story about a weird experience. These stories often had a narrator that framed the story, then let the actual teller of the tale take over, and in the end the narrator would return and wrap it up.

As a writer, I am known primarily in the horror world for things that don't quite fit into the normal approach to horror, but in the last few years I've had the bug to write more "traditional" tales, and I have written a number of them. The Dana Roberts stories are among the more traditional.

Unlike the psychic investigators I grew up reading, my investigator is female. All of the ones I read growing up, and as a young man, to the best of my memory, were male. Fiction was dominated by the male hero for a long-long time. I wanted to do a story with a female lead that was also a psychic detective, or in Dana Roberts' case, an investigator of what she calls the "supernormal." She doesn't believe in the supernatural, but she does believe in unknown worlds and mysterious puzzles that are caused by natural phenomena that we think of as supernatural. In this way, these stories owe more to Lovecraft than M.R. James. Strictly speaking, like the Mythos stories by Lovecraft, these are, in a way, science fiction, as there is supposed to be an explanation that would prove them to originate out of scientific knowledge yet to be discovered and confirmed. But, as with Lovecraft, the tone of the Dana Roberts stories is very much horror. In fact, one of the stories, "The Case of The Ragman's Anguish," is openly Lovecraftian.

Most of the stories I write have humor in them in one form or another. Even a lot of the darker ones. That is not exclusively true, but is a big part of what comes out when I write. Whistling past the graveyard.

I tried to make the Dana Roberts stories a bit soberer in tone than a lot of things that have come before by me, and I accomplished this for the most part. I also managed, at least in the first couple of stories, to use a narrator who introduced us to Dana, and like those stories I mentioned before, they would be told at a club.

After a bit, however, I found this framing device unnecessary for her tales. It was better when she told them directly without it, and when this collection was first conceived, I thought I would eliminate it from the stories where this method was used, but as I reread them for publication, I realized the concept was too integrated to be detached naturally. I would have had to rewrite the stories so much they wouldn't have been the original tales. I left the framing method, but didn't add it to the later Dana Roberts stories.

Meanwhile, back at the ranch, as they used to say, my daughter Kasey and I were asked to do a story together for a Christopher Golden anthology, and we did. Kasey created a character called Jana, began the story, and then we traded it back and forth by email, taking turns building and revising until the story was complete.

Working this way, we wrote a story titled "Blind Love," which was nutty as a squirrel's den. We liked it so much we decided to write another story about Jana, and we also decided to have her join up with Dana, to put humor in the adventures, and to give

Dana a kind of Watson-like partner. Like Watson, Jana is not without her own skills.

So, the first part of this book are stories about Dana, told by her, and in some cases, framed by an outside narrator.

"Blind Love" stands alone, but it's a great introduction to Jana. It allows for a better understanding of who she is for future stories, where she and Dana team up to solve what can only be described as very unusual mysteries from beyond the veil. But Kasey will have her say on Jana in her introduction, so I will leave that to her.

Included here, besides the original Dana Roberts tales and the stories that include Jana, is the first appearance of "The Case of the Ragman's Anguish," written exclusively for this collection.

My advice on reading these stories, due to a necessary similarity in structure, is not to read them all at once, but to read one daily, or one weekly, until you've read them all. I think that is the way to enjoy them best, but if you're a gobbler, and would prefer to gobble them down one after the other, I won't discourage you.

Will there be other tales of Dana and Jana?

Time will tell.

Joe R. Lansdale
Nacogdoches, Texas
September 8th, 2017

The Case of the Lighthouse Shambler

by Joe R. Lansdale

I guess you could say it's a kind of an organization, but we think of it as a club, but it's not just a men's club. Women come too. Or at least a couple do. And then, of course, there's Dana Roberts. She was our guest.

The club is simple. We meet once a month to chat and have drinks, eat a little bit of food. Sometimes we invite a guest. We always make an effort to have someone interesting, and not just someone to fill the slot. We'd rather not have a guest than have someone come in and tell us how to dry lumber or make strawberry jam.

Fact is, we vote on who our speaker is. When Dana Roberts came up, I didn't actually plan to vote for her. I didn't want a supernatural investigator there, as I find that kind of stuff silly and unbelievable, and mostly just annoying.

There are all the shows on TV about ghost hunters, and psychic kids, and so on, and they make me want to kick the set in. I guess it's good business, making shows where it's all shadow and innuendo. People saying they hear this, or they hear that, they see this, or they see that, and you don't actually see or hear jack. You just got to take their word for it.

Another thing, when they do have something, it's a blurry camera image, or a weird sound on their recordings that they say is the ghost telling them to get out of the house, or some such. I don't become more of a believer when they do that, I become less of one. The sounds just sound like one of the investigators getting cute, and the images look a lot like my bad vacation photos.

But the rest of the members pushed Dana on me, and I was outvoted, so on Thursday night, right after we had a general meeting, talking about a few things that had to do with the club, Dana showed up.

She was a tall woman in her forties, and though she wasn't what you'd call a model, there was certainly something about her. Her face was shaped nice and sharp by her cheekbones, and she had a wide full mouth, and eyes that looked right through you. She had shoulder-length blond hair. She looked to be in good shape, and in fact, looked more like a physical trainer than someone who chased spooks and such.

She went around and shook hands with everyone, and said thanks for inviting her. While she's doing this, all I could think about was that our club dues were paying for this. We always give a stipend for speakers, and sometimes it's pretty sizeable if the guest has some fame. I didn't know how much the treasurer had agreed to pay her, but whatever it was, I thought it was too much.

Dana Roberts is famous for her books, her now and again interviews on television. I will give her this, she didn't do TV interviews much, and she wasn't someone that was always popping up in the news or predicting this or that, or saying a body would be found near water or that the murderer has a name that has a J in it.

When it was time for drinks, we went into the big room, which is part of Kevin Dell's house and library, which is where we always retire to. There's no smoking at our club, and it's usually right about half way into our two to three hour talk or discussion, that we let the smokers go outside and suck some burning tobacco.

That was a bad rule, I thought, as it could break up a good presentation, but it was the way we maintained three of our members, and though I would just as soon see them go, Kevin, who was also our treasurer, liked their dues as much as anyone else's, 'cause it paid for our food and drinks and occasional guests.

Anyway, we're in the big room, and we're about to start, and Dana said something that sort of endeared me to her right off.

She said, "Now, if you watch all those ghost shows, and those people who predict the future, or find dead bodies, or missing people, then you'll be disappointed. I should also say I can't stand those fakirs. What I do is real, and the truth is, I don't care if you believe me or not. I'm just going to tell you about my most recent case, and you can take it or leave it."

There were some nods around the room, and Kevin said, “Certainly. Of, course.”

Then we settled into the chairs and the couch, a few seated themselves on cushions on the floor, and Dana took the guest chair; the most comfortable chair in the room. She leaned back and sipped her drink and looked at the ceiling.

“I’m going to tell this how it went, as best I can. Keep in mind, I don’t think of myself as a ghost hunter per se, nor do I claim to be psychic. I’m a detective. A detective of the supernormal. Most of what I encounter isn’t real. It’s a mouse in the attic, or some kids wanting attention by throwing plates or some such thing when people aren’t looking, scratching themselves and saying the devil did it.

“Let me say this too. I’m not religious. I don’t believe in God. I’m an atheist. But I do believe there are things we don’t understand, and that’s what I look into. I believe that religious symbols are often just symbols of power—as far as the supernormal is concerned. It’s not religion, or an exorcism, anything like that that effects the supernormal. It’s the power those things possess when they are used by those who believe in any kind of magic or religion that makes them work. The idea of religion has thought and purpose and substance, even if the religion itself is no more real than a three year straight win by the Red Socks.

“I like to give my cases a name when I write about them, and I gave this one a name too. It’s a little exaggerated, I admit, so I’m not entirely immune to the melodramatic. I call it, The Case of the Lighthouse Shambler. Cute, huh?”

With that, she took a sip of her drink and Kevin dimmed the lights. There was a glow from the fire, but it was a small light, and flickered just enough so you could see who was who in the room. Shadows jumped along the side of Dana’s face as she spoke.

***

Due to the bit of celebrity that I have as an author and investigator, the popularity of my books, I am often offered jobs that deal with the supernatural, or as I prefer, when it’s real, the supernormal. As I said before, the bulk of these turn out to be something silly, or a hoax, and because of that, I always send out my assistants, Nora Sweep and Gary Martin, to check it out. I don’t even do that if what’s being suggested to me sounds uninteresting, or old hat, or deeply suspicious, but every now and then I come across something that might be genuine. More often than not, it isn't.

But if a request hits my desk that sounds like it might be of some curiosity, I send them first to check it out. One of the queries was from a Reggie, whose last name I will not reveal. Reggie had a lighthouse he claimed was infected. Those were his words. In his email to my web site, which is how we obtain most of our queries, he said that the haunting, if it could be called that, had occurred as of late, and that he felt it more resembled the sort of things I dealt with than so-called ghost hunters. He added that he wasn't one who believed in life after death, or hadn't before all this, but was certain that whatever was going on was beyond his explanation, and that the lighthouse, which he had been converting into a kind of home, had only recently been subject to the events that were causing him to write for my assistance. It was intriguing, and I've always been prone to an interest in lighthouses. I find them an odd kind of structure, and by their nature, perched as they are on the edge of the sea, mysterious.

Anyway, I sent Nora and Gary over for a look, and then forgot about it, as I was involved in a small case that took me out of the country for few days, and was easy to solve. It turned out to be a nest of birds inside an air vent, and nothing supernormal at all. I collected my fee, which was sizeable, and disappointing to the couple who had hired me, who felt certain the wife's old uncle was responsible and was trying to speak to her from beyond the grave in a fluttering kind of way because he had died without teeth. The flutter, of course, was the beating of the bird's wings.

I won't give you the location of the lighthouse, as that is a private matter between myself and the client, but I will say it was located along the Gulf Coast, and had once been important for ships, but had long since been abandoned. For a time, it was a tourist site, but it drew few tourists, and then it was sold to my client, Reggie, who had begun to remodel it to make a home for himself and his soon-to-be wife. However, after a few days working alone in the place, breaking up the ground, and repairing an old stairway, he began to have the sensation that he was being watched, and that the watcher was, in his words—malignant. He didn't feel as if it were looking over his shoulder, but was instead at the bottom of the winding metal stairs and was looking up, as if it could see through the top floor and spy on him at work.

He had no reason to think this, other than sensation, but he felt that as the day wound on, as the night came closer, the watcher became more bold and more present, if you will. When it was just dark, Reggie heard a creaking on the metal stairs, which was startling to him, as he had locked the door at the bottom of the lighthouse. Next he heard a slow sort of thudding on the stairs. So certain was he that someone was there, he went out on the landing and looked down. He could see nothing, but he could hear a kind of labored, angry breathing, and he noticed that the metal steps leading up would take turns bending with pressure, as if someone heavy were climbing up, but there was nothing there. It frightened him so, he locked the door at the upper entrance—for he had built a wall and placed a door there for a bedroom—and backed away from it, waiting. Then there came a sound at the door like someone breathing heavily. This was followed by a light tapping, a delay, and then a scratching, not too unlike, he thought, a dog wanting in. And then the door began to bulge around the hinges, as if it were being pushed, and he felt for certain it was about to blow, and whatever was on the other side, whatever was pushing and breathing and scratching, would soon enter the room in a rush.

Well, there was a trap hole as well, in the middle of the room. He had built it and attached an old fire pole there for fun. He dropped through the opening and slid down the pole by way of exit, and looked back up. He couldn't see the landing, really, but he could see it partly, and there was nothing there. Nothing. When he got to the bottom of the pole, he was brave enough to go to the base of the stairs and look up. That was when he heard a kind of screech and an exhaust of wind, and the stairs began to quiver, and something, most assuredly, even though he could not see it, was hastening down after him.

He broke and ran, feeling certain the thing was behind him. Once, he glanced back and saw what he said was an unidentifiable shadowy shape, and then he came to a point where all of a sudden his fear was gone, and he slowed down and turned around and looked. And there was nothing there. It was as if there had been a line of demarcation between fear and sanity, and he had crossed it.

This was what Reggie told me in his email, and as I said, it was intriguing enough that I sent Nora and Gary for a look, and I went about my other business.

When I was back from Europe, I asked my assistants about the lighthouse. They had been enthusiastically waiting on me, and told me quite firmly this was the real deal, and that I would be interested, and Reggie seemed willing to let go of the proper fee to find out the cause, and if at all possible, banish it.

They had gone there during the day and placed talcum powder on the stairs that wound up to the top, to the light, which was still workable, and they had come back the next morning to find, as Reggie had said, someone, or something, had gone up the steps and left prints in the talc, though neither thought the prints were foot or shoe prints. They couldn't quite explain what they thought they were. They had photographs, and my first thought was that in some of these, they looked a little bit like the hooves of a goat. In other photos, the prints were quite different, and less comparative to anything I could think of.

The following night, they replaced the talc, locked the upper door, and stayed at the top. What followed for them was an event exactly like that Reggie had experienced, only they had seen the shadow of something through the crack under the door, pacing in front of it like an anxious parent waiting for a child to come home.

"It was a feeling like I have never experienced," Nora said. "And working for you, I've experienced a lot. But I felt, quite surely, that beyond that door was something purely evil. I know that's silly, and not particularly scientific, but that's how it was, and I was frightened to the bone."

Gary agreed. He said the door began to heave, as before when Reggie was there, and the two of them took to the fire pole and slid down. No sooner had they reached bottom, then whatever was at the top of the stairs shifted loudly, and came charging down the steps with a wild sound somewhere between a burst of breath and a screech, the stairs vibrating as it came, the steps seeming in danger of coming loose of their bolts.

"I think that whatever is there is building its reserve," Gary said. "That a night will come when it will come through that door, and going through the hole in the floor, sliding down that pole Reggie installed, will just not be enough. Whatever is there, wants whoever is inside that lighthouse to not be there. And my feeling is, once it builds its presence to a crescendo, something horrible will happen."

My assistants often experience incredible things, which is their job, but the way they talked, it was clear to me that they had been thoroughly impressed with the thing in the lighthouse, so we packed our bags, and on Reggie's dime, we flew out there, rented a car and drove the rest of the way to our destination.

***

In the daylight the lighthouse was interesting, but seemed far less than sinister. Of course, that is often the situation with these kinds of cases. You can't judge them quite as well in the day. There are certainly horrors that exist in broad daylight, but the bulk of the supernormal seems to prefer nightfall, if not particularly, the witching hour.

Reggie, as we planned, met us at the base of the lighthouse, shook hands, exchanged a few pleasantries, and then he gave me keys to the place, shook my hand again, as if he thought it might be the last time, wished us luck, and went on his way.

Since my assistants had already convinced themselves there was something in the tower, I didn't bother with the talc, or other measures of that sort, but instead sent them to town with a lunch order, and went to the top and looked around. The summit of the lighthouse, at least that part that was livable, had been remodeled as a bedroom, and the glass that wound its way about did nothing more now than provide a view completely around the circumference of the lighthouse. It was a lovely view, and I could see why Reggie would want to make this the master bedroom, turning other areas of the tower, eventually, into other living spaces. It would indeed make a unique home.

There was a bathroom slightly to the side, built into a kind of cubicle, so as not to be pressed against the glass and diminish the view. I went there and washed my face, more to understand what was what, and then examined the "fire hole" in the floor, and the pole that went straight to the bottom of the tower. I slid down it, and when I reached the floor, I looked back, noted that I could see through gaps in the stairs the upper landing, which was purposely pocked with holes so as to provide for the drip of water should it ever invade the upper quarters. A problem perhaps, if this was to be turned into a home, but not my concern. I'm a seeker of the supernormal, not an architect.

Climbing back up the stairs, I was suddenly accosted—that's the word that comes to me—by a feeling of anxiety. This is not new in my business, but as Nora and Gary explained, it was different here; stronger and more absorbing. I felt for a moment as if I might turn and bolt to the bottom and race out the door. Again, not all that unusual, but what was different was how hard I had to work to make myself climb to the top of the stairs. Usually, I can shake off those kinds of feelings with less effort than this took. I also felt an odd sensation as I climbed, near the bottom of the stairs anyway, on the left side, and that was a sensation of air that at first seemed cool, and then gave me a feeling akin to dry ice, which is so cold it can burn. My arm was freckled with goose bumps until I had gone up at least six feet from the floor.

In the top room, the sensation of fear did not go away, but it did subside considerably, enough for me to move comfortably about the room. Looking out the window, I saw that the light on the water was bright, and night was some time off, and it calmed me.

It seemed to me that whatever was here was not only dangerous, but somehow the stairs were its main area of strength. This didn't mean that it was weak away from the stairs, but the stairs were its prime location, and the area where its supernormal connection was most profound.

I decided not to spend the night in the lighthouse the first night, but instead sent Nora and Gary to the library, and any other source of information they could locate, to find out about the history of the lighthouse. I left the lighthouse several times during the day, and went back as it neared nightfall, and each time, I felt the presence in the building was growing more observant of my actions.

That night I watched the lighthouse from a distance, observing the upper windows, which were not lit up, and the light, which was no longer functioning. I tried to imagine how it had looked during its era of operation.

As the night fell, my vantage point from a nearby hill, where I sat with a cool drink in a lawn chair looking through binoculars, revealed to me a flash inside the upper darkness. I leaned forward. I saw it again. The flash moved before the window in a bobbing fashion, and then it was gone.

I had an idea that it had raced down the stairwell. I also determined from prior experience, that the light I saw would not be visible up close, and would in fact be the manifestation of the thing, if viewed from a distance. Up close and personal, it would be the presence itself that one would have to confront, lit or unlit.

That night, I retired to the hotel and read the information that Nora and Gary had provided for me, while they shared a room next door. They thought because they each had a bed in their room, that I believed there weren't any shenanigans going on. Actually, I suspected that they had been intimate for some time, and for reasons known only to them, didn't want me to know. I decided not to question their reasoning, or reveal my suspicions—which were founded on evidence—and I'll add to that statement that they are now married, so anything I'm telling you now does not matter, not that I cared in the first place.

In the notes they provided, there was nothing particularly interesting about the lighthouse. I read from a book on a history of the locale, to see if anything else might stand out as a catalyst for the thing on the stairs. Nothing jumped out at me. There had been a share of shipwrecks, in spite of the lighthouse, and there had been one famous one before its existence in the early seventeen hundreds.

That offered a note of interest. The problem was, there wasn't anything of detail on the wreck, other than an unnamed ship had collided with the rocky shoreline, and that on examination of the wrecked vessel, a man named Greenberg was located alive, and all others on the ship were found dead, and due to their condition, it was assumed they had been killed, and in fact cannibalized, as the ship had been becalmed for weeks at sea, and all food had been exhausted.

The article said Greenberg had committed the murders with an axe. When they took him off the ship, he said it had not been him who had committed the crime and the cannibalism, but was something else on the ship. A demon that he said lived in a brass jug—his words—and it was there now, and that it had been assigned to protect him when he did a good deed for an

Arab trader. He thought nothing of it at the time, and merely thought the jug given him was a nice item that he would sell when he arrived on the mainland. But the demon in the bottle seemed jealous and upset and chose to protect him, even when he felt he did not need protecting; the mere presence of anyone near drove the thing in the bottle to frenzy, and that its main purpose was to dispatch anyone nearby, so that it might return to the tranquility inside the jug. That was his story, and as you might judge, it wasn't taken seriously.

The ship was in terrible shape. It was searched, but no demon was found, nor was a brass jug located. Most of what could be salvaged was salvaged.

Nora and Gary's research showed that the ship dealt in antiquities, and that the crew was well experienced, and becalmed or not, there should have been enough food on board. The survivor was duly tried and hung, and that was the end of him. If he had a protecting demon in a jug, neither jug nor demon presented itself at his last moments as he stood on the gallows.

I think you might see where I'm going here, as I have discovered in my investigations that old trinkets or odd items, like a brass jug, might in fact have some connection to the supernormal. But since it was not recovered, and there wasn't any evidence of Greenberg being protected from even so much as a rope burn, there was little to go on.

***

I looked over maps and documentation to locate the exact site of the shipwreck, but there was nothing that could be fully determined. On a hunch, I went to the butcher shop and bought some soup bones and some animal skin, and a pint of calf's blood, and went to the lighthouse and began to search around the concrete floor near the stairwell.

I didn't necessarily expect to find anything, but I did satisfy myself, with a thermometer, that the air on the left side near the floor was quite cold and it wasn't my imagination. Still, the cool air there presented a sensation different from that of the garden-variety presence one sometimes encounters in these sort of spots; the kind of presence that is commonly called a ghost or spook.

I climbed the stairs with an uncomfortable consciousness of being observed, and made my way to the top room and closed the door. There, I set down the plastic bag containing the soup bone and skin, removed my shoulder bag and took out my tools, and went to work.

I first placed the bone on the floor, and placed the stretch of hairless animal skin beside it. I set up a camera on a shelf in the room, the sort sometimes referred to as a Nanny cam—a hidden device parents use to make sure their nannies are acting accordingly with their children. I then placed a mirror on the floor beside the bone and the skin, moved back, and drew a circle with blessed chalk. Now, the blessing isn't necessarily a Christian one. In this case, the chalk had been blessed by an African wizard who chanted over it with words of juju; to simplify, juju is an African term for magic and spells. I drew a large circle about ten feet in circumference with white chalk, and inside of it I drew around its edge in other colors of chalk, each blessed by different priests, wizards, rabbis, and so on, symbols of power. These symbols do not belong to any one theology, but are in fact, universal in the supernormal. I covered the inside of the circle with flour, not blessed, just plain flour, and then placed another soup bone and piece of skin in its center. I sprinkled more flour all around the circle so that it was next to the first soup bone and skin I had laid out, and then poured the flour on the floor as I backed toward the door and the stairway. I sprinkled it on the landing, stopped and looked down the stairs. It was not yet night, so I hadn't been followed up the stairway, and forced to exit by means of the fire pole, but I certainly felt the thing's attendance in the light house.

It could see what I was doing, I was sure, but if this thing was what I thought it might be, its nature and design would consign it to certain decisions. I went down the stairs, and I will tell you, quite frankly, it was hard to do. I found near the bottom that I was leaning away from the side where it was cold. But as a last test, I stuck my hand out in that direction, and felt the air hit me as briskly as if I had poked my arm into a meat freezer. I kept it there, and the cold turned so cold it felt hot, and my arm began to feel singed, as if I had been too close to a fire. I pulled it back before the heat became too intense, and the confirmation of the kind of cold that was there gave me yet another clue to what might be there.

I went out into the daylight, and I was grateful for the heat of the sun.

***

As I was, in a sense, gaining artillery range on my specter, I didn't stay in the lighthouse that night either. I felt I needed another night of information before I made an attempt to remove the thing. I knew too that if I was right, what was in the lighthouse, and why it was there, would make it a most deadly enemy. I didn't take this lightly.

Next morning, I took Nora and Gary with me, for they had been lying quite low in their bedroom, doing what you might expect. They were not altogether eager to go, which had nothing to do with facing danger, but had considerable to do with their libido.

Inside the lighthouse, I showed them the cold-hot spot, and then we went upstairs. The flour on the landing was disturbed, and there were marks in it that looked hoof-like in spots, and dog-like in others, and there were those other marks I had seen in their photographs that reminded me of nothing I could describe.

In the room, the flour was bothered, and in fact, it looked as if something had rolled in it. The bone and skin were there, but they had changed. The bone had grown meat on it, and the skin had grown fur. The mirror was cracked, and when I picked it up, the image of the intruder, as I expected, was still frozen in the glass.

I showed it to Nora and Gary, and I would try here to describe what we saw, but it was indescribable. But, I will come back to that later.

The circle was only slightly disturbed, and I could see where the chalk had been pushed at, but not actually broken. Inside the circle the symbols were as visible as when I wrote them, and the bone and skin there had not changed at all, except to putrefy a little. I had them removed, and refreshed the circle where it showed some minor contact, and then I examined the Nanny cam.

There was nothing present in the film but the flour being disturbed and the mirror cracking. Whatever had caused this was invisible to film. I knew that in person, it would not be invisible, but would have a very visible and menacing presence.

We went away and had lunch and waited until it was close to an hour before dark.

We went up the stairs, and this time the air was very cold and uncomfortable, in that dry-ice manner.

At the top, I had Nora and Gary get inside the circle and sit down, cross-legged. I sat with them. They had actually brought a sack lunch with them, with bottled Cokes, and though I started to admonish them for it, they had brought enough for me as well, so we all sat there eating fried chicken from a bag, drinking Cokes.

As we ate, I said, "It hasn't been deadly before, but tonight will be different. We have caught its image in the mirror. It can't tolerate that."

"You call that an image?" Gary said.

I said, "What we are dealing with is a jinn, or something like one. A demonic presence that resides in another dimension, and enters into this one by way of a device to which it has been confined. Like a brass jug."

"The Greenberg story," Nora said.

"Bingo," I said. "The demonic figure I'm talking about has the power to regenerate meat on bone, hair on flesh," I said. "But do not let that fool you. This is not a positive power in the universe, or the dimension from where it came. It hates being in the jug, or bottle, or container, but it's cursed to be drawn to just that. It can come out if called, or if the container is destroyed, but it must return to a container if one is presented to it."

"You mean if the jug were found, it would have to go back inside?"

"Exactly," I said. "There is an ancient line by an anonymous Arab wizard that reads something like, 'And when the mouth of the container is presented, and a request is made, then to its prison it must return.'"

"But we don't have the jug," Nora said.

"No, we don't. And that presents a problem. All I have is protection spells, and one juju spell that has proved powerful in other situations, and I hope will serve us as soundly this time out."

"Hope?" Gary said.

"Well," I said, "having not tried it on a jinn, having never dealt with one before, I must consign the idea to that area labeled: Speculation."

Long shadows had begun to crawl across the floor. The feeling of something observing magnified greatly.

"How did you know it was a jinn?" Gary asked.

"I was clued by the air at the bottom of the stair. Supernormal manifestations often present themselves by a chilling of the air, even in the hottest of places, but this spirit, its air is so cold it burns. That is the trait of a jinn, and they are often credited with the hot winds that blow across the deserts of the Middle East. That face you saw in the mirror, that is only a momentary presentation. It can shift its features, its shape. It is powerful. At some point, a commanding wizard, someone who understood dimensional spells, trapped this creature in a brass jug, and then he consigned it to the protection of someone he felt he owed a favor. Someone who unfortunately thought the idea of a jinn in a jug was all talk."

"That would be Greenberg again," Gary said.

"Absolutely," I said. "For whatever reason, the protector of Greenberg—this jinn—felt that it had to protect his master from, well, everyone. It didn't judge if they did anything to Greenberg or not. Its nature is ferocious, and it's a nasty sort of creature. It's possible it did what it did just because it could. So, it ran rampant on the ship, and my guess is somehow, after all the slaughter, Greenberg, its master, was able to have it go back in the jug, where it was stopped up tight."

"Like a fly in a Coke bottle," Nora said.

"Exactly," I said. "I'm surmising a bit, but after it was contained in the jug, the ship ran aground, having no one to sail it, and the damage the jinn did looked like axe murders and cannibalism. It wasn't. Greenberg told them the truth. But no one believed his story, and he was hanged for the crime. I don't think even he understood what he had. He popped the cork, the jinn came out, and started to 'protect him.' It was so full of passion and hunger and anger, it tore the crew apart. Greenberg most likely had been given a spell by the Arabic trader, and though he had thought nothing of it at the time, he remembered it, and by speaking it, he caused the jinn to return to the confines of the jug. But too late for the crew."

"Where's the jug?"

"Ah, and here I speculate again, though quite well, I venture to say. It was lost in the shipwreck, buried in the sand, and in time, sand was packed over it. The jug was sealed, and therefore so was the jinn. The lighthouse was built on top of the jug, and where Reggie reinforced the stair rail, near the bottom, he broke the concrete and the jug was underneath. He didn't see it, but it was there, and as he worked—"

"The stopper was popped free," Gary said.

"Yes, but it has been confined for some time, and it no longer had its master, so it has been learning on its own how to be free, how to use its own will. That's why it has only been a sensation, a sound, a glance, up until now. After I saw it had the ability to grow flesh on a bone, hair on skin, I felt it had come back to itself, so to speak. And with one of its many images trapped in a mirror, it will be angry; a jinn does like to show any part of its true self in a reflection."

"Being back to itself is not good, is it?" Nora said.

"No, it's not," I said. "There is little in the supernormal universe nastier than a jinn on the loose."

I looked outside.

"We should have evidence of that shortly, so I suggest you do not get outside the circle. Not a finger. Not a nose. Not a toe."

"Can it break through?" Nora asked.

"We will soon find out," I said, and removed a couple of thick incense candles from my bag, and lit them. The incense was supposed to contain powerful properties to combat evil. I hoped they in fact did. I had never before had the opportunity to use them.

It was then that we heard the footsteps on the stairs.

***

I could feel Nora close to me, shivering, or maybe it was me shivering, or the both of us. Behind and to my left, I could hear Gary. He was breathing like a horse about to make the grade.

Outside the door, we heard the jinn stop. We saw its shadow move along the floor, and slide under like an oil spill. The shadow quivered in the candle light. The jinn paused. Then the door started to buckle, and there was a sound like a wind blowing through a canyon, followed by a brisk scratching noise. From the vigor of the scratching, it was obvious that it had gained tremendous strength in just the few days we had been there. The room filled with a stench, like carrion, and it turned warm in the room, but my guess was, outside the circle, it was even warmer. I saw the paint on the walls beading.

Then the door sagged in the middle, creaked at the hinges, and blew across the room. It smacked into the field around our protective circle, bounced to the side, and skidded across the floor, hitting the runner at the base of the tall window glass. The circle, if it held, would keep out anything that was brought about by supernormal means. I tried to let that reassure me.

"You two," I said, "get behind me."

They didn't hesitate.

It came into the room in a whirl of shadows, and the whirl made dust rise up and twist about, and the dust hit the field around our circle as if we were behind glass. The jinn leaped right at us, so fast it made me jump. It hit the force field, bounced back, whirled in a tight spin of darkness, and came again.

This time the field wobbled and the chalk circle dented slightly. I reached into my bag and brought out the blessed chalk, and reached out to tighten the circle, and I felt it touch me.

I don't know how to describe it. It was a horrid touch. I know that sounds very... Lovecraftian, or Poe-like. What is a horrid touch? What does that actually mean? But I have no other words to describe it. I can only say it was like black electricity leaping through my bones, topping out at my skull to the degree that I thought the summit of my head might blow off.

And it had only been a touch. My finger was smoking and blistered from the burn.

Around and around it went, making the circle I had drawn. Out of the whirl, long fingers, spiked with nails like daggers, touched the field, and the field ripped. I pulled a paper from my bag and started to quote the spells the juju man had given me; they were written across the page in chicken blood and were easy to read even by candle light. My reading them made the jinn howl all the louder. I don't know if it was in anger or pain, or both.

It bounced again and again against the chalk wall, causing the chalk to dust slightly, and move. The circle was not holding. I had not only foolishly put myself in this bad position, but I had put my friends in the same position as well.

I kept reciting the juju spell, but it didn't seem to be working. I finally realized that I was showing fear, that my recital of it didn't have the African tone for the words; they sounded exactly like what they were—words read off paper and pronounced poorly.

I admit all this reluctantly, for I've faced many horrors, but this one was strong well beyond my expectations. I had never seen the chalk line start to break so easily. I closed my eyes, started to quote the words again, this time, not by rote, but with feeling.

When I opened my eyes, my heart sank. It hadn't mattered. The field was starting to fade, and the long fingers of the thing took hold of the tip of my shoe, and it was jerked off my foot and snapped into the spinning vortex. The room became dark. The light of the candles flickered, a sure sign that the jinn was breaking through. The air stank and it grew warm, like a campfire had been built all around us.

As it was tearing its way in, I attempted to draw the line with the chalk again, but each time I reached, it reached too, and finally it caught me by the tip of my finger. I tried to pull it back, but it had me in a snug grip, and in a moment I felt a burning, tearing pain that nearly made me faint. It pulled the tip of my finger off like it was snapping loose a damp piece of taffy. Blood dotted the floor with hot red splashes.

The chalk was buckling. The rip was widening. The field was about to break completely.

On instinct, for a weapon, I grabbed up one of the Coke bottles by the neck, just as this thing, this shape-shifting thing, plunged through the barrier. I swatted at it with the bottle, and in a rush, it turned thin and smoky, and was sucked directly into the bottle; all of him.

I quickly put the open bottle top against the floor, gently, and told Nora to roll up the paper with the juju spell on it, and she did. I took it, and with one quick move, lifted the bottle and jammed the paper inside. Then I grabbed up the candle, and ignoring what the hot wax was doing to my fingers, I packed the mouth of the bottle with it. The wax had another effect; it sealed off my finger wound.

The jinn roiled around inside the bottle like a lava lamp, but it didn't come out.

Nora said, "What happened?"

"I have to admit to an accident," I said. "It wouldn't have occurred to me. But remember the quote I told you that was anonymous, about the jinn? 'And when the mouth of the container is presented, and a request is made—'"

"Then to its prison it must return," Nora said, finishing off the line.

"I misunderstood. I thought it had to be the container it was placed in originally. But it's clear now. Once it was subject to a spell, if a container was put before it, it had to enter it. It didn't have to return to its original confinement, it just had to imprison itself. When I picked it up and brought it down, it was merely responding to its initial commands, given to it those long years ago."

"So, our jinn wasn't so bad after all," Nora said.

"Bad enough," Gary said.

I remembered I had considered scolding them for bringing a lunch and Cokes into a power circle. I decided not to mention that.

***

Not much more to tell. We put the bottle in a metal ice chest and covered the bottle in four or five inches of dry concrete, and put water in it, and let it dry for a couple of days on the landing of our hotel room. Day after it was solid dry, we rented a boat and motored out into the Gulf where it was deep, and dropped the closed chest full of concrete and the trapped jinn, into the depths of the water.

***

She leaned back, and said, "Well, that's it."

We all sat silent for a while. The smokers had forgotten to call time and go smoke. They had listened without interruption from start to finish.

Finally, I said, "It's a good story, but how are we to know it's nothing more than a story?"

"Oh," she said, holding her glass while Kevin refilled it, and then went over to turn on the lights, "you don't. Remember? I said it didn't matter to me... But...."

She reached inside her coat pocket and brought out something small and round.

"This is the mirror in which the jinn's image was trapped, and considering I thought you might ask something like that, just for grins, I brought it with me."

"It's easy to fake things," I said, but then my mouth fell open.

She held the mirror toward us, and all I can tell you is what Dana said before. There's no way to truly describe the image that had been trapped inside that broken mirror. It sent chills down my back, and in fact, the whole room for a moment seemed as if it were made of ice. None of us questioned its validity.

Another thing. As Dana held the mirror out, I noted that the tip of her index finger on her right hand was missing; where the tip should have been there was a glistening wink of bone.

She smiled, put the mirror away, then without another word, downed her drink, rose from her chair, and departed, leaving us speechless.

The Case of the Stalking Shadow

by Joe R. Lansdale

(For Kasey Lansdale)

I've mentioned Dana Roberts before, though with less kindness than I do now, and if anyone would have told me that I would be defending, even supporting, someone who in layman's terms might be known as a ghost breaker, or a dealer in the supernatural, I would have laughed them out of the room.

It should also be noted that Dana does not consider what she does as dealing with the supernatural, which she believes is a term that often assigns some sort of religious aspect to her work. She believes what others call the supernatural is an unknown reality of this world, or some dimensional crossover that has yet to be explained, and if truly understood would be designated as science.

But, here I go trying to explain her books, which after her first visit to our club I have read extensively. That said, I should also note that my conclusions about her observations, her work, might be erroneous. I'm a reader, not a scholar, and above all, I love a good story.

The first time she was with us, she told us of an adventure she called The Case of The Lighthouse Shambler. At the end of her tale, or her report, if you take it as fact—and I do—she showed us something trapped in a mirror's reflection that was in my view impossible to explain away. She was also missing the tip of her right index finger, which went along nicely with the story she had just finished.

Her visit to our club was, without a doubt, a highlight.

Though I suppose I've gotten a little out of order, I should pause and tell you something of our group. It now stands at twelve—three women and nine men. Most of us are middle age, or better. I should also mention that during our last meeting I recorded Dana's first story for our gathering, unbeknownst to her. My intent was to do so, and then replay parts of it to our treasurer, Kevin, with the intent of obvious ridicule and a declaration that money spent on spook hunters as guests were wasted dues.

Instead, I was so captivated with Dana's story that I went home forgetting I had recorded her, and, of course, Kevin had heard it all first-hand and had been as captivated with her adventure as I was.

A few weeks later I was finally brave enough to call Dana's business, which is registered simply, DANA ROBERTS, SUPERNORMAL INVESTIGATIONS, and tell her what I had done. There was no need for it, as she would never know, but I harbored a certain amount of guilt, and liked the idea of having contact with her, and encouraged her to come to the club again.

To my relief, she found my original skepticism more than acceptable, and asked if I might like to transcribe my recording for publication in her monthly newsletter. I not only agreed, but it appeared in the April Online Magazine, DANA ROBERTS REPORTS. And so, here is another story, recorded and transcribed with her enthusiastic permission.

The night she came to us again as a speaker, she was elegantly dressed, and looked fine in dark slacks and an ivory blouse. Her blond hair was combed back and tied loosely at her neck, and she wore her usual disarming smile.

She took her place in the large and comfortable guest chair, and with a tall drink in her hand and the lights dimmed, a fire crackling in the fireplace, she began to tell a story she called The Case of The Stalking Shadow.

It follows.

***

Since most of the events of the last few months have turned out to be hoaxes, or of little interest, and because I am your invited guest, I decided tonight to fall back on one of my earlier cases, my first in fact, and the one that led me into this profession. Though, at the time I didn't know I was going to become a serious investigator of this sort of thing, or that it would require so much work, as well as putting myself continually in the face of danger. I've done more research for my current job than I ever did gaining my PhD in anthropology.

Mistakes in what I do can have dire consequences, so it's best to know what one is doing, at least where it can be known.

I was not paid for this investigation. It was done for myself, with the aid of a friend, and it happened when I was in my late teens. In the process of my discovering my lifelong occupation, I nearly lost my life on more than one occasion, for there were several touchy moments. Had this particular case gone wrong, then I would not be here today to entertain you with my adventures, nor would my friend and cousin Jane be alive, wherever she may be right now.

Simply put, I come from what must be defined as a wealthy family. There were times when there was less wealth, but there was always money. This was also true of my close relatives, and so it was that my Aunt Elizabeth, on my father's side, invited us each year to her home for the summer. It was a kid event, and children of both my mother's and father's siblings were gathered each year when school let out to spend a week with Aunt Elizabeth, whose husband was in oil, and often gone for months at a time. I suppose, having no children of her own, she liked the company, and in later years when her husband, my then Uncle Chester, ran off with a woman from Brazil, it became more clear to me why she looked forward each year to a family gathering, and why she surrounded herself with so many other activities, and spent Uncle Chester's money with a kind of abandon that could only speak to the idea of getting hers while there was something to be got.

But, that is all sour family business, and I will pass over it. I'm sure I've told too much already.

The year I'm talking about, when I was thirteen, my Aunt and Uncle had moved from their smaller property upstate, and had bought what could only be described as a classic estate, made to look very much like those huge British properties we see frequently in older movies and television programs. It was in America, in the deep South, but it certainly had the looks of a traditional upper-level British residence, with enormous acreage to match. In the latter respect, it was more common to America's vast spaces. One hundred acres, the largest portion of it wooded, with a house with no less than forty-five rooms, and a surrounding area dotted with gardens and shrubs trimmed in the shape of animals: lions and tigers and bears.

It was overdone and overblown. For a child, those vast rooms and that enormous acreage was a kind of paradise. Or, so it seemed at the time of that initial gathering of myself and my cousins.

To get more directly to the point, after arrival, and a few days of getting to know one another—for in some cases our lives were so different, and things had changed so dramatically for each of us in such a short period of time—it was necessary to reacquaint. We were on the verge of leaving childhood, or most of us were, though there were some younger. For me, this year was to be particularly important, and in many ways I feel it was the last year of what I think of as true childhood. Certainly, I was not grown after this year passed, but my interests began to move in other directions. Boys and cars and dating, the whole nine yards. And, of course, what happened changed me forever.

But this summer I'm talking about, we spent a vast amount of time playing the old childhood games. It was a wonderful and leisurely existence that consisted of swimming in the pool, croquet, badminton, and the like. At night, since my Aunt would not allow a television, we played board games of all varieties, and as there was a huge number of us cousins, we were often pitted against one another in different parts of the house with different games.

One night, perhaps three days into my visit, my cousin Jane and I found ourselves in a large room, alone, where we were playing chess, and between moves she suddenly said, without really waiting for a reply: "Have you been in the woods behind the estate? I find it quite queer."

"Queer?" I said.

"Strange. I suppose it's my imagination, and being a city girl. I'm not used to the proximity of so many trees."

I didn't know it at the time, and would probably not have appreciated it, but those trees had been there for hundreds of years, and though other areas had been logged out and replaced with "crops" of pines in long rows, this was the remains of aboriginal forests. Jumping ahead slightly, the trees were not only of a younger time, but they were huge and grew in such a way the limbs had grown together and formed a kind of canopy that didn't allow brush and vines to grow beneath them. So when someone says there are as many trees now as there once were, you can be certain they are describing crop trees, grown close together, without the variance of nature. These trees were from a time when forests were forests, so to speak.

Anyway, she said perhaps a few more words about the trees, and how she thought the whole place odd, but I didn't pay any real attention to her, and there was nothing in her manner that I determined to be dread or worry of any kind. So, her comments didn't really have impact on me, and it wasn't until later that I thought back on our conversation and realized how accurately impressionable Jane had been.

There was something strange about those woods.

***

After another day or so, the pool and the nighttime games lost some of their appeal. We did some night swimming, lounging around the pool, but one moonlit night, one of the younger children amongst us—Billy, who was ten—suggested that it might be fun to play a game of tag in the woods.

Now, from an adult standpoint, this seems like a bad choice, mucking about in the woods at night, but we were young, and it was a very bright night, and though deeper into the acreage the trees were as I formerly described them, up close to the house they were spread about more. There were adequate shadows for hiding, but they were less thick there, and grew in an odd manner, as if the soil were bad. There was no canopy overhead, but instead there was plenty of openness to let in the moonlight, which made the area more appealing for the sort of game we planned. But what I'm trying to point out here, is how distinctly different these trees were from the ones I told you about before. That said, I now realize these trees were even older, far older, but were of a totally different nature.

We decided a game would be delicious. We chose up teams. One team constituted eight cousins, the other seven. The game was somewhere between hide-and-go-seek and tag. One team would hide, the other would seek. If an adversary, for want of a better name, were discovered, they could run and hide again. The trick was to chase them down, tag them, making them a member of the hunting team. In time, the idea was to tag everyone into the Number Two Team, and then the game would switch out.

How we started was, Number Two Team was to stay at the swimming pool while Number One Team had a fifteen minute head-start into the woods. It was suggested that the more open part of the woods was to be our area, but that no one should go into the thicker and darker part, because that was a lot of acreage and more difficult. Oddly enough, we would have been better off to have played there, instead of where we ended up.

At the signal, we shot off like quail, splitting up in the woods to hide, each of us going our own route. It was every cousin for themselves.

I went through the trees, and proceeded immediately to the back of the sparser woods and came to the edge where it thickened. The trees in the sparser area were of common variety, but of uneven shape. They didn't grow high, but were thickly festooned with sickly widespread branches, and beneath them were plenty of shadows.

As if it were yesterday, I remember that as soon as I came to that section of trees, I was besieged by an unreasonable sensation of discomfort. The discomfort, at this point, wasn't fear, it was more a malaise that had descended on me heavy as a wool blanket. I thought it had to do with overextending myself while on vacation, because even though young, I was used to a much more controlled environment and an earlier bedtime.

The trees seemed far more shadowy than they had appeared from a distance, and there was also an impression of being watched. No, that isn't quite right. Not of being watched so much, as of a presence in the general locale. Something so close, that I should be able to see it, but couldn't. Something I should be able to see, but instinctively felt I didn't want to.

I marked this down to exhaustion, and went about finding a good place to hide. I could hear the seekers beginning to run toward the woods, and then I heard someone scream, having been tagged immediately. I chose a place between two trees that had grown together high and low in such a way as to appear to be a huge letter H placed on a pedestal; the trees met in such tight formation they provided a near singular trunk and the bar of the H was an intermingled branch of both trees. I darted behind them, scooted down, and put my back against the trunk.

No sooner had I chosen my spot, than it occurred to me that its unusual nature might in fact attract one of the seekers, but by then, I felt it was too late and pressed my back against the tree, awaiting whatever fate might come.

From where I sat, I could see the deeper woods, and I had an urge to run into it, away from the grove of trees where I now hid. I also disliked the idea of having my back against the tree and being discovered suddenly and frightened by the hunters. I didn't want that surprise to cause me to squeal the way I had heard someone squeal earlier. I liked to think of myself as more mature than a child's game to begin with, and was beginning to regret my involvement in the matter.

I sat and listened for footfalls, but the game went on behind me. I could hear yelling and some words, and I was bewildered that no one had come to look for me, as my hiding place wasn't exactly profound.

After a while, I ceased to hear the children, and noticed that the moonlight in the grove, where the limbs were less overbearing, had grown thinner.

I stood up and turned and looked through the split in the H tree. It was very quiet now, so much in fact, I could almost hear the worms crawling inside the earth. I stood there peeking between the bars of the H, and then I saw one of the children coming toward me. I couldn't make out who it was, as they were drenched in shadow, but they were coming up the slight rise into the ragged run of trees. At first, I felt glad to see them, as I was ready for my part in this silly game to be over, and was planning on begging off being a seeker. I felt I could do this quite happily and conveniently, and the teams would then be Even Steven, as my father used to say.

However, as the shape came closer, I began to have a greater feeling of unease than before. The shape came along with an unusual step that seemed somewhere between a glide and a skip. There was something disconcerting about its manner. It was turning its shadowed head left and right, as I would have expected a seeker to do, but there was a deeply ingrained part of me that rejected this as its purpose.

Closer it came, the more my nervousness was compounded, for the light didn't delineate its features in any way. In fact, the shape seemed not to be a shadow at all, but the dark caricature of a human being. I eased behind the trunk and hid.

A feeling of dread turned to a feeling of fear. I was assailed with the notion that I ought to run away quickly, but to do that, I would have to step out and reveal myself, and that idea was even more frightening and oppressive. So, I stayed in my place, actually shivering. Without seeing it, I could sense that it was coming closer. There was a noise associated with its approach, but to this day, I can't identify that noise. It was not footfalls on leaves or ground, but was a strange sound that made me both fearful, and at the same time, sad. It was the kind of sound that reached down into the brain and bones and gave you an influx of information that spoke not to the logical part of your being, but to some place more primal. I know that is inadequate, but I can't explain it any better. I wish that I could, because if I could imitate that sound, most of this story would be unnecessary to tell. You would understand much of it immediately.

I spoke of shivering with fear, but until that day, I didn't know a person's knees could actually knock together during the process, or that the sound of one's heart could be so loud. I was certain both sounds would be evident to the shadow, but I held my ground. It was fear that held me there, as surely as if my body had been coated in an amazingly powerful glue and I had been fastened and dried to that tree with it.

Eventually, I steeled my courage, turned and peeked between the trunks of the H tree. Looking right at me was the shadow. Not more than a foot away. There wasn't a face, just the shape of a head and utter blackness. The surprise caused me to let out with a shriek—just the sort I'd tried to avoid—and I leapt back, and without really considering it, I broke around the tree and tore through the woods toward the house as if my rear-end were on fire.

I looked back over my shoulder, and there came the thing, flapping its arms, its legs flailing like a wind-blown scarecrow.

I tripped once, rising just as the thing touched my shoulder, only for a moment. A cold went through me as it did. It was the sort of cold I imagined would be in the arctic, the sensation akin to stepping out of a warm tent, soaking wet, into an icy wind. I charged along with all my might, trying to outrun the thing I knew was right behind me. It was breathing, and its breath was as cold as its touch on the back of my neck. As it ran, the sound of its feet brought to mind the terrors I had felt earlier when I first saw it making its way through the woods; that indescribable sound that held within it all the terrors of this world, and any world imagined.

I reached the edge of the woods, and then I was into the clearing. I tried not to look back, tried not to do anything that might break my stride, but there was no stopping me. I couldn't help myself. When I looked back, there at the line of the woods, full in the moonlight, stood the thing waving its arms about in a frustrated manner, but no longer running after me.

I thundered down a slight rise and broke into the yard where the topiary animals stood, then clattered along the cobblestone path and into the house.

When I was in the hallway, I stopped to get my breath. I thought of the others, and though I was concerned, at that moment I was physically unable to return to those woods, or even the yard to yell for the them.

Then I heard them, upstairs. I went up and saw they were all in the Evening Room. When Jane saw me, her eyes narrowed, but she didn't speak. The others went about joshing me immediately, and it was just enough to keep me from blurting out what I had seen. It seemed that everyone in the game had been caught but me, and that I had been given up on, and that switching the game about so that the other side might be the pursuer had been forgotten. Hot chocolate was being served, and everything seemed astonishingly normal.

I considered explaining all that had occurred to me, but was struck with the absurdity of it. Instead, I went to the window and looked out toward the forest. There was nothing there.

***

Jane and I shared a room, as we were the closest of the cousins. As it came time for bed, I found myself unwilling to turn out the light. I sat by the window and looked out at the night.

Jane sat on her bed in her pajamas looking at me. She said, "You saw it, didn't you?"

She might as well have hit me with a brick.

"Saw what?" I said.

"It," she said. "The shadow."

"You've seen it too?"

She nodded. "I told you the woods were strange. But, I had no idea until tonight how strange. After the game ended, the others thought it quite funny that you might still be hiding in the woods, not knowing we were done. I was worried, though..."

How so, I thought, but I didn't want to interrupt her train of thought.

"I actually allowed myself to be caught early," Jane said. "I wanted out of the game, and I planned to feign some problem or another, and come back to the house. It was all over pretty quick, however, and this wasn't necessary. Everyone was tagged out. Except you. But no one wanted to stay in the woods or go back into them, so they came back to the house. I think they were frightened. I know I was. And I couldn't put my finger on it. But being in that woods, and especially the nearer I came to that section where it thinned and the trees grew strange, I was so discomforted it was all I could do to hold back tears. Then, from the window, I saw you running. And I saw It. The shadow that was shaped like a man. It stopped just beyond the line of trees."

I nodded. "I thought I imagined it."

"Not unless I imagined it too."

"But what is it?" I asked.

Jane walked to where I stood and looked out the window. The man-shaped shadow did not appear, and the woods were much darker now as the moon was beginning to drop low.

"I don't know," she said. "But I've heard that some spots on earth are the homes of evil spirits. Sections where the world opens up into a place that is not of here."

"Not of here?"

"Some slice in our world or their world that lets one of us, or one of them, slip in."

"Where would you hear such a thing?" I asked.

"Back home, in Lansdale, Pennsylvania. They say there was an H tree there. Like the one in these woods. I've seen it in the daytime and it makes me nervous. I know it's there."

"I hid behind it," I said. "That's where the shadow found me."

"Lansdale was home to one of the three known H trees, as they were called."

This, of course, was exactly what I had called the tree upon seeing it.

"It was said to be a portal to another world," Jane said. "Some said hell. Eventually, it was bulldozed down and a housing project was built over the site."

"Did anything happen after it was torn down?" I asked.

Jane shrugged. "I can't say. I just know the legend. But I've seen pictures of the tree, and it looks like the one in the woods here. I think it could be the same sort of thing."

"Seems to me, pushing it over wouldn't do anything," I said.

"I don't know. But the housing division is still there, and I've never heard of anything happening."

"Maybe because it was never a portal to hell, or anywhere else," I said. "It was just a tree."

"Could be," Jane said. "And that could be just an odd tree in the woods out there." She pointed out the window. "Or, it could be what the one in Lansdale was supposed to be. A doorway."

"It doesn't make any sense," I said.

"Neither does a shadow chasing you out of the woods."

"There has to be a logical explanation."

"When you figure it out," Jane said, "Let me know."

"We should tell the others," I said.

"They won't believe us," Jane said, "but they're scared of the woods. I can tell. They sense something is out there. That's why the game ended early. I believe our best course of action is to not suggest anything that might involve those woods, and ride out the week."

I agreed, and that's exactly what we did.

***

The week passed on, and no one went back in the woods. But I did watch for the shadow from the backyard, and at night, from the window. Jane watched with me. Sometimes, we brought hot chocolate up to the window and sat there in the dark and drank it and kept what we called The Shadow Watch.

The moon wasn't as bright the following nights, and before long if we were to see it, it would have had to stand underneath the backyard lights. It didn't.

The week came to an end, and all of us cousins went home.

***

There was an invitation the next summer to go back, but I didn't go. I had tried to dismiss the whole event as a kind of waking nightmare, but there were nights when I would awake feeling certain that I was running too slow and the shadow was about to overtake me.

It was on those nights that I would go to the window in my room, which looked out over a well-lit city street with no woods beyond. It made me feel less stressed and worried to see those streets and cars and people walking about well past midnight. And none of them were shadows.

Jane wrote me now and again, and she mentioned the shadow once, but the next letter did not, and pretty soon there were no letters. We kept in touch by email, and I saw her at a couple of family functions, and then three years or so passed without us being in communication at all.

I was in college by then, and the whole matter of the shadow was seldom thought of, though there were occasions when it came to me out of my subconscious like a great black tide. There were times when I really thought I would like to talk to Jane about the matter, but there was another part of me that felt talking to her would make it real again. I had almost convinced myself it had all been part of my imagination, and that Jane hadn't really seen anything, and that I misremembered what she had told me.

That's how the mind operates when it doesn't want to face something. I began my studies, with anthropology as my major, and in the process, somewhere, I came across a theory that sometimes, instead of the eye sending a message to the brain, the brain sends a message to the eye. It is a rare occurrence, but some scientists believe this explains sincere ghostly sightings. To the viewer, it would be as real as you are to me as I sit here telling you this story. But, the problem with this view was, Jane had seen it as well, so it was a nice theory, but not entirely comforting.

And then out of the blue, I received a letter from Jane. Not an email. Not a phone call. But an old-fashioned letter, thin in the envelope, and short on message.

It read: *I'm going back on Christmas Eve. I have to know.*

***

I knew exactly what she meant. I knew I had to go back too. I had to have an answer.

Now, let me give you a bit of background on my Aunt's place. She and her husband separated and the house and property were put up for sale. I knew this from my mother and father. They had been offered an opportunity to buy the house, but had passed due to the expense of it all.

Interestingly enough, I learned that Jane's family, who had later been offered the opportunity, could afford it, and plans were made. Jane's father had died the year before, and a large inheritance was left to Jane's mother. No sooner had the house been bought, than her mother died, leaving Jane with the property.

Perhaps this was the catalyst that convinced Jane to go back.

I acquired Jane's phone number, and called her. We talked briefly, and did not mention the shadow. It's like our conversation was in code. We made plans; a time to arrive and how to meet, that sort of thing.

Before I left, I did a bit of research.

I didn't know what it was I was looking for, but if Jane was right, her hometown of Lansdale, Pennsylvania was supposedly a former home to an H tree. I looked it up on the Internet and read pretty much what Jane had told me. As far back as the Native Americans there had been stories of Things coming through the gap in the H tree. Spirits. Monsters. Demons. Shadows.

As Jane had said, the H had been destroyed by builders, and a subdivision of homes was built over it. I looked for any indication that there had been abnormal activity in that spot, but except for a few burglaries, and one murder of a husband by a wife, there was nothing out of the average.

***

Upon arrival, at the airport I picked up my rental car and drove to a Wal-Mart and bought a gas can, two cheap cigarette lighters, and a laser pointer. Keep in mind, now, that I was doing all of this out of assumption, not out of any real knowledge of the situation. There was no real knowledge to be had, only experience. Experience that might lead to disappointment, and the kind of disappointment that could result in a lack of further experience in all matters. I had that in mind as I drove, watching the sun drop in the west.

When I arrived at the property and the house, it had changed. The house was still large and regal, but the yards had grown up and the swimming pool was an empty pit lined at the bottom with broken seams and invading weeds. The topiary shrubs had become masses of green twists and turns without any identifying structure.

I parked and got out. Jane greeted me at the door. Like me, she was dressed simply, in jeans, a tee-shirt and tennis shoes. She led me inside. She had bought a few sandwich goods, and we made a hasty meal of cheese and meat and coffee, and then she showed me the things she had brought for "protection" as she put it.

There were crosses and holy water and wafers and a prayer book. Though I don't believe that religion itself holds power, the objects and the prayers, when delivered with conviction, do. Symbols like crosses and holy water and wafers that have been blessed by a priest who is a true believer, contain authority. Objects from other religions are the same. It's not the gods that give them power, it is the dedication given them by the believer. In my case, even though I was not a believer, the idea that a believer had blessed the items was something I hoped endowed them with abilities.

On the other hand, I bore great faith in the simple things—like gasoline and fire starters.

Shortly after our meal, we took a few moments to discuss what we had seen those years ago, and were soon in agreement. This agreement extended to the point that we admitted that we had been, at least to some degree, in denial since that time.

Out back we stood and looked at the woods for a long moment. The moon was rising. It was going to be nearly full. Not as full as that night when I had first seen the shadow, but bright enough.

Jane had her crosses and the like in a small satchel with a strap. She slung it over her shoulder. I carried the gas can, and had the lighters and laser pointer in my pants pocket. By the time we reached the bleak section of woods and the H tree was visible, it was as if my feet had anvils fastened to them. I could hardly lift them. I began to feel more and more miserable.

I eyed Jane, saw there were tears in her eyes. When we were to the H tree, I began to shake.

We circled the tree, seeing it from all angles. Stopping, I began to pour gasoline onto its base, splashing some on the trunk from all sides. Jane pulled her wafers and holy water and crucifixes from her bag, and proceeded to place them on the ground around the tree. She took out the prayer book and began to read. Then, out of the gap between the trees, a shadow leaned toward her.

I tried to yell, to warn her, but the words were frozen in my mouth like dead seals in an iceberg. The shadow grabbed her by the throat, causing her to let out with a grunt, and then she was pulled through the portal and out of sight.

***

I suspected there would be danger, but on some level I thought we would approach the tree, read a prayer, stick a cross in the ground, set the tree on fire, and flee, hoping the entire forest, the house, and surrounding property wouldn't burn down with it.

I had also hoped, for reasons previously stated, that the religious symbols would carry weight against whatever it was that lay inside that gateway, but either the materials had not been properly blessed, or we were dealing with something immune to those kinds of artifacts.

Now, here comes the hard part. This is very hard for me to admit, even to this day. But the moment Jane was snatched through that portal, I broke and ran. I offer as excuse only two things. I was young. And I was terrified.

I ran all the way to the back door of the house. No sooner had I arrived there than I was overcome with grief. It took me a moment to fortify myself, but when that was done, I turned, and started back with renewed determination.

I came to the H, and with a stick, I probed the gap between the trees. Nothing happened, though at any instant I expected the shadow to lean forward and grab me. I picked up the bottle of holy water that Jane had left, hoping it might be better than a prayer book, climbed over the communal trunk, ducked beneath the limb that made the bar on the H, and boldly stepped through the portal.

***

It was gray inside, like the sun seen through a heavy curtain, but there was no sunlight. The air seemed to be fused with light, dim as it was. There were boulder-like shapes visible. They were tall and big around. All of them leaned, and not all in the same direction. Each was fog-shrouded. There were shadows flickering all about, moving from one structure to another, being absorbed by them, like ink running through the cracks in floorboards.

Baffled, I stood there with the bottle of holy water clutched in my fist, trying to decide what to do. Eventually, the only thing that came to me was to start forward in search of Jane. As I neared the boulders, I gasped for breath. They were not boulders at all but structures made of bones and withering flesh. The shadows were tucked tight between the bone and skin like viscera. I stood there staring, and then one of the bones—an arm bone—moved and flexed the skeletal fingers, snatched at the air, and reached for me.

Startled, I let out a sharp cry and stepped back.

The structure pivoted, and a thousand eyes opened in the worn skin. It was a living thing made of bone and skin and shadow, and it slid along, a gray slime oozing out from beneath it like the trail of a slug.

I bolted in what I hoped was the general direction I had come, but directions were confused. I wheeled and flung the holy water violently against the thing, but the only reaction I got was a broken bottle and water leaking ineffectually down its side. As it pivoted, I saw sticking out from it a shape that had yet to become bone and dried skin. It writhed like a worm in tar. Then it screamed and called out.

It was Jane, attached to the departing thing like a fly stuck to fly paper.

***

Other mounds of bone and shadow and flesh were starting to move now, and they were akin to hills sliding in my direction. They were seeking me, mewing as they went, their sliding giving forth that horrid shuffling sound I had heard years before from the running shadow. The sound made me ill. My head jumped full of all manner of horrid things.

I realized escape was impossible. That no matter which way I turned, they were there.

Now the shadows, as if greased, slipped out of gaps in the bones and skin, moved toward me, their dark feet sliding, their arms waving, their odd, empty, dark faces, turning from side to side.

I knew for certain that it was over for Jane and myself.

And then I remembered the laser pointer in my pocket. I had brought it because shadows are an absence of light, and if there is one thing that is the enemy of darkness, it is the sharp beam of a laser.

That said, I was unprepared for the reaction I received when I snapped it on. The light went right through one of the shadows, making entry into it like the thrust of a rapier. The shadow stopped moving, one hand flying to the wound. The beam, still directed to that spot, clipped off its hand at the wrist. It was far more than I expected; my best-case plan had been that the light would be annoying.

I knew then that I had a modern weapon to combat an ancient evil. I swung the light like a sword, and as I did, the shadows came apart and fell in splashes of inky liquid that were absorbed by the gray ground. Within moments, the shadows were attempting to leap back inside the structures, but I followed them with my beam, discovering I could cut flesh and bone with it as well, for what had once been human had been sucked dry of its essence, and was now a fabric of this world.

As I cut through them, the bones were dark inside, full of shadow, and the skin bled shadows; the ground was sucking them up like a sponge soaking up water.

I darted to the beast that held Jane. It was sliding along at a brisk pace. I grabbed one of Jane's outreaching hands and tugged. I was pulled to my knees as the thing flowed away. I didn't let go. I went dragging along, clinging to Jane with one hand, the laser with the other.

Eventually, I lost my grip, stumbled to my feet, and pursued the monster as it moved into a gray mist that nearly disguised it. A shadow came out of the mist and grabbed me. When it did, an intense coldness went over my body. It was so cold, I almost passed out.

I cut with the laser. The shadow let go and fell apart. I had split it from the top of its head to the area that on a human would have been the groin.

I ran after Jane. The mist had become so thick, I almost lost her. I ran up on the creature without realizing it, and when I did, its stickiness clung to me and sucked at me. I was almost lifted off my feet, but again, I utilized the laser, and it let me go.

Aware of my determination, it let go of Jane too. She fell at my feet. My last sight of the thing was of it moving into the mist, and of bony arms waving and eyes blinking and shadows twisting down deep inside of it.

I pulled Jane upright, and it was purely by coincidence that I saw a bit of true light—a kind of glow poking through the mist.

Yanking her along, we ran for it. As we neared, it became brighter yet, like a large goal post. We darted through it and fell to the ground in a tumble. Making sure Jane was all right, I cautioned her away, and stuck the laser in my pocket.

I pulled out one of the cigarette lighters I had bought. Shadowy arms reached through the gap in the trees, into the light. The fingers snapped at me like the fangs of a snake. I avoided them with an agility I didn't know I possessed.

The shadow came through in all its dark glory. I bent low and clicked the lighter and put the flame to the spot where I had poured gasoline. A blaze leaped up and engulfed the shadow and rolled it up into a ball of fire.

With a shaking hand, I went around to the other side of the H tree, put a lick of flame to it. Coated in gasoline, it lit, but weakly.

I flicked off the lighter and grabbed up the can with its remaining gas and tossed it toward the fire. The flames fanned up the gas stream and almost reached the can before I dropped it and the blaze ran into it and the can exploded.

My ears rang. The next thing I knew I was on the ground and Jane was beating out tufts of fire that had landed on my pants and the front of my shirt. It was pure luck that kept me from catching ablaze.

We watched as the tree burned. Shadow shapes were visible inside the H, looking out of the gray, as if to note us one last time before the fire closed the gateway forever.

***

The tree burned all night and into the next morning. We watched it from where we sat on the ground. The air was no longer heavy with foreboding. It seemed... how shall I say it... well, empty.

I feared the flames might jump to the rest of the trees, but they didn't. The H tree burned flat to the ground, not even leaving a stump. All that was left was a burned spot, dark as a hole through the center of the earth.

***

Jane and I parted the next morning, and for some reason we have never spoken again. At all. Maybe the connection at that time of our young life, that shared memory, was too much to bear.

But I did hear from her lawyer. I was offered an opportunity to buy the house and property where the H tree had been. Cheap.

It was more than I could manage actually—cheap as it was—but I acquired a loan and bought the place. I felt I had conquered it, and buying it was the final indicator.

I still own it. No more shadows creep. And that spot of woods where the tree grew, I had removed by bulldozer. I put down a stretch of concrete and built a tennis court, and to this day there has not been one inkling of unusual activity, except for the fact that my tennis game has improved far beyond my expectations.

***

Finished, Dana leaned back in her chair and sipped from her drink.

"So, that's how I got my start as an investigator of the unusual. Beyond that revelation, I suppose you might want me to explain exactly what happened there inside that strange world, but I cannot. It is beyond my full knowledge. I can only surmise that our ideas of hell and demonic regions have arisen from this and other dimensional gaps in the fabric of time and space. What the things did with this stolen flesh and bone is most likely nothing that would make sense to our intellect. I can only say that the shadows appeared to need it, to absorb it, to live off of it. However, their true motivation is impossible to know."

With that, she downed her drink, smiled, stood up, shook hands with each of us, and left us there in the firelight, stunned, considering all she had told us.

The Case of the Four Acre Haunt

by Joe R. Lansdale

We were at the club's Christmas Eve party. In the past, the organization had been all male, but though we had changed with the times, few women came to our meetings, perhaps finding them boring. But on Christmas Eve we always had parties, and even before the club moved with the times, women were invited to this specific shindig. The rules were simple—no presents, no children, just adults, drinking and eating and singing, and later, if anyone had a good Christmas story, they were allowed to tell it. Usually there was time for one good long story, and that was it.

On this night Dana Roberts had accepted our invitation, not as a storyteller, but as a visitor. As you may know, I have chronicled some of her adventures, those told at the club by her. I started out as a non-believer, but have come to accept that not only is Dana Roberts a bestselling author, but an author who is writing from true experiences.

There are a few doubters among our group, and I should add that no one was more of a doubter than me when she was first invited to the club as a guest speaker. But most have fallen over into her camp, because she is not only convincing, she has provided in some cases circumstantial evidence to go with her stories.

But none of this is either here or there. I merely mean to report that on this Christmas Eve, after the festivities died down, someone called for a story. This was our common practice, and sometimes a story was told from what was said to be personal experience, or occasionally one was read aloud from a book.

No one had a book, and no one volunteered a story, though Robert came forward and told a slightly risqué joke about Santa Claus and an elf that went over like the proverbial lead balloon.

I turned and looked at Dana, who was sitting in a chair near the Christmas tree. In fact, we were all looking at her.

She looked up, said, "What?"

"You know what," I said. "A story."

Dana nodded. "Well, I don't know that I have a story, but I have an account, a somewhat disturbing one."

"All the better," Robert said. "Someone needs to clear the air of that joke I told."

"That's certainly true," Dana said, and we all laughed.

"Move to the storytelling chair," I said.

She rose to go there, and I poured her a glass of wine. By the time I brought the wine to her, she was comfortably positioned in the storytelling chair, and this is the story she told.

***

This took place on Christmas Eve, and there was a bit of a repercussion on Christmas Day, but it started earlier than that. About mid-December of four years back. I am often asked to check out haunts in my business as investigator of the supernormal, but this request was not strictly speaking a job. They were dear friends of mine, though in the last few years our contact had been less, our jobs and personal pursuits having taken us in different directions.

But on the day it began, a phone call started it. Karen, my dear friend, asked if I might like to have lunch, and I agreed that I would. We met at a small restaurant downtown, one of those cozy places that have a reputation for good food and a certain amount of decorum.

Anyway, when I arrived, Karen already had a table, a booth actually. It was at the back of the restaurant, in a somewhat dark section. We had made our plans a little past the normal time for lunch, as the restaurant's major traffic was from the off-work lunch crowd who had to eat and hurry back to their jobs. It was a perfect time, and there were only a few people in the restaurant, and no one near us.

We started out with the usual pleasantries, talked about old friends, and old stories and things that were funny that had happened to us in the past, and then I asked about Jim, her husband.

"He's not doing too well," she said.

The sound of her voice was so sinister, at first I thought she might be referring to some terrible illness, but that was not the case.

"Neither of us are doing well," she said.

My view then changed to a concern for their marriage. I think she saw that in my eyes. She said, "It's not us, dear. It's our house."

"The house?"

Their house had been built on a four-acre tract to their specifications, and it was a two-story nicety with a two-acre front yard packed with flowers, and a two-acre back yard packed with trees, and a little park. I had never been inside, but I had seen it from the outside, and once spent an afternoon in the backyard park visiting with Karen while the house was being built.

Now, considering my profession, my next consideration was that she was talking about a haunting. I have made it clear here before, and in all my books, that I do not believe in ghosts in the classic sense, and that I think there are a number of explanations that are more scientific. Less spirit realm than dimension realm, but this time, well... I'll just let the story unfold and save my analysis. You have asked for a story, not an opinion, and to be honest, I'm not sure what my opinion is in this case.

Anyway, Karen said, "There is something in that house besides us, and it's not rats, and it's not mice, and it has an air of evil about it."

This sounded so melodramatically simplistic; I could barely contain a smile.

"How so?" I said.

"I can't describe it accurately," Karen said, "but simply put, the last few months the nature of the house has changed. Not visually, but... It's just not right, and I have this awful feeling that it's growing worse. As I said, Jim senses it, and he knows it too, but he hasn't been quick to admit it. You know how he feels about what you do—"

"That it's all hokum pocus, and that I'm misguided, but sincere," I said.

"Yeah," Karen said. "That's it. But I know he is uncomfortable there, and he even mentioned something about selling, and moving to a place closer in town. He's never talked like that before, and a few months before he was very happy with the house."

"He doesn't want to admit that he's a little scared?" I said.

"I think that's it."

"All right," I said. "How about you invite me over for dinner, or a game of cards, something, and perhaps I can take the measure of the house."

"I think you might want to stay awhile," Karen said. "I think it would be a way you could feel what we feel, or perhaps explain it away. We have a room at the top of the stairs. You could stay there if you like, but that's where the problems seem most intense. I'm not certain, but I often find the door open, and once I went into the room and found all the furniture rearranged. To put it mildly, I was confused, chilled, and frightened."

I nodded. "It could be a poltergeist, but that's usually associated with children."

"You know Helen is in college, and we don't have any children at home, and no one nearby who has children."

"It's not exclusive to that," I said, "and it involves telekinesis more than it involves spirits from another world."

"Whatever the case, that is just one of many things," Karen said, "and the thing that bothers me most is that it's the unseen things that make me feel the most horrible. I can't stand to be in the house alone. I go out shortly after Jim leaves in the morning for the office, and I stay out until it's time for him to come home. I do my design business on my laptop at the library, or the coffee shop. It's easier that way, as I'm less distracted. In the house, when I'm working, I have the most uncomfortable sensation of someone looking over my shoulder, following me around the house. Of course, when I look, no one is there."

"Besides the rearranging of furniture and a feeling of discomfort," I said, "have there been other events?"

"Perhaps too many to name," Karen said. "And some of them could be my imagination. I'm hoping they all are, though the furniture, that's not an easy one to explain."

"No," I said, "but I have had cases where I discovered that my client, in the middle of the night, sleepwalked and rearranged furniture, and was totally unaware of it. They were their own ghost."

"I don't sleepwalk, that I'm aware of," Karen said, "but I'm more than willing to hope that is exactly what happened. The problem is, it was mid-day."

"You discovered it mid-day, if I understand you correctly," I said. "But it could have been something you or Jim did the night before in your sleep."

"But how could Jim or me move furniture, including relocating a bed with a heavy mattress in the middle of the night, and one of us not hear it? It stretches my imagination more than a ghost. Other things are glimpses of someone moving about in the house. Darting suddenly past doorways, and once, when Jim was late at work, I was in the kitchen, which seems to be the most comfortable place in the house these days, and when I went to the sink to run myself a glass of water, I could have sworn that I not only saw my reflection in the kitchen window, but that behind me, where there's the opening into the main foyer, I saw a figure pass by quickly."

"What kind of figure?" I asked.

"It moved very fast," she said. "But it seemed like a man, perhaps wearing a black coat. The coat flared out as it went; or so it seemed. It was just a glimpse. I picked up a tenderizing mallet and forced myself to go check, but when I got to the foyer, there was nothing. It could easily have darted into one of the rooms along the hall, including the storage closet, but my bravery ended there. I didn't go any further. The foyer was chilled and shadowy, which it shouldn't have been, as I had every light in the house turned on because of the discomfort I felt, and it was not a cold day. I couldn't force myself to go a step farther, and went back to the kitchen."

"Which didn't feel like the rest of the house?" I said.

"It didn't," she said. "Thing is, the house has become miserable. I don't want to stay there any longer, and I think with only a word, I could get Jim to leave the house for good. But damn it, we built that house on that good piece of land, and if you can help me remove whatever the problem is, I'd like to stay there. I, of course, will be more than willing to pay any fee you normally receive."

"Don't be silly," I said. "Let's make arrangements and I'll check it out."

***

We did in fact make arrangements, and I went over for dinner on a cold, late December night. It was a clear night and the stars were as bright as if they had been polished. I pulled in the drive and looked at the house. It was not an old house, though it was made of older lumber and stone. It had none of the appearance usually associated with haunted houses and spirits. It looked like a large, nice, two-story house with dormant flowerbeds and a two-acre backyard of tall pine trees. It was built on the outskirts of town, but there was still a very bright yard light, and the porch light was on, anticipating my arrival. Lights were on downstairs and up; yellow beams gleamed out of all the windows. It had the air of a well-loved home.

I climbed out with my bottle of wine in a gift-wrapped sack, walked up and rang the bell. Karen let me in with much enthusiasm, and Jim greeted me as well. I gave them the wine and we immediately retired to the kitchen. I had not visited Karen and Jim since this house had been finished, and I knew Jim was not entirely aware of why I had been invited, but considering their circumstances and my profession, I doubted he was totally in the dark as to why I was there. I assumed he knew it was more than just a friendly visit. Still, I decided not to mention my conversation with Karen until an appropriate time. I had no intention of ruining a nice evening, and a visit with old friends that I had been away from for far too long.

On our way to the kitchen, I glanced across the foyer, which was decorated with a Christmas tree—though the holiday was still a few days off—and into the open dining room. There was a long plank table covered in a light blue tablecloth, and the positions where we were to sit were prepared with dinnerware. I could see to the far left of the dining room a broad opening that bled into a living room. Stairs were visible directly across from the foyer. They proceeded up to a brightly lit hallway and onto the second floor. As I said before, the house seemed to be lit up with every light available.

The kitchen was warm with the heat of the stove where our dinner cooked, and the light there seemed almost loving. There was a small table with stools around it, and we seated ourselves and Jim took the wine and opened it and poured it for us. For the first hour, our conversation was typical of friends who had not seen each other in a while. Catching up on our activities, continuing from where Karen and I had left off in the restaurant, with me avoiding any details of previous adventures, making sure there was not an allusion to the subject that was truly at hand. I kept all of my conversation on simple matters of who I was dating at the moment, or had been dating. I did talk about my travels, but only in a kind of tourist manner, not mentioning that many of my overseas activities had to do with my peculiar line of work.

Karen and Jim told me about their life. Karen was doing well as a designer, and Jim's law practice, specializing in probate law, the clarification of wills, was doing a tremendous business. After a while the talk slowed down. The dinner was ready, and we all helped bring the food to the table in the dining room, sat down and prepared to eat.

It was shortly after this that things changed.

***

As we ate, a shadow walked, not flowed, across the table. That's it; simple as that, a shadow. It was a jagged shadow that had some kind of silhouette reminiscent of human shape; a tall, hook-nosed man clothed in a flared coat. It walked on the tabletop from one end to the other with a heavy tread that made the table shake. The very air around it vibrated in the manner of cold gelatin shaking on a plate, and like the gelatin, the air was cold, arctic cold. The food I had just eaten felt uneasy in my stomach.

We all turned our heads to look as it stepped off the table and moved quickly toward the stairs. Instead of proceeding up the stair steps, as someone's shadow might, it came to the rail, and wrapped its shadowy arms and legs around it, and began to slither up the banister in a rapid, serpent like manner. At the top of the stairs, where before it had been bright with light, it was dark as the inside of a croaker sack now, and it was into this darkness that the shadowy shape slipped. If it hadn't been so bizarre, it would have almost been comical. I can say that now, in retrospect, but in the moment of the occurrence, it was anything but humorous.

After it enveloped itself in the shadows, the shadows went away, but I can't for the life of me define that moment. They were there in one instant, gone the next, and the top of the stairs was as bright as before.

I heard Jim let out his breath, and slide his chair back. Karen reached out and took his hand. Jim said, "Dana, I'm glad you're here."

***

Dinner ended at that moment, at least the semi-formal part of it. Some of the food was carried into the kitchen and placed on the little table. Bread was pulled from the cabinet, and we made sandwiches with the chicken, and coffee was boiled. In the kitchen the atmosphere was different. It was akin to a feeling that we were encased in a castle, and outside there was a bear at the gate. Certainly ferocious, but as long as we were where we were, we were safe.

I filed this feeling away for further consideration.

We talked as we ate, and Jim said, "I've tried to deny it for some time. I even thought it was my imagination, as it's been mostly a feeling, and things Karen has told me... and forgive me dear. I thought perhaps you were stressed, or... I don't know."

"No need to worry about that," Karen said, touching his arm. "Go on. Finish."

"But this is the first time I've actually seen... What would be the word?"

"Manifestation will do," I said.

"Yes," he said. "There was the furniture moved about in the upstairs bedroom, but I thought that was, and forgive me, hon, but I thought that was sleepwalking on Karen's part, though I thought it unusual I hadn't heard her in there going at it, and certainly there was the size of the bed. But what other explanation could there be? Sometimes I can sleep quite deeply. Or maybe I sleepwalked. I just couldn't accept anything else. Until now."

He paused and sipped his coffee. I saw that his hand was shaking; so much he had to use the other to steady his cup. Eventually he took a sip and set the cup down.

"You being here, Dana, actually helps me to embrace the idea more easily. I have for some time had the unfathomable sensation of someone being in the house. I marked it up to the newness of the place, hearing unfamiliar sounds of wood shifting, the wind fluttering through the trees out back, causing leaves to shake and boughs to wobble. Thinking I saw something move out of the corner of my eye, only to turn and find nothing. Have you ever seen anything like this?"

"Not exactly," I said, "but like it, yes. What it means, I can't say. All of these so-called hauntings have certain similarities. What we saw a few minutes ago was a bold threat."

"Threat?" Jim said.

"Yes," I said. "It somehow knows who I am and what I do, and it may even fear me a little. It doesn't want to leave. It wants you to leave. So it's decided to reveal itself in a bold manner, hoping to frighten you off."

"It's working," Karen said.

"You said 'so called' spirits," Jim said. "What do you mean?"

"I believe they are less spirits of the dead, than they are dimensional worlds that slip into ours. I think this explains ghosts, demons, goblins, the devil, gods and imps, and so on."

"But," Jim said, "in the end, it really doesn't matter what the cause is, does it?"

"I suppose not," I said.

"And it can't hurt us, can it?"

I hesitated. "Most of the time, no."

"Most of the time?" Karen said.

"Often these things, whatever they are, are benign," I said. "But not always."

"So you've encountered some that are dangerous?" Jim asked.

I nodded. "I have. All manner."

"Are we safe?" Karen said.

"I don't think so," I said.

***

"The kitchen seems so calm," Karen said.

I nodded. "Sometimes certain parts of a house are possessed, for lack of a better word, while other portions are not. It is occasionally due to there being a dimensional break in one area. There are times when that restricts the unwelcome visitor from another location. From time to time it's certain protections. Crosses. Spells. It doesn't really have to do with religion, it has to do with human intent. When people make these sort of holy items, be they of devil worship, Christian, Muslim, or any sincere source, they take on power. It is a natural power given to us by nature, I believe. But we manifest it best through talismans. We think it is our religion, or our god, or our demons that protect us, when it fact, it is our deep-down well of intent. Even then, that's not always enough. I use a variety of talismans, and I have had them all blessed by true believers."

"But you're not one?" Karen said.

"Not in what they believe, but in the strength of their beliefs," I said. "Not having that foundation, I can't bless things myself, so therefore I can't just create talismans. It sounds odd, I know. However, that's how I see it, and I've had just as much success, or lack of success, with items of Christianity, devil worship, you name it."

"So we're safe here?" Jim said.

"Right now it seems that way," I said. "But it can change. It could just be coincidence, or there could be some powerful reason you are safe here, but not elsewhere in the house. Perhaps, in time, the kitchen will no longer be off limits. It could gain strength. There are a lot of factors."

"Should we stay here?" Karen asked, squeezing Jim's hand.

"I don't think so," I said. "If I have your permission, I'd like to bring in my crew, see what we can find, and see too if we can deliver you from it. Either send it back from where it came, or destroy it. I would suggest just leaving. Walking from here to the door and driving away to a motel for the night. Pick up some things at a store tomorrow, and prepare to dig in for a while."

"How long a while?" Jim asked.

I shook my head. "I can't say. And understand, I also can't say for sure the house is dangerous, but I suggest we err on the side of caution."

We tipped our coffee quickly, and walked out of the kitchen toward the door. And I do not exaggerate in the least when I say that that walk from the wide open kitchen to the front door, a matter of ten feet, felt as if it took a week. The air in that part of the house had become heavy as lead, and there was that horrid feeling of being watched, and of something most unkind being close by. The air tasted like copper.

Once we were outside, I bid Jim and Karen goodbye, and when their car lights were out of sight, I went to my car and got out my bag, which looks like an old-style doctor's bag, and stood looking at the house. I could have called my assistants, but I wanted to check a few things first, to see if we were up against something truly dangerous, or if I was in fact overstating the case.

I was only a little surprised when I looked up to see that the top floor was no longer lit, and that it was so dark it appeared to have been dipped into a syrupy gloom. It was almost as if this thing, whatever it was, had been waiting on me to show up. As if it knew who I was, and it wanted a challenge.

I took a deep breath and went back inside.

***

Just inside the door, the air was still heavy and foul, but it had gone from chill to being cold as the arctic. It was as if during my brief absence a furious blizzard had blown through and left icy air in its wake. I pulled a sweater from my bag and slipped it on. It only helped a little.

Except for the lighting having gone out everywhere but the kitchen, it all looked the same. The table in the dining room was still partially set, and the stairs were cloaked in shadow. I bent down and got out a book of prayers from many different religions, and read aloud from them. Upstairs, I could hear clanging and banging, and finally a loud moan that shook the house, and almost shook my resolve.

I stayed steadfast in the foyer, however, and read through the prayer book, which took some time, and all the while I did it, the house shook and things clunked upstairs and there was that horrid moaning that grew louder and seemed to climb inside my flesh and shake my bones. At the end of the prayers there came a scream like a banshee falling off a cliff. I had made a number of copies of the prayer book, all designed so that I might rip out the pages. I also had with me a small bottle of roll-on glue I could use to stick the pages to the wall, furniture, what have you. I took my little flashlight from the bag and gripped it between my teeth, began my investigation by pushing one of the prayers against the front door, and then as I walked, I placed others against the wall and on the landing of the stairs as I attempted to start up.

I took only one step before stopping. I have dealt with many things, but in that moment I knew my prayers had actually done nothing to contain the powers of this entity. They had only served to aggravate it. How I knew this I can't explain, but I honestly believe had I chosen to go up those stairs then, secure that I had somehow, even if temporarily, bound this terrible creature, I would have been walking into a trap of my own overconfidence. There was a moment when I even thought I heard the thing upstairs breathe with a sigh of anticipation. What I would have walked into had I continued to the upper landing is beyond my knowing, but I am certain it would not have been pleasant.

I managed to swallow without the little flashlight in my teeth going down my throat, tore a page from the book, applied the roll on glue, and put it on the stairway, dead center. When that was done, I stuck a page on either side of that step, then retreated to the kitchen. It was like stepping out of an icy climate into a tropical one. The kitchen was warm, the light golden. Fear oozed away from me like sweat. I took the light out of my mouth, turned it off, and sat down on one of the stools because I had to. I took off the sweater, which now felt too warm, returned it to my bag, and tried to gather myself.

In a short time I knew it was best I leave this house, and not return until daylight, when the powers of these kinds of things were usually less powerful. I would need more than my little black bag for this, and I would need my assistants.

As I sat there, I caught movement out of the corner of my eye, in the darker part of the house. When I glanced up, there was nothing solid, though I swear the darkness in there rippled like oily water for a moment. This was followed by a sound akin to rats, or an infestation of thumb-sized cockroaches rambling about within the walls. Then, there was silence.

I walked to the edge of the wide opening that led into the foyer, glanced toward the front door. I noticed that the page of prayers I had stuck there was still in place, but there was a difference.

I turned on the flashlight, and carrying it in one hand and my bag in the other, I walked briskly toward it. Again, it felt like a long walk, and the air was not only colder than before, it had become fouler, like the stench of road kill. At the door, I examined the prayer. It had been written over in a color that can only be described as shadow.

It read: MINE.

I tore the page off the door and went out into the much warmer air, climbed into my car and drove away at a brisk rate of speed.

***

I put my assistants, Nora and Gary, to work right away, asking them to use not only our sizable library, contacts and the internet, but to go downtown and use newspaper files and city records as well; things that might not be in our vast collection, or readily available by using the computer. My idea was to see if there was any written record of strange doings in the area where the house now stood; they might be stored away somewhere that had not seen the light of day for some time.

While they went about this chore, I drove over to the hotel where Jim and Karen were staying. It was a nice hotel, and they offered me breakfast and coffee. We ate and I told them what I had experienced, showed them the prayer page with the note that had been written over it. The writing was fading. It was my guess that the page would soon be only a page of exotic prayers from a variety of sources.

"What do you make of it?" Jim said.

"The obvious thing is that whatever is in the house," I said, "and I have no doubt that whatever is there is dangerous—wants you out. I think it wants me out more than you."

"You?" Karen asked.

I nodded. "It knows of my capabilities, if I may so immodestly mention them, and it sees me as a bigger threat. It realizes my intention is to remove it from the premises."

"Can you remove it?" Jim asked.

"So far, I'm batting a thousand. So, yes, I think so. But at the moment I'm trying to determine exactly what it is I'm dealing with. I would ask a few things of you."

"Anything," Karen said, "if it will get what's in the house out of it."

"First off, stay away from the house. I know how inconvenient it is, but truthfully, without being too melodramatic, I think you made your exit just in time. Whatever is in the house is becoming stronger, more possessive of its territory. So you must stay away. Second, you have to give me carte blanche to be at your house, with my assistants, as frequently as I need be."

"Granted," Jim said.

"And one last thing," I said, "if you think of anything different that occurred in your lives around the time of this haunting, or before, or at any time, I would appreciate you letting me know. Sometimes the smallest, most inconsequential thing can initiate these events. It doesn't have to be a big thing, anything unusual."

"Of course," Karen said.

I looked at Jim. He seemed to be thinking on the matter. "Yes, certainly," he said.

After our visit, I met up with Nora and Gary at the office. Gary, nestled in one of the comfy chairs, his feet on a cushioned stool, said, "We've looked at so many records about this county and city, I think I could write a history. But as to the property in question? Nothing unusual."

I glanced at Nora. "Same," she said.

"Very well," I said. "It's not always necessary to know the source to get rid of this sort of inconvenience, but it helps. I think the next step is we move to the house for a few days and see if our unwanted visitor presents itself again, which I'm sure it will."

When we arrived in the middle of the day on Christmas Eve, the house lights were all on, brightly shining, upstairs and down. I had left so abruptly, I hadn't bothered to turn them off. The air was no longer chill, nor did it have the horrid smell I had previously encountered, but the air was stale; it was a dry unpleasant aroma, halitosis of the house.

The kitchen became our command center. We brought sleeping bags, food—though Jim and Karen assured us that anything in the house was at our disposal—and other items we needed, including some equipment like infra-red digital video-recording devices, and so on. Our stay might be only a few hours; it might be a few days. It depended on how well things went.

The kitchen had a short hallway that connected it to a bathroom down the way, and though it was small, it seemed to be within the area of security, so it was convenient, having a sink and toilet. If we needed a shower, it would have to wait.

As we set up, hauled our needs in from the van we used for these cases—we called it our Scooby Doo van—I said, "Don't become too lax. It's here. And it's waiting. The daylight may weaken its powers, but it doesn't mean they're eliminated."

"We have done this before," Nora said.

"I know," I said. "But there's something about this case. Something that makes me feel overly cautious. Stay alert."

***

I stood at the bottom of the stairs and looked for the prayers I had left. There were only shreds of them lying about. Still, I could tell things were different now than the night I was there. At this time of day the thing's powers appeared weaker, or perhaps it was merely out of range, in some dimensional hole.

"All right," I said to myself. "It begins."

At the top of the stairs we set up the recording devices. Unique video cameras, sensitive to movement, infra-red, and with terrific sound. They were designed so that they stuck easily to the walls and clung there like spiders. We put one at the top of the stairs looking down, another at the bottom looking up.

When we had the video cameras arranged, we went into the bedroom, the one where Karen said the furniture had been rearranged. The furniture was all in its place now. It was a large room and the bed was huge. We moved the bed away from its spot to a corner of the room. It was a difficult thing to do, and assured me that no one had sleepwalked in the middle of the night and moved it about.

In the center of the room, I drew with voodoo-blessed chalk a circle with a pentagram inside. It was a very large symbol, so large we were able to pull the bed back and place it inside the circle of protection. I then made sure that the pulling of the bed had not destroyed any part of the circle. For added protection, just above the doorway to the hall, I drew a smaller pentagram with the same chalk. I took cursed wax (let me remind you again, I use curses as well as blessings) that had been made from the bodies of ancients—please don't ask how I came by it—and used it to seal the bottom and top and edges of the doorway, the edges of the window panes, for there were two windows in the bedroom, one on either side of where the bed had been placed.

I positioned one video-recording device on the wall, looking across the bed toward the bedroom entrance. I shook out some old bones from my kit. They were said to be the bones of a powerful wizard down New Orleans way. I also had what is sometimes called a Mojo Hand, which is the withered hand of a dead man, the tips of the fingers arranged with bits of blessed wax that can be lit to make a five point candle. I moved a small end table inside the circle, next to the bed, and positioned a cigarette lighter on the table next to the Mojo Hand. On the other side of the bed, on the floor about a foot out, but still some ways from the chalk edge of the circle, I arranged the bones.

After this was prepared, I took out a bottle of holy water from the bag, as well as several books of prayers, and placed them at the end of the bed facing the door.

"Don't you think you're a bit overly prepared?" Nora said.

"No such thing," I said. "You need to learn that. You can't be overly prepared. And in this case, I'm not sure we're prepared enough."

"You really think it's that powerful?" she asked.

"I do," I said.

I even drew a series of small pentagrams that led off of the larger one that led to the bathroom. I thought it necessary for obvious reasons. Even ghost hunters have to pee. I drew a pentagram halfway around the toilet and up against the wall, drew another on the wall behind the toilet. I thought that if some horror were to take me, I would not want it to be at that moment, if I could possibly prevent it.

***

We removed our shoes and all three of us sat up in the bed, waiting. Gary had brought a paperback and was reading it. Nora dozed, and I just waited. I tried to imagine all manner of scenarios and how I would handle them. Finally it seemed as if my mind slipped into a kind of grayness, and I lay down and dozed beside Nora.

When I awoke it was because of the air in the room. It had become heavy and uncomfortable to breathe. I sat up in bed, aware of a sensation of something outside of our realm focusing all of its energy on this room. It was uncomfortable. Gary was still sitting on the bed with his book, but now it was on his knee and he was looking off toward the hallway. He turned and looked at me and swallowed.

Nora sat up and gave me a glance, said, "I take it back. I'm not sure you brought enough stuff."

"You can sense it?" I said.

"I know I can," Gary said, tossing his book on the floor.

"Yes," Nora said, "and it is horrible. It's coming up the stairs."

None of us knew this by witness, but we all knew it by instinct, perhaps a primitive instinct imbedded in our brains as a form of warning, protection. Slowly, something was making its way up the stairs. Why it had been in the lower parts of the house and not the upper where it was stronger, I can't say, but up the stairs it came, and I could feel its strength growing.

"It's in the hall, near the door," Nora said, by way of running commentary.

"Be quiet, and focus," I said. I leaned out and picked up the lighter from the nightstand and lit the mojo hand, sat back and waited.

It was indeed at the door. It breathed heavily outside of it. The knob began to turn slowly, but the lock held. The door was pushed at; a hard shove that made the wood groan. And then there was a pounding, as if whatever was out there had fists the size of my head. The pounding rattled the door and shook the very air in the room, which had turned cold and stale, the way it had been that night in the foyer. Our breath came out in little white clouds.

Then the hammering stopped. I couldn't hear the breathing either, but I knew it was not gone.

The way we were set, the backyard light came through the bedroom windows and streamed across the floor and fell against the bedroom door. I could see the trail of wax at the bottom of the door, and along its top and sides. The wax at the bottom of the door began to vibrate, and then it became thin, as if melting, and before long there was a crack of light at the bottom of the door. The shadow of an arm reached quick under that crack and kept reaching, way, way out, until it came to the edge of the pentagram. One long dark finger of shadow lifted and pecked at the edge of the barrier. There was a shock sound and a zip of blue lightning. A roar came from the thing outside the door. The shadow hand and arm fled back beneath it, and was immediately followed by a terrible thrashing against the door. The lock snapped. Wood flew. The door swung open, and...

I wish I could describe it as well as I saw it. It was more than a gloomy shape now. It had the general countenance of a human being, but there was something bestial about it; a flash of teeth wiped by shadow, burning eyes dropped down deep in a face so dark, a pit would be considered a bright place to be. The stench that came off of it was like a blow. The mojo hand's five lit points flickered out.

The thing came through the door as if shot from a cannon, not touching the floor, not running, not moving like anything alive, but like a dart of frozen smoke. It hit the edge of the pentagram and there was a flare of blue and red flame that licked up and covered the fiend so that I could see it more clearly. The dark face was of an old man with hard, bony features that housed an intense anger; or rather, it barely housed it, and it was easy to understand in that moment that the anger of this thing was its foul engine. I knew then something else. For the first time in my experience I had encountered a true spirit, a ghost, a specter of someone formerly alive. Not an astral projection. Not a thing from another dimension, but a thing from a spirit world I had previously denied. The wraith of someone so full of anger and hatred, its anger and hatred had lived beyond the grave and had become horridly toxic and able to withstand death.

It came again. It hit hard and harder at the pentagram. The chalk line began to waver.

I reached in my bag and pulled out a bottle of holy water and stood upright in the bed just as it broke through. I had only taken the cap off, when it grabbed Gary by the leg, and flung him as effortlessly as it might a chicken through the air and into the wall near the doorway. He smacked hard, fell against the floor, and didn't move. Nora shrieked.

I flung the water from the bottle with a flick of my hand. The shadow burst into flames and blasted backwards as if blown that way by hurricane force; the flames licked around it and over it, and then they were gone, leaving it still there in all its hard and terrible darkness.

This time it dropped down to the floor, thin as the edge of a knife, and went under the bed. The bed rumbled and rumpled underneath my bare feet. There was a bump in the center of the bed, and the blankets rose up, then a sharp and shadowy finger tore through the mattress. Then its whole shadow-hand was through, then its arm. It grabbed my ankle. It was as if I had been gripped in a vice and it burned like dry ice. I flung the last of my Holy water down on the gripping hand. It snapped loose. I staggered back. Nora was striking the thing with the book of prayers, slapping the book against it with all the effect of slapping an elephant on the rump with a paper fan.

The bed rose up and flipped backwards. I hit the wall as the bed rocked over and tumbled to the left, trapping Nora under it. I blinked, and in that short time, its face was right against mine. Oh, what a horror. I can't describe. I can't. I can only tell you that of all the things I've faced, in that moment, I may have been the most frightened.

"Mine," it said, and its breath was as if from a dumpster. I rolled rapidly, trying to get away from it, but it snatched my ankle again and began jerking me across the floor. It slung me into a wall so hard I was stunned, if not unconscious. For a long moment, I couldn't place where I was. By the time I determined I was near the bathroom door, I was grabbed by my shirt collar and dragged toward light.

***

It was Nora. She had me and was pulling me across the pentagram. I thought that my body might be disturbing the chalk, but I was too weak to get to my feet, and too stunned to protest.

In a moment, I found myself in the bathroom, saw that she had dragged Gary there ahead of me. My feet were in one of the smaller pentagrams I had drawn as a pathway, and my butt was in the bigger one, my back was resting against the toilet itself. Gary was still unconscious, placed sitting up, just inside the pentagram, his back touching the one I had drawn on the wall. Nora perched on the closed toilet lid like a harpy, clutching one of the prayer books in her hands. She was reading rapidly from it, trying to hold back what was about to rush through the doorway.

As it came in a dark wind-rustling rush, it shrieked, and was then knocked backwards as if it had been nothing more than a dark sheet yanked back by someone strong.

I managed to stand. I stepped quickly to the light switch and jerked it on.

It was at the door again. It happened so abruptly, I leaped back with a little shriek I'm not exactly proud of. The old man's face was clear now, and there was such a look of anger and disappointment on it, I almost felt sorry for it. Almost.

Then, it was gone as if it had never been.

I'm not sure how long we remained in the bathroom, or how much time I spent trying to discover why we were protected there, and why we had not been safe in the bedroom with its greater protections. By the time morning came, I felt that I had the answer. All I had to do then was verify it.

When it was solidly day we no longer felt its ponderous presence. It was like having an elephant lifted off our chests. Gary was sore, but up and around, and I was limping, but I felt good enough to help gather what equipment it was necessary to collect, and then we were out of there.

I'll be honest with you. I never had any intention of coming back. At least not as an explorer in that terrible house.

And that was our Christmas morning.

***

For the record, we looked at the digital recordings. The stair recorders were for me one of the most disconcerting. It took a bit of straining of the eyes, but in time, there was a dark whirl of shadow, and then the shadow collected into human-like form, and it walked in an odd manner to the stairs. It didn't bother with the steps. Like a lizard it clutched the railing and slithered up with a speed that belied human abilities. At the top of the stairs the shape became nothing more in the video camera than a wall of shadow. And then it was out of sight. There was the sound of pounding on the door, the breaking of the lock and door, all the sounds that had gone on in that room.

As for the video cameras in the bedroom itself...

Nothing but darkness. Perhaps it had become too intense by that time to be recorded by digital means. I don't know exactly, but in the bedroom there was nothing of it, just the tossing of Gary across the room, the turning over of the bed. But unlike outside of the room, what was causing all of it, what we had seen, was not visible on our devices.

Sometime later, on the upstairs recorder, it was seen again. Making a kind of elongated, shadowy, old man shape; it gripped the banister, and moving head first, with that lizard-like assurance of before, down the banister it went. When it came to the bottom, it leapt off into...

...nothingness. Not even shadow.

It was gone.

This video camera showing was at our office, and I had invited Jim and Karen to watch. When it finished, I turned and looked at Jim.

"Heavens," he said.

Karen said, "It's hard to believe. Why couldn't we see it in the bedroom?"

I told them what I expected, that it may have been due to the intensity of the thing. I really didn't have a true explanation.

I gave Nora and Gary a look. They took note of it and left the room. I turned back to Jim. "When I talked to you about anything you might know that might help this investigation, you hesitated. I caught it then, but the other night, in the bathroom, it came to me. The bathroom and the kitchen, all of the house on that side, are not affected by this thing. There has to be a reason. I don't know exactly what that reason is, but I think you do. I'm not accusing you of anything. But I believe you had a thought cross your mind, just a thought, but it wasn't something you could hold onto. Or it was just so wild you couldn't embrace it. Am I right, Jim?"

Jim nodded. "Yes."

"For God's sake, Jim," Karen said. "What is it?"

"Garren McDowell," he said. "I did his will. The face on that thing on the video. It's his. I've seen his photograph in the records given to me. That's him."

"But there's more to it than that, isn't there?" I asked.

Jim nodded. "Yes. No one in his family wanted anything to do with him. He hadn't really left anything to anyone anyway. It was a complicated mess, but somehow I was able, through a tremendous amount of legal wrangling, to save the property for his heirs. Only thing was, when it was finally decided they owned it, none of them wanted it. His niece, who I suppose is in her late twenties, said she only wanted it so she could burn the house and raze the land with a bulldozer. There was one problem, however. I hadn't been paid."

"Let me guess," I said. "You took the land in payment."

"I did," he said.

"I remember," Karen said. "You mentioned it."

"I didn't think all that much about it, but there were some peculiarities. I had been forced to do similar things in the past, but the niece said something peculiar when I explained that I had not been paid, and that she should sell the land to pay my fee. She said, 'He has done all he will ever do to me now. I'm glad to be shed of him and anything that's his. You keep it and sell it.'

"I gave it a day, thinking she might just be angry at the old man about something. But it was more than anger; it was far deeper than that. I had my suspicions as to the cause, but now that he was dead, there really was nothing to say. I made the proper arrangements and the property became mine.

"I owned it before I saw it. It was the only payment I was going to get, so I had accepted it sight unseen. I drove out to take a look. It was about twenty acres covered in trees, but the ugliest trees you can imagine. No pines, all hardwoods, but the soil there must have been bad, because they were all twisted and stunted. The house was at the end of a gravel road. At the time, I thought it was silly, but merely seeing it made me a little ill, akin to looking into a pit and seeing that a terrible massacre of children had taken place there. I can't explain exactly why I use that analogy, but it's the one that came to mind then, and it's what I am reminded of now. I thought what I was feeling was due to something I had eaten that morning, but after you telling me what happened to you and your assistants, and seeing his image on camera... Well, the house was huge and well made, with wonderful lumber. It had been carefully crafted, but the house itself was built in an irregular style, as if it had been added onto by someone with no sense of symmetry or common sense. I took the key and unlocked the door, and went into the foyer. There were a number of antiques that I thought I could sell, and I continued to marvel at the materials that had been used to build the house. But the place made me uncomfortable. There was a huge stairway with nice railings and I decided to go up the stairs and take a look around, but I only got halfway up and couldn't continue.

"I quit. I felt that at the top of those stairs something was waiting. At the time, I concluded it might be a wild animal that had found its way inside. Maybe something rabid. Okay, let me add this. I considered it might be more than an animal. But it was a fleeting feeling. I turned around and went out of there quickly, locked the door and drove away. I never went back. I sent some people in to get the antiques, but I had to send three different moving companies to get it all. Each one did a bit of work and then quit on me. At the time I thought it odd, and of course, I had had peculiar experiences in the house, but since I credited that to my imagination, I didn't put it all together; wasn't ready to accept there was something really wrong with the house."

"But there's more to the story, isn't there?" I said.

"Yes. When we were building our house, I remembered the fine lumber in that one, and I had the house torn down and used the wood here. I told you about it, Karen. About it being lumber from a property I had ended up with."

"I remember," she said.

"By then," he said, "I had dismissed the unusual feelings I had in the house. Shoved them to the back of my mind. We used that lumber to build our home."

"But not all of the house," I said.

"Some of the old house was spoiled by weather and termites. It had to be burned. The workmen, they told me they found all manner of odd books in the house, leather bound, and asked if I wanted them. I'm a fanatic for books. I love them. But for some reason I knew I didn't want those. I told them to burn them, and as far as I know, they did. The lumber we used was good for most of the house, but—"

"The kitchen area, the bathroom above," I said, "that was a different source."

"Correct," Jim said. "Right from the lumber yard."

"That's part of the answer," I said. "I don't know the old man's history, but I can guess that it was one of debauchery. I can guess that those books were on dark subjects. And I can be sure that the house he lived in had soaked up his soul. So when you built your home, you brought him with you."

Karen shook as if cold.

Jim said, "Another thing. For no reason I can explain, when I got back to the office that day, I found the few photographs of Garren McDowell that had come by way of his niece, along with a large number of papers, and burned them in the trashcan. I have never had an urge to do such a thing before, but that day I did. I burned them and felt good about it."

"What do we do?" Karen said.

"I'll be straight with you," I said. "There is only one thing to do."

***

On a bright, early January morning, Jim and Karen went into the house with a large number of hired hands and hastily carried out what little they wanted, leaving the furniture, a large number of clothes, dishes and a variety of other items. They refused to sell the house, not wishing to pass along Mr. Garren McDowell to anyone else.

I asked if they might make a deal with me. I got it for a song, not because I drove a hard bargain, but because they refused to have me pay very much for a house that was dangerously haunted.

Not long after I took ownership, there was a huge fire. Arson, it's thought. I won't say anymore on that matter, lest it cause me problems. But once it was burned to the ground, I had the entire place bulldozed, trees and all, as they had almost overnight become sickly, weak, and stunted. I drive by the land from time to time, and if I so much as see a sprig popping up, I cut it down and dig out the roots. I never intend to build there or allow anything to grow that might house that horrible man's spirit.

Even now, I can't quite decide if I won that battle, or have merely stalemated Garren McDowell.

***

Dana finished her tale and leaned back in her chair. She had been leaning forward as she talked.

She said, "Now, after that dark story, I think we should indulge in the Christmas spirit."

No one disagreed. Dana was the first out of her chair, heading toward the bar. The night went quickly, and even with drinks and conversation on other matters, Dana's tale lingered.

At one point I thought of a couple of things I might like to ask her about her story. Some points that I wanted her to expound on, but when I looked for her, she had already left.

The Case of the Angry Traveler

by Joe R. Lansdale

When Dana Roberts arrived she went straight away to the storyteller chair and sat down and took the drink offered her. She was certainly her usual attractive self, but there was about her an air of exhaustion. Without any fanfare, she launched straight away into her story.

As was the custom, I recorded it and then typed up the transcript. I call it the Case of the Angry Traveler. Melodramatic, I admit, but there you have it.

This is what Dana told us.

***

I received a call from a friend of mine—we'll call him Frank—who works as an exterminator in a large city. I won't name the city, since this tale will be published, and I won't name my friend or any of his associates by their real names. I will provide names, but understand, they are contrived so that those involved shall remain nameless. The exception to that will be the names of my assistants, which are correct. All of you here, of course, know who they are from at least one of my previous narratives.

On a blustery fall day when I was at home with a mild case of the common cold, sitting up in bed with a lap tray, sipping coffee, the phone rang. It was my friend the exterminator.

Perhaps I should also explain that big city exterminators are not at all what you might think. They certainly do not fit the stereotype of a greasy man in overalls with a rattrap slung over one shoulder, a string of dead rodents being dragged behind him on a chain.

It is actually, at least in the city I'm talking about, a respected business. Someone has to take care of the vermin, and my friend is a specialist, well trained in the science of insects and rodents, all manner of animals, reptiles, etc., that might pose a problem to residents of the city. In many cases, a simple trapping is all that's necessary. He has told me numerous accounts of removing large reptiles, pythons in particular, from numerous homes and apartment complexes in the city. Often he removes them from toilets, as from time to time they arrive there from the sewers below, as do rats. It sounds like an urban myth, but I assure you it has happened, and will happen again. He kills the rats, the snakes he often gives to zoos or research centers. But, that is neither here nor there, other than to let you know that Frank is a professional. So, when I got a phone call from him asking for my help, I was surprised.

"I believe I've come across something new," he said, "and I was wondering if you might be willing to lend me a hand."

"To chase rats?"

"No. It isn't a rat. As I said, it's something new. Something most peculiar and it might lend itself to your particular talents."

"My talents?"

"Yes."

"You mean you are dealing with the supernormal? Your pest is supernormal?"

"To be honest, I don't know, but I suspect that could be the case. Perhaps, in the long run, it will turn out to be quite normal, but so far the common methods of removing pests have failed, and this particular pest seems to be more than a little vicious."

He had piqued my curiosity, I must say. I sat up straighter in bed with the phone in one hand, my cup of coffee in the other. I sipped the coffee and put it on the tray and leaned back into my pillows.

"Tell me about it," I said.

"Three days ago I was asked to check out an apartment on the Upper East Side. I was directed to the toilet of a small, but well cared for home, and in the toilet I found a large rat. He had come up through the drains. They can swim well and are fantastic survivors, so this unto itself isn't unique.

"Anyway, I dispatched the bugger and took him away. There was something odd about the critter though. He was nine inches long, not counting tail. That is a big rat. A uniquely large rat. I was curious enough to take photos of it and carried it back to the laboratory. I decided to perform a rodent autopsy. When I cut it open, I was surprised to find a small piece of a human finger. The finger tip and the nail to be exact."

"My goodness."

"Not exactly what I said in the moment of discovery, Dana, but the sentiment is there. I immediately contacted the police. They came and took it away, and the police lab technician, who is a friend of mine, called me the next day to tell me that the finger was fresh, meaning that it hadn't been taken by the rat too long ago, and that it had come from an elderly man, most likely malnourished and dead when the rat had its lunch."

"A homeless person, perhaps," I said, and as soon as I did, I somehow felt snobby.

"A strong possibility," Frank said. "Perhaps he crawled down in the sewer, as many do, to find a place to sleep, or rest, died, and a rat came along and bit off a portion of his finger."

"It's intriguing," I said, "but I don't see how this has anything to do with me. It sounds like you have a dead body to find. Or the police do."

"I'm coming to that, Dana. Bear with me. So, we try and trace the possible path of the rat, and since it came up through a sewer pipe, and found its way into a home, that isn't easy. That small piece of human flesh had set something uncommon in motion.

"Soon, I was aiding the police, and we were searching the sewers. They are quite deep and very complex, and many of the routes below were constructed at an earlier time. And there are areas beneath where the old city was. Large areas. This means there are buildings down there."

"Buildings?"

"Exactly," Frank said. "There are shops and alleys and even houses of a far earlier time. Recently, ruins below those known ruins were found. The ruins I knew about were from the eighteen hundreds, with some remnants from the seventeen hundreds, but these were earlier yet. Much earlier. Quite crude. Mud buildings. Narrow cobblestone streets, damp with dripping moisture from above. Archeological layers of civilized development.

"The upper sewer paths have lights. Limited, but there are lights for construction, and for me to be about my job, and for archaeologists to noodle about. But the lower cities, the recently discovered ones, are not lit. I saw them first by flash and head-lamp."

"And this all has to do with the finding of a piece of human finger inside a slightly oversized rat?"

"It does," he said. "I determined from my own investigation the likely area in the sewer where the rat had come from. An area where the above locations provide sufficient waste from restaurants and homes to allow the sort of diet that might lend itself to such a large sized rodent. A rat that would be willing to come topside for that kind of nourishment. It could easily have gotten into a pipe, looking for a short cut, and ended up in a toilet.

"It also struck me, that if I were a homeless man, and I were struggling to survive, that like the rats, I would visit this area as well. Meaning the spot that provided the better hand outs, and the superior toss outs in the dumpsters."

"But didn't you say the finger indicated that he was undernourished?" I said.

"Better nourished than he might have been, is my guess," Frank said. "Not as well nourished as the rat, but better than he would have been without access to those dumpsters. And maybe he hadn't been visiting the area long. It was all a guess, Dana. Anyway, I went there and looked around.

"The weather was cold, and it occurred to me without too much use of the brain cells, that a homeless person might be desperate to find a warm place to sleep. Of course, our missing man could have died anywhere, but I was just following hunches, aided by a bit of logic, so the truth is, I wasn't expecting to actually find the remains of our missing man.

"Just as I was about to leave, I spied a grate in the alley wall, about three feet behind a large dumpster. I removed the grate and looked into the darkness. I chose this spot, because the grate came loose easily, and I could tell without too intensive an examination that someone had been removing it and replacing it; the wall was scraped considerably from this action, and the screws that should have held it in place had been removed. The only thing that contained it was its snug fit.

"I had my head-lamp, and I fastened it on, and before entering, examined the blueprints I have of below. When I had put them to memory, I folded them up and placed them in my fanny pack, and entered the opening on hands and knees.

"Inside there were a number of rags, and I deduced these had been placed there as a kind of mat for the knees. The way the opening was, you had to crawl along for about ten feet before it widened, and there was a manhole without a lid that led down into the sewer. It was dark there, and unless whoever was crawling along had a light, or they knew the way by experience, it could easily turn out to be a death trap. It was quite a fall without service of the ladder.

"I carefully took hold of the damp metal ladder and went down. The smell was foul, not only from the sewer, but from the odor of unwashed human bodies. When I was down there, I saw a number of people get up and move away. They had been sleeping along the edge of the sewer, on the concrete on flattened cardboard boxes, and I could only imagine what foul diseases they might contract from doing so. But, on the other hand, up above it was cold. Here, at least, along the concrete runs on either side of the sewer there were places to lie and there was a roof overhead and it was reasonably warm. None of them carried lights, but they moved easily and swiftly through experience and an acquired ability to see better in the dark than someone like me, fresh from the sunlight above. Of course, there were a few lights in the ceiling of the sewer, the ones I told you about. But they were pretty dim. I was glad I had my head-lamp.

"The people said nothing to me, and I said nothing to them. I was just some government worker, and they had no trust of me, and considering how they were often treated, I didn't blame them. I know there are some who would rather not work, and would suffer the greatest of indignities to avoid such, but for the most part I doubt this is true. It's hard to imagine that there are that many people eager to be homeless. It's hard to imagine anyone looking forward to each day being one of hunger and hardship and disappointment. Being homeless has a poor career arc.

"I hadn't intended to go deep, so I hadn't brought with me my protective mask with breathing device, but I was now certain that my rat had found his dead victim in this vicinity. I knew too that this was not far from where there was an opening to the older cities, and finally to the oldest city below; the one I had recently discovered and documented. That said, it was not an area that had been explored with any enthusiasm. Archaeologists might have it on their list, but due to finances, there was little provided for them to accomplish much. Nothing more than to visit what I had found and take a few photographs, some notes, and move on.

"Anyway, more on a hunch than for any good reason, I started along the concrete landing, and finally I came to where the wall was split by an old alleyway that had not been covered up completely. Workers had tried, but the earth there was weak, and it wouldn't hold the concrete. It kept breaking open.

"I took to the alleyway, and went along it, looking at the old city, the one built in the eighteen hundreds. I entered one of the houses, and realized I had been there before, but had arrived this time by a different route. I removed the blueprint and studied it in my head beam to make sure, and within moments I was certain I was correct. I was near the other gap that led down to the older city. Village, actually.

"I searched for perhaps three hours, and was about to give up, when I saw something familiar. It was the way two old shops came together. It was what I was looking for. I entered one, and at the back, through a break in the wall—a break caused by time and the pressure of above—found the opening I was looking for. The trail down-sloped even more dramatically than the other that led from the eighteen hundreds to the seventeen hundreds. I followed the path and it went down and turned and twisted, and became quite steep. I should add that though I have called it a trail, it was merely an accidental rip in the earth.

"I suppose there was more in my mind than the rat and the finger. I felt the need to explore. It was my thought that in a short time no one would be allowed down here, and that these older versions of the city would be off limits, though how that would be regulated was beyond me. I had a hard time envisioning the police force patrolling the area, or there being hired guards willing to stay down here in the dank with the homeless and the rats and the stink. Still, I wanted to see what I had discovered again before it was closed off for safety reasons, or archaeologists did in fact find the money they needed and occupied it on a daily basis.

"But, to come to why I am calling you. I went down there to the lower location, the oldest one, and looked around. There was peculiar writing on the walls and on the old mud buildings. It was nothing like anything I have ever seen. I found something else, as well. Bones and bodies."

"Of humans?"

"Yes," Frank said. "There were also some very large and peculiar tracks. I reported it and took the police there. Some of the remains I found were old. But there were fresh corpses as well. One that was somewhere between flesh and bones was missing the tip of its finger."

"Your rat's lunch," I said.

"Correct. But I should add that besides a finger, it was also missing a head and leg. The other bodies and bones were of a similar nature. Ravaged."

"Jesus," I said. "So what did the police do?"

"Not much they could do. Like I said, they came and looked and found that there were bites and claw marks on the bodies and the bones, and I assured them the bites and claw marks were too large for rats. They altered the idea from rats to dogs. This seemed equally unlikely, but I couldn't change their minds.

"I showed them the strange marks on the walls and buildings, the odd tracks. They dismissed the marks as graffiti by homeless people, and the tracks they said were not tracks at all, as they didn't match anything they could identify. Bottom line was the police department felt they had more important matters to attend to than the deaths of homeless people, and the whole matter was quickly dropped. And that is why I need you. I'm certain that what killed them isn't any known animal, or anything human."

***

I arrived in the city early the next morning. Frank met me at the airport. He looked as sleek and energetic as always. He drove me to the hotel he had arranged. I quickly checked in and put my luggage in the room. Then I went downstairs and he drove me to his office where he showed me photos he had taken underground. They had been taken in poor light, but they were intriguing. There were several of the bone and body heaps they had found. Some of the remains were nothing but gnawed bones, while others held strips of withered flesh, all of this piled among ragged clothes. Some were missing heads and limbs. Looking at some of the closer shots of the bones, the skulls, it was obvious to me that what had chewed and clawed them was neither rats nor dogs.

The tracks were long and flat. There were holes at the tips of the tracks that looked like claw marks, or some rather large and nasty, bony toes. The heels of the tracks were perfectly round and deep.

Frank showed me where he had consulted numerous wildlife books and websites, and explained to me he had even talked to experts on tracks, sent them the photos. None could identify them. All they could determine from the impressions in the photos was that whatever had made them was large enough to cause a severe indention, and was bipedal.

I immediately decided we would need certain equipment. Lights, motion cameras, some basic supplies. I went around renting certain items, buying others. This took Frank and me a full day. During this time, I called my assistants and had them prepare to fly in.

Nora Sweep and Gary Martin had been with me for some time. They had recently married, though Nora had kept her maiden name. They were experienced and reliable. I had a feeling right from the start that this was a situation that would call for considerable assistance, and along with Frank, they were just the ones to supply it.

It was with considerable anticipation that I went to bed that night, and I arrived at Frank's office fifteen minutes early. I had to stand at the doorway for ten minutes before he arrived, five minutes early. He had required help with the equipment and supplies, and had hired two huge men to help carry the items down below.

Everything we had brought, for the most part, was either easily folded or easily bagged, and with all four of us carrying our share, we managed to work our way through the narrow passages, down to the crack in the old walls, to the more ancient structure below. It was odd to descend into history like that, and to think that different civilizations, or different phases of it, were laid out in that manner. It was exciting, to say the least.

We wore construction-style helmets with lights, and we carried flashlights as back ups. Of course, we had serious lighting equipment with us as well, but it was packed away and of little use while in progress.

When we finally arrived, the first thing we did was set up one of the lights with its small but powerful battery. We used this to work by while we laid out our camp.

We chose an adobe style hut without a roof and worked our way through the tight round opening that served as a doorway, and put our supplies in the center of the room. It was cool down there, but I will admit to you that I had a feeling of unease.

Perhaps this was the nature of the situation. The isolated dark. But I have been at my work for some time, so I think I am authentically sensitive to feelings of supernormal dread. I use the word supernormal as opposed to supernatural for the simple reason that I believe that the supernormal indicates that things we call supernatural have some natural explanation that is only unnatural to us because we have yet to learn the true nature of its cause. That has always been true in my experience. But, that is neither here nor there. Simply let me say that I was immediately struck by an air of oppression. I asked Frank if he felt the same, and he agreed that it had been that way each visit before, and if the mystery had not been so great, so tantalizing, he felt he might not have returned. Even our two burly assistants admitted to feelings of unease.

While Frank worked on establishing positions for the cameras, I went outside the hut and looked at the tracks with a flashlight and my head beams. There were a lot of them. So many, in fact, you couldn't help but step on some of them. Many appeared fresh in the dried dirt, while others were older and had been made when the ground was damp. That was something I noted, that from time to time the ground was damp. I wouldn't have liked to have been trapped there if some conduit from above was going to drop tons of sewer water on our heads, or some stream from below were to rise and wash us away.

Examining the tracks in person made me even more uneasy. It was one thing to see digital photos of them, but to be able to kneel down and put my hand inside of them was another matter.

That afternoon Nora and Gary arrived and were ushered down by an assistant of Frank's, Raymond we'll call him, who after delivering them to us, along with another decent-sized battery for our equipment, went topside with the two men who had helped carry the lights. They were in quite a hurry. I think they felt what I felt, a kind of oppression and a sensation of being watched, or at least a feeling that something, by some method or another, was aware of our presence.

I introduced Frank to Nora and Gary. Frank didn't say it, but I got the impression he was surprised they were so young looking, like magazine models who had given up on fashion. I knew that any misgivings he might have about their age and experience would disappear once we set to work.

The amount of markings on the walls were astonishing. They were not all clearly visible, however, and even those that were, baffled me. I am fairly well versed in a number of older writings, hieroglyphics and such, but these markings, though somehow familiar, I couldn't decipher. Nora, who specializes in just that sort of thing, was also unable to deduce their meaning. These inhabitants most likely disappeared long before ships from Europe gave rise to the people who built the cities above us, old and new. We went about our research, and I was surprised to check my wristwatch and find that hours had passed, when it had only seemed like a few minutes. By saying this, I'm not trying to assign anything amazing or mystical to that fact. I'm merely demonstrating to you that we were well absorbed in our research. What we were doing was taking more photos, and even rubbings of the markings on the wall. We filed these away in a satchel, and then walked among the ruins.

It was not a large place, this village. All the roofs, which I presume had been thatch, or animal hides, were long gone now, but the walls stood thick and sturdy. Extremely thick.

We walked along narrow streets, nothing more than worn paths actually, using flashlight and head-lamp beams to guide our way. We walked and stared in awe at all that was there. Eventually, we came to the largest structure we had encountered, and were shocked to discover that it had a roof, and that it was made of ancient timbers that had petrified. Our thoughts were that they had not petrified here, but had been relocated here already in that condition. The timbers were covered by large slates of clay, one slate on top of another so that the roof was about two feet thick and solid as rock. The walls to the house were even thicker and more solid than the others. There was one doorway, a kind of mouse hole. To enter, you had to get down on your knees and crawl through.

I volunteered, but Frank made the point that it was he who brought us here, and though he had no problem with me having the first discovery, he did have a problem with me entering into a strange, perhaps dangerous place first. That being the case, Frank was the first one through the mouse hole.

After a tense moment the beam of his light poked out through the hole and he waved us inside.

***

Although it was some trouble, we moved our entire camp from its previous place to this hut. I liked the idea that it had a roof. It gave me a greater feeling of security, even if that feeling might be false. We set up lights on the outside of the hut, and on the inside. Frank had placed our cameras at the rear corners of the hut, and near the opening. There were both night-vision and common digital cameras that would record in low light. Then we set out to explore.

Our decision was to follow the narrow path that wound amongst the hard mud buildings. We did this, and finally we came upon a split in the old clay walls, a split that was an avenue of sorts. Narrow, and shiny as if polished by something, it went deep and far, slanting gradually. The air was dense with an aroma of decay.

I'm uncertain how far we went before the tunnel narrowed to the point where we could no longer move four abreast, but instead had to go one at a time; it continued to slope downward and the stink in the air increased. I decided it was gas from the sewers.

We came to what was nothing more than a large hole in the wall. I peeked in, dipped my head. The light on my helmet revealed a tremendous drop off. I thought I could hear water below, but after a moment, whatever sound I heard stopped. I decided that what I had actually heard had not been water at all, but a kind of rustling. Bats, perhaps. Beyond the beam on my helmet there seemed nothing but a wall of darkness.

"The end of our path," I said.

We worked our way back the way we had come, moving slower as our ascent was obviously more tiring than our descent had been. It was not a horrid climb, but after our long journey to arrive at the drop off, and with the air being thin and foul, it took its toll. When we were back at what I now thought of as base camp, I was somewhat relieved. The air still stank, but something had gone out of it, a kind of skin-crawling rottenness.

Inside the large, roofed hut we sat in its center with a battery powered heater to warm us. Before it was comfortable as far as temperature went, but now I found myself not only pulling on a light jumper from my pack, but feeling quite grateful for the heater Frank had brought.

"It's like a cold wind," Gary said, "only there's no actual wind. It's just colder."

I nodded. I didn't say it, but I knew what he was thinking, and for that matter, what Nora was thinking. It's often a phenomenon from beyond our dimension—what some call the spirit world, and what I frequently call the unknown or the supernormal.

"I think," I said, "I should lay out some of our protection."

I was referring to what some would brand witchcraft, but what I thought of as items in tune with the supernormal. I have found that crosses and swastika shapes—turned in the opposite direction of that the Nazis used—and certain powders and minerals, etc., contain powers that can hold dimensional and astral visitors at bay. I'm uncertain why this is, but I've found that religious reasons have nothing to do with it. A cross for example has no effect on vampires. Yes, I have encountered one, and perhaps someday I will tell you about that case, but to stay on course, what I am trying to say is there are powers in certain objects and concoctions. Humans often assign religious reasons to their power, but I don't believe this to be correct. It's the object itself, something about the shape, or its source. Prayers from any dedicated religious leader have power, but it is not the power of a god; it's the power of conviction.

Still, powerful as many of these symbols and concoctions can be, they are not universal. What may work against a so-called ghost, may not work against a bloodsucker or a lycanthrope, and so on. Not all denizens of dimensional netherworlds are affected by the same methods. It's always something of a crapshoot. That being the case, I put at the door of the hut a row of black candles, made from the fat of corpses. I assure you, I came by these by quite legal means, but this is not the time and place to dwell on that explanation. They were thick, black candles, mixed not only with corpse fat, but with a number of herbs and chemical sprinklings. Each wick was a spell wrapped in paper and then waxed to burn slowly. The candles were designed to last for hours, days even. I waited to light them.

After placing those at the door, unlit, I took a willow branch from my pack. It too was coated with corpse fat, except for the portion that I allowed as a kind of handle; it was wrapped in cord made from corpse hair. Again, I assure you, I came by all these devices legally. I waved it about and over our heads and recited spells from a number of cultures, hoping this would in fact give us protection. I wrote a few spells in Arabic on paper and placed them in small bottles and set them at the four corners of the hut.

They too were designed to seal us off from anything supernormal that might want in.

When I was finished, I lit the candles, and then sprinkled around us a concoction of herbs and ash from paper on which spells of the strongest kind had been written out by means of a goose feather quill and ink made of human blood and urine. I know, it sounds unpleasant, and is, but it's a necessary and powerful deterrent to angry things from beyond.

Oddly enough they have to be angry. A comfortable and pleasant traveler from the dimensional worlds that border ours is totally unaffected. Why? I can't say. Only those that would do harm respond to it, and sometimes, even they do not. So, as you can see, everything I was doing was nothing more than trial and error.

I finished by using the wand to draw a large circle around us. I followed this with another circle within that one, and warned everyone to stay tightly inside during the time that we were calling night. I decided that it would be best to turn off all the lights but one, and that one would be one of the lights inside our circle. It was powered by the same battery that gave us our heater, and it was on a six foot stand and could be swiveled about with a lever that projected from the back of the light's base.

After I completed my protections—or so I hoped they would be—Frank produced an automatic pistol, said, "And in case the mumbo jumbo fails to work, I've got this. Nine rounds."

"If the mumbo jumbo fails to work," Nora said, "then you might want to hope that a certain part of your anatomy is well greased, because that may be where this thing inserts that pistol."

"Still," Frank said, "it makes me feel better to have it. I mean, really, does any of this stuff work?"

"You asked me here because you know me, and you know what I do. It's worked in the past. Mostly."

"Mostly?" he said.

"There are no absolutes," I said.

Frank nodded. "Fair enough. I suppose being down here, feeling as if there is something out there... knowing there has been. Thinking back on those photos and those footprints, somehow I find it difficult to put my faith in a few candles and circles and bottles with paper in them."

"For this world, they are pointless, and will have no effect. But for the other worlds, which are the ones we're dealing with, they may prove our salvation."

"And what if it turns out to be of this world?" Frank asked.

"Then," Gary said, "maybe it'll be a good thing you have your pistol."

Frank sat for a moment considering. "I apologize for pulling you into this Dana, you too Nora, Gary."

"Nonsense," I said. "It's what we do. And besides, whatever is down here, it should be stopped. Nothing says it will consign itself to this area forever. It might decide to come topside."

"So, what do we do now?" Frank asked.

"We roll out our sleeping bags and wait," I said.

"And exactly why are we doing that?" he asked.

"Because it feeds on people," I said. "We are people."

"We're bait?" Frank said.

"That's about the size of it," Nora said, nodding as she did, tossing her hair.

"Is that a good thing?" Frank asked.

"Not if it breaks through the protection," I said. "Listen, Frank. You brought me here to figure this out, but you don't have to stay."

"No... that's all right. I can't leave you here. I don't want to be here. I won't kid you. But I'm staying."

I nodded. "Very well, then." I glanced at my watch. "My suggestion is that we take shifts sleeping, and that we keep guard two at a time. That way if one of the two gets sleepy, the other is there to rouse them. Say four hours per pair."

"And if both of the guard team get sleepy?" Frank said.

"Then we just may have a problem," I said, and I got up to light the candles in front of the mouse-hole door.

***

I'm going to pause here to state that I have often been frightened in my work. It comes with the territory. But when it came my time with Nora, the second shift, I felt a sensation that went more deeply than fright. It was a kind of haunting in my bones. Frank and Gary had endured their shift without incident or comment, but within fifteen minutes of Nora and I taking a sitting position on our sleeping bags under the light, I began to feel almost nauseous with discomfort. I looked at Nora. I didn't have to say a thing. She just said, "Yeah. Me too."

Within moments, the air became colder and the stench we had smelled down that long tunnel to nowhere became evident and so thick, you could almost saw it into blocks. The flames from the candles at the door fluttered.

There was a shuffling, like an old man dragging a bum leg. It moved along the path that led to our hut, and the nearer it came, the dimmer the light above us seemed and the more the candle flames guttered. For a moment I considered turning it off altogether, so as not to attract whatever was outside, but I knew that would be a pointless endeavor. Whatever was out there, if it was of the nature I suspected, it would find us anyway, and it wouldn't need a light, and a light wouldn't deter it.

I reached in my bag and took out one of the vials of powder I had. It was harmless to living humans, but as sharp as acid to most things from beyond. But therein was the problem. Most things. I had no idea what I was dealing with. I only hoped it shared certain characteristics with past supernormal denizens, things some called demons or spirits or haints.

The shuffling became louder, and soon it was obvious that whatever was out there was right next to our location. I glanced toward the open mouse-hole door, trembling, waiting.

"Shall we wake the others?" Nora said.

"Gently."

Nora touched them and whispered them awake, warned them to silence. Now all four of us were sitting up on our sleeping bags, watching the mouse hole.

I couldn't see anything, but I was overcome with a feeling of dread, and an awareness of something being at that opening. Then, in the candlelight, I saw the dust just outside the door form into one of those unique footprints, and without meaning to, I let out my breath, causing all of us to jump a little. I hadn't even been aware that I had been holding it.

Then the footprint was overtaken by a smudge. It took me a moment to figure it, but I came to the conclusion that our invisible stalker had bent down and put what might be a knee in the smudge of its print. The dirt there shifted and the candles were knocked aside, some of their flames going out. I knew then, as I was sure the rest of them knew, that whatever invisible horror was there, it was crawling inside.

***

Frank lifted his revolver. I said, "Save it."

The power of the candles was no power at all. The invisible thing came into the room. Its footprints in the dim light proved that. There was a roar. So loud and so awful it shook my brain inside my skull. The air crackled with electricity. The light in our circle blinked. The monster was charging the circle, breaking through all of the exterior spells like a determined bull crashing through an electrified fence.

"Jesus," I heard Frank yell, and he fired a shot. He couldn't help himself. In fact, he fired twice. The air crackled. There was a blue and green and red burst of fulmination that formed around whatever it was, gave it a kind of outline, a shape. I can't really describe that shape accurately. If I could, it wouldn't be a shape readily recognizable. All I can say is that I couldn't see the whole of it, but the colorful, electric-like outline of it alone was enough to wither my hopes. It was over ten feet tall and there were arms tipped with claws. There were even a couple of flashes that revealed its prominent, wide, toothy mouth.

It was a momentary display, almost subliminal, but it was enough to chill the blood. It moved through the magic defenses until it came to the first invisible wall, meaning the outline of the circle. It hit that wall with a sound like an eighteen-wheeler going off a cliff.

The circle was powerful enough that it knocked the thing back. I could tell that by the flames and electrical shocks, the shifting of the invisible creature's footprints in the dirt just outside the barrier.

It came again. Another clash, and this time I saw the circle give a little. Dirt shifted, the shape wobbled.

I thought, Oh hell. This is it. It's going to break the circle and tear us apart.

***

Obviously, I am here, so I was not torn apart. But it did break the circle. It took three more rushes, and on the third one the circle folded in on itself and broke. The air filled with smoke and crackling light, and then we could see it. See it well. It was only for a moment, but longer than before. It was even more strange and horrible than I had originally thought. It carried its stink with it, like a battering ram, and that came inside the second circle, but the creature did not.

The second circle, the smaller one, held.

I stood up then. The vial of powder in my hand. I had already twisted off the lid. I yelled out a short spell, and tossed the powder.

The powder went outside the circle and hit the beast. There was a bellow so loud it knocked me down. The thing clawed at the air, leaving fiery marks that hung in space for long moments. I struggled to my feet, tossed another handful of the powder. Another bellow. But a lesser one this time, because the thing was moving away, and swiftly.

It was no longer visible. There were no more sparks. Just a shuffling sound as it dropped to its knees, or rather what passed for them. It wormed its way so violently through the mouse hole that a chunk of the wall broke loose, widening the path.

Then there was silence and the stink floated away and the air was still.

"It's gone," I said.

"Are you sure?" Frank said.

"Yeah," I said. "It's gone."

"How can you be sure?"

"Guess I can't absolutely," I said. "But from experience... It's gone. Feel how the air has warmed, relaxed. The smell is gone. I know, that's not a very good explanation, 'relaxed air,' but it's the best I know how to describe it."

"No," Frank said. "I feel it. But what was it?"

"It's a spirit of sorts," I said. "The hot astral remains of something dead."

"Hot astral remains?" Frank asked.

Nora said, "Yeah. It's what we call a malignant entity. It's what remains of something that once lived, and it's not happy, and it is out to make us unhappy."

"Will it come back?" Frank asked.

"They usually do," Gary said.

"When will it come back?" he asked.

"I don't know," I said. "It took a good hit, but so did my protections."

"Can you reinstate them?" Frank asked.

"She can," Gary said. "But my suggestion is we grab a few things and run like bastards. At least for now. We need some consider time. This thing is powerful."

"Agreed," I said. "Thing is, whatever that was, it was just probing the protection. It might decide it can bull its way through. And it might be right. If it is... well, not good."

***

It seemed like a long trip to the surface. We went past a number of homeless people, shuffling about in the near dark. I thought of our equipment down below, and I thought of that thing. These people were at its mercy if it chose to ascend. Or, if they went below.

I considered trying to warn them, but it occurred to me they might think we were merely trying to hide or protect something they could use to survive. It could only lead to curiosity, and them exploring below, perhaps bothering our equipment, which we had abandoned. So I chose not to. I hoped they thought we were the same as them, survivors in the wilds of the city.

When we came to the surface, it was surprising to find that it was mid-day. We ended up trudging our way to Frank's office, stretching out on the couches there, and on pallets on the floor. Each of us slept, the combination of the intense drain of adrenaline, the effects of fear.

Hours later, I awoke and found Frank was in the examination room with Nora. This was where Frank dissected rats and the like. They were sitting at his long worktable, and Nora was talking excitedly.

Nora saw me, said, "Well, sleepy head. How you feeling?"

"Not as good as you," I said. "I must be getting old."

"No. It's just that I've discovered something," she said. "It's the excitement giving me energy."

"Something good?" I asked.

"Interesting. Come over and look."

She had a small digital camera. It was one of the cameras from below.

"You were quick getting that," I said.

"I went back and got all the cameras when I woke up," she said. "I slipped off while you three slept. I was afraid you wouldn't let me go otherwise."

"I might not have," I said. "It's probably safe right now, but I couldn't say it's safe for sure."

"Look here," Nora said, and leaned over and gave me the digital camera. "It's ready to go. Just touch the button."

I held the camera and propped my elbows against the table, watched as the invisible force entered the hut and began to tear at our protections, move the circle, then retreat when I threw the powder from my container. I noted how some of the powder hung in the air, clinging to the invisible thing. That immediately gave me an idea, but it was one I tucked away for later.

"I have more," Nora said, taking the camera, placing it aside.

I pulled a stool up between Frank and Nora and saw that what she had was a run of printed photographs and a chart she had made with a swath of butcher paper and a ballpoint pen.

The photographs were of the wall markings.

"I looked at these more closely," Nora said. "They actually are familiar. At the time I didn't think so, and that's because there's a different flavor to them than I expected."

"What kind of flavor?" I asked.

"They are reminiscent of Mayan writings, as well as a number of South American markings. But my guess is they are the forerunners of their writing, so it looks a little different. It would be like the difference between print and cursive. Not literally, but that's the idea. Slightly different emphasis here and there. But I've started doping it out. It's pretty fantastic."

"Why am I not surprised," I said.

"Because an invisible monster tried to kill us?" Frank said.

"Okay," I said to Nora, "tell us what you have."

Nora's face was flushed with excitement. "I can't say it's entirely accurate. My translation, I mean."

"But you think it is?" I said.

"Yes. I think it is. Simply put, what's down there is the spirit of an extraterrestrial."

I gave Nora a look. "Even for us, that's kind of... out there."

"Out there is right," Frank said.

"I know how that sounds," she said, "but is it really any more fantastic than other things we've experienced?"

"Yes," I said. "I think it is."

Right then Gary came into the room rubbing the back of his neck. He said, "What did I miss?"

"Nothing yet," I said. "Nora has discovered she can read the markings below, and that she thinks our problematic monster is the spectral remains of an alien. The outer space kind."

"You're yanking my leg," Gary said.

"No," Frank said. "She's not."

Gary took a stool at the worktable.

"Here's what I got," Nora said.

***

Nora's chart was a breakdown of the markings. Once she showed me how it was similar to Mayan writings, and also how it differed, it began to fall in place.

From what Nora made out, the story in the markings was that once in the long ago, a space ship (yeah, actually, a space ship) came here from dark beyond. It may have been an intentional landing, or an accidental landing, but it came. Nora showed us the markings, which looked like a shooting star to me, and I said so.

"Yes," Nora said, "and my first thought was that it was referring to a meteor or comet. But the rest of the story is about how beings came out of the star."

"It could be symbolic," Gary said.

"It could," Nora said. "But it fits the rest of the story. It seems that beings, human-like from the drawings, came from somewhere out there, and landed here when it was little more than a prehistoric tribal gathering. They interacted with man... and see this?"

Nora was pointing to one of the photos taken of a marking on a wall below. It was a crude marking that didn't really look like anything to me. "Okay," I said. "What about it?"

"Really look at it," she said.

I really looked at it. Nothing.

"Oh," Frank said. "I see it."

"See what?" I said.

Gary said. "I'm with Dana. Out in the wilderness here. It doesn't mean squat to me."

"It's one of the tracks," Frank said. "One of the tracks we saw down below."

I leaned over and looked again.

"I see it now," I said.

"Thing is," Nora said, "this was a marking that has been rubbed out. Not by time, but intentionally. And it's not the only one."

Nora bent down and pulled a satchel from under the table. She opened it and took out the rubbings we had made of the wall markings.

"I started studying these things, and realized the markings were picking up shapes that had been sanded down, but some of the impression remained. You have to look at this in a strong light. Frank, can you push that light over?"

Frank slid the desk lamp closer. Nora shuffled through the rubbings, picked out one, pushed it under the light.

"I've outlined this one a little, to make it more visible."

I studied it carefully. A chill moved along my spine and I felt the hair on the back of my neck rise. It was a shape that I can only describe as being insect-like. If an ant had two legs and strange feet, it might look something like that. Something like it, not exactly like it. It had bulging eyes and long arms with claws on the tips. Parts of it I had seen during the attack on the circle.

"There are a lot of these in the rubbings," Nora said. "All of them had been scrubbed out with something, but not all the impressions were gone. They just got the surface, muddled them a bit, but the rubbings brought them out.

"And there's a history here. Once I caught on to the writing, it all started to fall together. Actually, it's easier to read, more sophisticated in a way than Mayan or Aztec writing. I think these prehistoric ancestors were advanced. Perhaps the star visitors had something to do with it. I don't know. But, in time, the humans wanted any memory of these things removed. The aliens, and I don't know any better name to call them, seem to have been here for some time. The markings go back a long ways. It's odd, but the earliest are the sharpest and the most advanced. They became considerably more crude as time went on. I think it's because of those things."

"The aliens," Frank said.

"Yes, and no," Nora said.

"That's a safe answer," Gary said.

"From what I understand, and there are gaps, and things I can't decipher, but it seems a race of beings came here from the stars, and among them were a race of other beings. Workers. Drones."

"Like bees or ants," I said.

"Like that," Nora said. "Thing is, these things revolted."

"Good for them," Gary said.

"Going to have to say yes and no again on that one," Nora said. "Seems the aliens, and the indigenous peoples, now most likely the same people, as I'm sure they had by this time intermixed—"

"Meaning we're all from Mars?" Frank said.

"I don't know about Mars," Nora said. "But if this is right, it's likely that our DNA, or a lot of DNA, is mixed with the star travelers'. I call them that because I like to say star travelers. It has a nice ring to it."

"The rest of it," I said.

"The rest as I understand it," Nora said. "And there are a few guesses here. But the human/alien mix lost out in a battle to these drones."

"Oh, come on," Frank said.

"I know how it sounds," Nora said, "but that's what it says here."

"Maybe these were our first science fiction writers?" Gary said, nodding at the photos of the wall markings.

"Except that we've met one of these critters," I said. "So they're not fiction."

"The population came to worship the drones, but the drones started dying out. My guess is they couldn't reproduce. Maybe they were all of the same sex, or had been neutered, or, well, I don't know. But they died out. The last one long ago. Somewhere around then the whole civilization, such as it was, fell apart. Or at least their records did. They could have left. Disease. I don't know for sure."

"But how could that drone still be alive?" Frank asked. "It would be ancient."

"It's not alive," I said, because right then I got it. "It's no different from other situations we've been in. This is the spiritual residue of one of those things. For some reason that spirit has survived. My guess is it's trapped in that area, tied to the place because that's what it knew in life. Just like so-called ghosts in houses."

"We've encountered a few of those," Nora said.

"It's a ghost?" Frank said.

"In a manner of speaking," I said. "It's a residue."

"An awfully spry residue," Frank said.

"Correct," I said. "Not everything that dies leaves a spirit. It's not about heaven and your soul, or any of that. It's about circumstance. Sometimes, for whatever reason, a residue of something living remains. It can be benign, unable to actually interact with us on this dimensional plane. I think our spectral visitor is from another dimensional plane and we call it a ghost because it slips back and forth. Or sometimes it's trapped in between. The worst ones are the ones trapped here completely as a spirit. Their spirits have substance. And if they're angry—"

"They can hurt you?" Frank said.

"Exactly," I said. "And the spirit of this ant drone from the stars—"

"Star traveler," Nora said.

"Very well," I said, "Star Traveler, is as angry and powerful as they get."

"So we get more potions and light the candles again?" Frank asked.

"We may have to do that," I said. "Probably will. But I think this thing is stronger than the spells I have. Maybe it's because it's from... out there. I don't know. I had a feeling that if it had pushed harder, it would have come through all my defenses, and we wouldn't be here now looking at wall rubbings and photos. What we have to do is find out why it's still here."

"You're sure it will come back?" Frank asked. "It won't just fade out?"

"Not as long as it can kill," I said. "It feeds off fear, death, anger, passion, that sort of thing. It may have lain dormant for centuries. When that old village was discovered, and people began to go down there, it sensed it, gained strength. And with the killings, it's stronger than ever. It saps up a life force like a kid sucking chocolate malt through a straw."

"And it'll come back at the same time of day?" Frank asked.

"Usually does," I said. "It's possible it has other times it can break loose, but we know for sure the time we met it. We'll use that as our guide."

"Then we have more than one chance to get at it?" Frank said.

"Probably," I said. "But it has more than once chance to get at us. And I think it may be able to take the wear and tear a lot better than our human flesh can."

***

Two days later we started back down.

I had prepared new protections, and Frank hired the two burly men again, as guards and helpers. They wore side arms this time, though I knew the guns would most likely be useless.

I could also tell they were both still reluctant to go down there, but too proud to let on they were having feelings of insecurity. Truth is, I would rather they have stayed behind. Their method of dealing with this thing would be of the natural order, and that wasn't going to cut it. I tried to explain to them just what to expect, but they looked at me in a way that said: Talk on, lady. We know you're crazy, but we're getting paid, so talk on.

Frank's assistant, Raymond, came as well. He carried down for me two large cans of bright red paint and a flamethrower; one of those things with a tank and arm straps. After delivery of those items, he quickly went topside. He wasn't having any part of what was down there. It was all instinct on his part, and it was a good instinct.

We camped in the roofed hut again, and I was pleased to find that everything was as we had left it, except for the cameras that Nora had brought up, and now brought down again. Word had most likely gotten out among the homeless that the farthest place down below was not a good place to be; that there was someone, or something, down there.

This time I drew the circle bigger, and thicker, and filled the drawn line with some of my powders. I had been able to find most of the ingredients without too much work. Nearly every city, if you have the right contacts, and know who to ask (and I do) have people who carry and use and sell those kinds of things. Often out of their houses, frequently out of the back of herb and novelty shops. Anyway, I pulled out the protections I needed and set about making the hut as secure as I could manage. We set up four infrared cameras, two in the back corners of the hut, two in the front corners. Nora used the stands we had left down there, fastened the cameras to them, pushed them tight against the hut wall and taped them securely to the adobe with good ole Duct Tape to protect them from falling over.

Secretly I had brought buttons of peyote with me to chew. Too much of it and I would have been useless, but a bit of it, under stressful, and supernormal circumstances, would heighten my connection to whatever was visiting us from the border between dimensions.

I also had a handful of flares inside my safari pants pocket, a lighter, and matches. I wanted to be well-armed with fire and light, two of the stronger nemeses of the supernormal.

We had timed our arrival to coincide with our previous adventure, and I had timed it so that our protections would be in place and we would be within the circle several hours before the thing showed up. These sorts of "hauntings," if you will, nearly always take place at the same time. It is rare that the pattern is broken. The only thing that might disturb the pattern is us. Once we were discovered, our dimensional monster was much freer to work outside the box. In fact, our meddling, if we failed, could make matters worse. It could give the thing such a rush of energy, it might be able to completely move into our realm, no longer be confined to its spot down below.

Inside the smaller of the two circles I drew, I had everyone find a spot and insisted they stay there. I had Frank explain to the two guards that they were being paid to do as I said, not as they wanted. I felt this was necessary after my preliminary conversation with them. I had him tell them that the spot I assigned them in the circle was their spot until further notice. If they thought I was crazy, they might at least respond to Frank who was supplying them with payment. The guards were, by the way, named Jake and Fritz, and both looked to have come from the same mold. Burly, with a shaved head. The biggest difference in them was Jake wore a mustache and small beard, while Fritz was clean-shaven. Both had faces that looked to have been chiseled out of stone. Still, tough or not, I could detect their nervousness, and I noticed that their hands never strayed far from their holstered weapons.

Once we all had our positions, the light turned on inside our main circle, our head beams strapped to our foreheads, I carefully slipped the peyote buttons into my mouth and began to chew slowly. Gary and Nora glanced at me and knew. We had on one other occasion needed such an aid. I thought it best Frank and the other two not know, lest they think I was drug-crazed, or was putting myself into a condition where I would be useless. I was Frank's anchor, the one who knew the other worlds, someone with experience. He had enough worries without fearing I wouldn't be able to hold up my end.

The peyote was bitter. I picked a stick of beef jerky from our supplies and nibbled on it, giving excuse to my constant chewing. I drank from a bottle of water, then checked my watch numerous times, sometimes within seconds of the previous checking. I wanted to have the peyote in my system before *it* arrived.

I said, "It has a certain time period in which to do mischief. If we can hold it off during that time, when that time passes, then we have a chance to find its source. It will leave a kind of residue that I think I can follow."

"But how?" Frank asked.

"Leave that to me," I said.

I glanced at Fritz and Jake. They were both looking at me in a way that made it clear they thought I was an idiot, and that Frank was a bigger idiot for believing in me.

"When it starts," I said to them, "it will be unlike anything you have ever experienced. My assistants and myself have been witness to this. We know it's real. I understand you doubt me. But when it happens, when it starts, stay inside the circle. If you step out of it, even into the outer circle, I can't promise you protection. And while I'm at it, I can't promise you complete protection even inside this circle. So, if you want to go, now is the time to go."

Jake looked at Fritz. Fritz nodded. Jake looked at me, said, "We'll stick. But if you don't think guns will do anything, why the flame thrower?"

"Fire," I said. "For whatever reason, fire seems to work against all manner of evil. Dimensional, spectral, you name it. If it has bad intentions, and it's in our dimensional frame, it can taste fire. That doesn't mean fire always stops it, but it usually works."

"Usually?" Jake said.

I managed to grin. "There are no absolutes, as I always say."

"What about the cans of paint?" Fritz asked.

"I'm hoping that will become evident," I said, pulling my clasp knife from a pocket in my safari pants. I flicked out the blade and slid it under the tops on the paint cans. With a flick, I removed the lids.

I looked at my watch. It was almost time.

***

It was much as before. The air turned stale and stank to high heaven, and this was soon followed by a kind of electricity in the air, as if we had suddenly sat down near a power plant. We could hear it coming, and it seemed to be moving faster than before, with anticipation. As I have said, the spirit—and I use that term for lack of a better one—had a time-block in which it worked best. Why that is, is hard to determine. Sometimes it has to do with its previous life, when the host of the spirit was most active. Or when certain events happened that led to its demise. But though there was a normal time frame, and the thing had a kind of pattern to follow, it also could deviate somewhat within that pattern. It could gain greater strength. It could become so strong that the rules that governed it could suddenly no longer apply. It could begin setting its own rules. Bottom line was we needed to destroy it.

So it came, and we sat, and we fidgeted. I heard Jake let out his breath loudly, realized he had been holding it. I realized then that I was holding mine as well, and was in fact becoming a little light headed. I let my breath out, softly. The noise outside the hut grew, and then it slowed, and I knew that it was at the doorway. That it was most likely bending down, looking inside, seeing us sitting here. I wondered if it understood what our intent was? I wondered if it feared us? Perhaps it had no real thoughts outside of finding us, destroying us, and feasting on our life force.

I felt sick to my stomach. I felt my eyes water. My body was trembling. This was not only due to fear, but to the peyote. And then I saw that footprint in front of the doorway, clearly outlined in the dirt, in the light of the candles I had lit. As before, I saw the footprint smudge over with the print of its knee as it knelt. The candles were knocked over. If their magic had any effect at holding the creature at bay, it was negligible.

"Oh, hell," Gary said, without even realizing he was speaking.

I unscrewed the cap on my powders, put them in front of me. I glanced at the flamethrower and gently eased the tank onto my back by sliding my arms through the straps. I made sure the cans of paint were well within reach. Everything seemed too close, and too far away at the same time.

As the thing stood we saw its footprints in the dust again. We saw this because the light in the middle of the circle was bright enough to reveal it. That was when I realized I could see a wavy-line image of the thing. It was the peyote. I had entered the realm that is thought of as the spirit world, but is in fact either dimensional, or inter-dimensional, which seems to be some place in between where you can shift either way instantly.

Everything was bright and the stink was stronger than ever now. Spinning around the thing I could see all manner of vibrating lights. There were images that fled past it, and over it, and through it. Images of men in simple outfits made of cloth and skins; there were others, alien forms that looked almost human, and alien forms that looked like our intruder beast; they were present, and they were not. Those images were its memories, a clutter of this and that. The beast itself was of both worlds, and was invisible to the others in the hut, but solid and dangerous, nonetheless.

It moved closer and closer, but due to the peyote, it all seemed to be happening in super slow motion. This thing, this poor thing. I could feel its hate and anger, confusion and pain. It made my stomach churn and filled my head with images.

It had come out of the blackness between the stars, come out of it riding in a spacecraft controlled by its masters. It had come down from that deep blackness and crashed into our planet. Trapped here, it continued to be a slave, along with those like it. In time the drones rose up and the drones became the masters. Then the drones died out, one by one. They were long-lived, but like mules, sterile; the offspring of two kinds of creatures on a far away world, bred for work, brought here to our world by spacecraft and default. They had taken over as the masters, but long-lived as they were, without a way of procreating, they ceased to be. Finally, there was just the one. This one. Perhaps a child when it first came to our world.

The people who were now a mix of human and alien life forms similar to our own, the drone's former masters, and finally its servants, rose up against the last drone, and it fled. Fled back down that tunnel and—

Then the images, the sensations stopped. I was adrift in a murky sea of thought and fear. Time came unstuck. It was moving. It was working its way through our protections. I could see those protections, bright walls of power—yellow and green, red and blue, like colorful strands of wire. But this thing was ripping through them. The circle pushed back, like a snake writhing away from heat. I stood with my container of powder, and flung it. It was like acid hitting the wavy shape of the creature. It recoiled. Then it lunged forward. I tossed the powder again. It recoiled once more, regrouped.

I grabbed up one of the paint cans, sloshed the paint in the thing's direction. The paint splattered on the monster, splashed on the adobe floor. Now our attacker was visible in splotches. I grabbed up the other can and tossed it low down. It hit in such a way that part of the creature's peculiar legs and feet could now be seen. I did this thinking that making it somewhat visible might supply the others with a modicum of confidence. This may have been a mistake, because Fritz stood up and started firing his revolver. Paint flicked up from the thing but it didn't go away.

"Forget the gun," I said. I pulled the nozzle of the flamethrower free of its clip on my back, and pointed it. Before I could cut loose, Fritz and Jake were both firing. And now Fritz panicked, made a break for it, trying to make an end run around the thing, darting his way toward the exit.

It moved fast. It grabbed Fritz. There was a flurry of red paint and then red blood as Fritz was torn asunder and his insides hit the wall of the hut and blew apart in bursts of intestines and gore. In my peyote-filmed eyes, the blood and the paint were much alike. They formed into small balls of red and dropped like a broken strand of ruby beads. They fell slowly, and then suddenly, they fell fast. The paint and blood drops striking the ground were loud as tom-tom beats.

The destruction of Fritz happened so fast, there was no time for him even to let out a yell. And Jake, now he was outside of the protection, maybe attempting to go to Fritz's aid, maybe attempting to find a path to escape. He fired his handgun in rapid succession, until it was empty. It was like tossing peas at the paint-blotched behemoth. It froze in its spot, as if trying to determine if those pistol pops meant anything. Jake started back-pedaling, trying to get back inside the circle.

It was too late.

As he turned to run, the thing swept low and grabbed his ankle and whipped him over his head as easily as if he had been a wet rag, and then snapped him like a towel, slammed him into the roof of the hut, then into the wall. Blood sprayed like a spring rain, drenched us.

I know this sounds as if it took a while, but I can only tell this as fast as I can tell it. Fritz and Jake were both dead before you could blink your eyes twice. I had the flamethrower at the ready, but it had all gone down so quickly, and with Fritz and Jake in the way, I had hesitated to use it. Now I squeezed the trigger, cut loose.

In my peyote-rich state the flames appeared to reach out like a fiery finger, then the tip of the finger plunged apart, and the fire was not red, but all the variations of red—pink and rose, orange and rust. The flame curled and licked and tasted. There was a noise that sounded like something between a dinosaur scream and an eighteen-wheeler locking its brakes.

Flames crawled all over it, as if trying to find a proper place to lie down. Our monster, wearing a coat of fire, lunged forward, completely through the first circle. The circle at the edge of my feet wavered a little. Nora dropped down, and using the blessed wand, drew a stronger line to replace it. But the line didn't hold. The thing grabbed her by the wrist.

She yelped. Gary grabbed her arm, tried pulling her back. Frank was on his feet. He picked up the empty powder bottle and threw it in the direction of the flames. It was like tossing spit on a house fire. Useless.

I gave the flamethrower another burst. The flames formed the shape of our attacker, crawled over its body until it was a writhing torch.

The monster weakened. Nora broke free. Gary yanked her back. She clutched her wrist. It was bleeding. It was a bad wound.

The inner circle wobbled.

"Oh, hell no," Frank said, seeing it collapse.

"Stand firm," I said, and cut loose with another burst of fire.

This time the screech was even more powerful than before. I could see it in the flames, see its tongue slashing in its wide-toothed mouth, hear the paint crackle like someone wadding up dried leaves.

Then I could see its memories buzzing around it like spectral bees, flowing in and out of its narrow eyes, images and shapes and impressions too strange to describe, the actual manifestations of hurt and betrayal. Even in that moment, knowing if I failed that it would tear us apart, I felt sorry for it. The peyote not only allowed me to see into its spirit world, its past, its thought imagery, I could actually feel all that it was, and all that it had been, and there wasn't a moment of satisfaction there.

In that instant, its will broke. Our circle had held. The creature leaped backwards, still looking at us with those narrow eyes. It wheeled, jumped, flailed, and clawed, bouncing off the wall and clamoring up it like an electric spider. It clung to the roof like a bat, smoking from the flames. An instant later it dropped to the ground near the mouse hole, slammed its huge fists against the wall, knocking it apart. It shoved itself through the gap it made, and it was gone, leaving behind the smell of burnt flesh and paint, and a whiff of gray smoke.

***

Immediately, the air warmed. The stench moved away from us. Much of our fear departed with it.

I stopped, looked at Nora.

"You okay?" I said.

"Forget it," she said. "For heaven's sake. Stop it. Stop it."

I nodded. "Frank," I said. "Get Nora topside. And Gary, you go with her."

"I wouldn't do it any other way," he said.

I stepped out of the circle. Frank grabbed my arm. "Is it safe?" he said.

"Right now. Yes. But it won't be, later. I have to finish this."

"I should stay," Frank said, and he tried to look at me like he meant it.

"You should do as I say," I said. "And you should call the police."

"What do I tell them?" he said.

"Whatever it is," I said, "they won't believe you."

Gary grabbed Frank's arm. "Come on. Now."

They went out of the hut and headed for above ground. I turned toward the tunnel we had investigated earlier. I could see a trail of smoke drifting out of it, the equivalent of Gretel's crumbs, and I could follow it. Besides, I had some idea to where it was going.

***

The tunnel was full of its stink and the air was as chill as an ice tray. Tendrils of smoke drifted past me as I went. The peyote was still doing its trick. The smoke appeared heavy, like strips of cotton suspended in amber.

I had turned on my head-lamp, using it to light my way. I was holding the flamethrower before me, wondering how much fuel was left in the tank.

The smell diminished and so did the smoke. The air warmed slightly. This meant either the spectral alien had gotten far ahead of me, or its time had run out and it had been whisked back to the dimension from which it came. If that was the case, it would be more difficult to track it. A part of me was glad for that thought. Finding it with no real protections outside of the flamethrower might be disastrous.

It was all I could do to keep going. It was all I could do not to think about the size of that thing, what its claws had done to poor Fritz and Jake.

Finally the tunnel narrowed and I came to the pit. I could smell smoke rising up from below, but it was faint. I got down on my knees, leaned over into the darkness, moved my head around to get a better look at the drop-off with my head-lamp. I pulled a flare from my pocket, broke it against the edge of the pit, and tossed it. It went flickering downward, like a falling star. In that momentary glow, I saw something I had not noticed before. About six feet down, there was a kind of trail that wound off to the right and moved around the pit in a circle, around and around. A crude circular staircase where the stair steps were little more than bumps of rock. It was slick looking, as if someone had wiped it down with buckets of snot. I discovered there was a fragment of a step where I was kneeling, but the rest of it, and any steps that might have gone with it and matched up with those below, were gone. It made sense that our astral visitor was somewhere at the end of all this, down deep in that pit.

I gathered my nerve, swung a leg over the edge of the pit. My foot dangled into nothingness. The flamethrower suddenly seemed very heavy and awkward. I clung to the step fragment with aching hands, lowering myself as low as I could before I dropped, hoping to hit those slick looking steps and not go sliding off into a bottomless dark.

I took a deep breath and let go. I fell and hit close to the pit wall. My feet went out from under me, but I landed on my knees and didn't slide very far. I stayed on solid rock. The nozzle on the flamethrower came loose and clattered backwards, but of course it was on its hose, so I didn't lose it. My knees ached as bad as if they had been hit with an iron bar.

I got my feet under me and looked over the edge where I could have gone. My head light didn't show me much down there, the dark was too thick to penetrate.

I gathered up the flamethrower nozzle and slipped it in its place, and kept descending. The steps were very slick, and there were squirts of water coming out of the walls. It stood to reason that all of this had been sealed off by shifting rock and time, but that recent water activity had changed things. Had opened up what had been closed, and perhaps that connection to the outside world had caused this thing's spirit to stir.

I kept going down. I paused once and looked up. There was darkness up there, but it seemed lighter than below. Finally the steps ceased, and the ground became flat. I could see something shiny in my head beam, but it was impossible to make it out. I pulled one of the flares from my pocket, struck it against the rock wall. It hissed awake, brightened. I tossed it.

In the light of the flare I saw an amazing thing.

***

Rock and metal twisted together. The metal was bright and the rock was dark. Slowly I realized what I was looking at in those flickers of light, the remains of a huge spacecraft. It had come down from the heavens long ago, collided and slid and ended up here as part of the earth. A civilization of sorts had built up around it. Time had covered it up. I stood there looking at it for a long time. In spite of everything, it was awe-inspiring. It was crumpled in spots, like wadded aluminum foil. The rock jutted into part of it, and it seemed to be all of one, a mighty and magnificent sculpture made by an insane artist.

The flare went out.

I walked toward the craft, following my head beam. I went along until I found a gap in the ship's wall, a rip from collision. I eased inside, turned my head to move the light about. There was all manner of dirt piled along the sides of the gap and inside of it there were ridges of it, piled there by collision and time. I went deeper in, saw bones of all manner strewn about, big ones, little ones; the remains of humans and drones, and beasts that no longer existed.

There was writing on the metal walls. The kind of writing I had seen on the upper dirt walls. It was dark and crusty looking. My stomach lurched and the air began to move, and it had color. It was a color beyond the spectrum of the rainbow. It was a color out of space and time that could be seen as well as felt. Hell, I could taste it. In the waves of color there were memories, the monster's memories, and they hit me like a fist.

In the waves I saw the ship. I saw the drones, down below in the lower hatch. They all wore a strand of shimmering metal around their necks. And I knew that it was some sort of advanced form of containment. In those necklaces of shiny metal there was what we of lesser knowledge would think of as magic. But it was technology that confined the drones so they could be used as the star travelers wished. And I saw those humanoid aliens too. They swirled around me like clouds. I grew weak. I had to squat to breathe the better air close to the floor.

Gathering myself, I stood up and moved along. The presence of the thing was stronger. I unhooked the flamethrower. The ship became narrow. I was in a hall. I trudged down it, the flamethrower before me. The hall turned right and I turned with it. I stepped out into a vast room full of decks of controls, dull and dusty in the glow of my head beam.

Above it all, against what had once been the view shield, now busted out and replaced by rock, was the monster.

I had been wrong about its long dead spirit. This wasn't just its corpse. It was alive. It was pinned, crucifixion style, to the rock. It was pinned there by great bolts through its neck and arms and legs and torso. Bolts that should have killed it, but hadn't. It writhed there and made a noise like a lost pup. Its long beak of a head was dipped, and its body was trembling. It looked like a bundle of withered sticks in a series of bags. It had long bird-like claws for feet and hands. It appeared to be partially petrified. It wore one of those control necklaces I had seen in my vision. And it lived.

It turned its head so slowly at first I was not sure it was moving at all. I saw its eyes, sunken and dark, a brittle spark flashed there, hatred and anger.

I caught movement out of the corner of my eye. I turned, and there was the paint-splotched specter. It flowed out of the shadows toward me, moving rapidly.

I lifted the flamethrower, but it sailed by me, toward the thing pinned to the rock. It moved there quick and smashed up against it and was absorbed. The peyote's magic wiggled inside my head, flooded me with understanding. I knew then that the last of its kind had not been killed. It had been punished. It had been pinned here centuries ago, its control necklace freezing it in place.

It had hung there all that time, like Prometheus on his rock, somewhere between living, somewhere between dead. A drone designed to work with little food or water, a beast of burden that could live for centuries on little more than air. It had dangled there in pain as the civilization it had been forced to build died out, or moved on. The last of its kind, displayed like an ornament. Now it was ragged and angry, so angry that over the centuries that anger had turned into a wraith, an astral projection reaching out in blind revenge.

But now, its astral self had returned to its source. Had given up the ghost, so to speak. At least for the moment. Perhaps to recharge its anger, its ability to project.

I stepped closer, looked up at it. Never have I seen such sadness. It wasn't a kind of face I recognized. Inhuman, strange, but a tired and defeated thought projected from it, heavy as an anvil. It clumped around inside my head, like a fat workman moving furniture.

I knew what it wanted.

It wanted it all to end.

It wanted to be past pain and anger.

It didn't want to live another century or more before it finally came completely apart, or the earth moved and tore it asunder. It didn't want to live another day, another hour, another minute, another second.

I lifted the flamethrower, and just before I pulled the trigger to make the fire jump, the feeling of anger and hate went out of the air, and it nodded its head as if in anticipation.

***

There's not a whole lot to tell now. I did what I sensed it wanted. I burned it until there was nothing left but blackened bones. I knew that would end whatever astral projection it had created inside its tortured brain. All it really wanted was peace.

As for the rest, well, the peyote wore off. I climbed up and out. The cops came down. I had to go back down there with them. They had safety harnesses and all manner of gear this time. It was an easier go. They saw everything, including the space ship and the charred remains of the angry traveler. They were startled, of course.

We had more evidence. Our cameras had caught the paint-splotched thing at work, tearing Fritz and Jake apart. No one in a position of authority wanted to digest that.

It was decided by the law that it just wouldn't be talked about. Story they told was Fritz and Jake died in an accident while helping us explore. That was the official line. Although there may be a true file stored somewhere. Our cameras were confiscated. There was talk of prosecuting us, but they couldn't decide what for. They let us go.

A final note. They sealed off the old ruins with explosives.

That's all right. I know what happened. So do Frank and Nora and Gary. It's fresh in our memories. It's only been three weeks.

By the way, Frank retired the day after it all came down. Rumor is he's moved somewhere warm and he no longer exterminates. I got stiffed. Frank never paid me for my work. I haven't heard from him since.

***

Finished, Dana stood up from the storyteller chair, went to find a drink. Several members tried to talk to her about her story, but she wasn't talking back. She said simply that she had told it, and now she was through. They could believe it or not.

She concluded her visit with a bit of small talk, finished her drink, and went outside. I went out with her. There was a big black car waiting for her. A man and a woman were outside of it, leaning on it. They were a good-looking pair. The woman's arm was in a sling and her hand was in a cast. The man opened the back door for Dana, and she slipped inside.

Before he could close the door, I said, "Will you come back? Will you tell us more of your adventures?"

"It could happen," she said, and the man closed the door. He opened the door for the woman whose arm was in a sling. She worked herself into the front passenger's seat. He went around to the driver's side, got in, and drove them away.

Introduction: Jana and Dana

by Kasey Lansdale

When I was a kid, I read anything weird or mysterious I could get my hands on. It started with R.L. Stine's *Goosebumps* series, and evolved into all the Nancy Drew mysteries. I loved a classic mystery, and especially a female sleuth. Not much there has changed. A few years back, I was on radio tour and the like, and I ended up in Boston, Massachusetts. It was a place I had always wanted to go, and I knew a large contingency of writers, and specifically horror writers, lived in that area. Maybe because it gets so bleak up there in the wintertime, who knows.

Nonetheless, I found my place in the group quickly, as they welcomed me with open arms. The leader of the group, more like social director, if you will, is Christopher Golden. We hit it off (which, let's be honest, if you don't get along with Christopher, it's likely you), and when the opportunity to return as a musical guest at the annual NECON Convention arose, I jumped at the chance and headed to Rhode Island. There, I met, or re-met some of the people I feel closest to today.

So I tell you this story, to explain how I became involved with the Dana Roberts series.

There was an anthology being put together called *Dark Duets*, from Harper Collins, edited by Christopher Golden. He invited my father to write a story for that collection, which he declined. My father is many things; a collaborator, overall, is not one of them. This collection involved each author to team up with another, and create the darkest tale they could conjure up. Christopher, however, is not one to take a "no" easily. It can be said it's part of his charm. So when I received an email from him with the anthology breakdown, followed up with the information of it being a "duets" piece, I called my father and asked if I could be the other half of the duet. To which my father also said, no.

I too, do not take no easily.

I love a good mystery, as I said, but I also read a lot more straight fiction, or women's fiction, as it's called, than horror. I like horror, I dabble, but I have always considered myself sort of "Lansdale Light."

I had this character that I really loved, who was working her way through another project I was writing, and I wondered how she might do in the horror world. One thing led to another, and she and I, Jana is her name, wound up with about five pages that I then sent to my father.

Remember when I said my dad is many things? Well, he's a sucker for a story, among others. After I hit send, I just waited, told Christopher to wait too, and sure enough, a day or so later, there was an email in my inbox where Dad said some semblance of my being evil, which I am, and then followed that up with another five or so pages. Success.

The book released and the story was there, and it was definitely a story of lighter tone than the rest, but it was a good story, and one I am still really proud of. I also knew that anyone familiar with my father's work would be able to tell that I really had a hand in this, as the voice was mine, and Dad was good about keeping that theme. It isn't too hard, as he and I are pretty similar in a lot of ways, even in our writing styles and pacing and voice. I'm not sure how much I just absorbed, or how much was intentional, but there are times it's hard to tell our work apart.

Then there are other times, when I think I really have hit on something, and I realize I've only laid the foundation, and he comes back in and weaves it into a thing of beauty. But that's why it works. That's why, when he asked me if I wanted to take that character from "Blind Love," Jana, and put her into a Dana Roberts casebook story, I said absolutely yes. And so we did. We had Jana team up with Dana in the story, "The Case of the Bleeding Walls."

Putting those two characters together completely changed the tone of the Dana Roberts books. It went from being intentionally stiff and in the style of a men's club storytelling, to goofy, fun, but still downright scary coming from Jana's point of view. No matter the situation, Jana tends to have a lighter, more compassionate take on things. Her empathy often extends to those who don't deserve it, and to those Dana gives no time of day. Jana is funny, brave, quick witted, and kind. She's who I want to be, and on a good day, am.

Anyone who has spent any time with me knows that the Jana character is very similar to my personality in real life. I was grateful that Christopher took a chance on a story that was a little offbeat, and in edits once, he said he'd debated about having us kill Jana, though I'm glad he held off, giving us the freedom to see what her next adventure might be.

Dad really wanted me to be involved with the Dana Roberts series specifically, because he felt that this tone of more natural ghost storytelling was closer to the things I was interested in, and enjoyed writing, and I loved that these two women were the strong lead characters, just doing what they do. Nowadays, more and more you get female led stories, movies, songs, etc. But it's still not even, and the respect level overall is still not the same in many cases for females. It's better though, there's no doubt about that.

I saw recently at the California State Capitol, in Sacramento, that back in the early 1900's, there were fifty male employees at the Governor's office, and two female. I'd say we've come along way from that, and being able to write about Dana and Jana in this way, as smart, successful, likable characters that also happen to be female, well, it's something I am proud to be a part of.

Each character has her strong suits, and it's less about what either one has or doesn't have, but how the skills they each possess help out one another. One hand washes the other, you might say.

Dana didn't even realize what she was missing until Jana came along, and though there isn't a hugging, bubbly, loving relationship between the two of them, there is a friendship, and a respect, and a different kind of bond between them that Dad and I tried to channel from Sherlock Holmes and John Watson. Sherlock is decidedly the brains of the operation, but without Watson, it just isn't the same. Watson, in many ways, is the heart. I'm thrilled to see these stories come together, including the Dana Roberts tales written by my father, before myself or Jana came along. It's a fun departure from what many know in the Lansdale universe, and I'm honored to be a part of it, even in a small way.

I do hope that Jana and Dana will have more opportunities to work together, not only because I am a fan of these two, but because it means I'll get another opportunity to write something new with my dad. That's fun for me, not only because it's on the job training by one of the best, but it's a way to take something we do together, and memorialize it forever. I'll always have that character, and that connection to family, and I hope that the reader can feel not only the heart of the characters, but that of the Lansdale clan.

Blind Love

by Kasey Lansdale and Joe R. Lansdale

I don't believe in love at first sight. Lust at first sight, maybe, but love? Not so much. That strikes me as a crock, and because of that, I can't believe I let my friend Erin convince me to go to an Eye Gazing Party with her, a kind of modern day hippie's answer to Speed Dating.

What you do is you go into a room with all these other sad, dateless men and women, a timer is set, and you sit down at a table and gaze into each other's eyes for two minutes without speaking. When you've done that with everyone in the room, you're supposed to choose the person you felt a burning eye connection with, go sit with them for a second round, and this time you can talk, having hopefully made a soulful bond by previous eyeball connection.

I, on the other hand, feared the first two minutes might only involve observing distracting mucus and a bulbous, red sty.

Not Erin. She was all in, high as a kite about the whole thing. It reminds me of when she went through her massage therapy phase, where the massage is applied through psychic power. You're not touched. The masseur or masseuse waves their hands over your body and channels some kind of energy from beyond the veil, or pulls it up from Mother Earth, or some such thing, and sticks it in your back through the enchanted power of healing hands.

I injured my back once during a sex act with a gymnast. He proved agile, but had all the personality of a pommel horse. It was a onetime experience in which I was assured certain positions would bring me unique pleasure, but instead brought me a bad back and three sleepless nights due to embarrassment and pain.

Erin assured me her masseur could pull out the ache, if not the embarrassment. What he pulled out of me was forty-five dollars and an hour out of my life. I went home with the pain I came in with.

Bottom line is she's the kind who reads her horoscope for real, believes there are special numbers in her life, and that constipation is a sign of energy clog instead of pizza, tacos, and an abundance of cheese. We even did nude skydiving once—well, there was the parachute. It was supposed to free our inner-self. She swore to me. We ended up with several seconds of fear, skinned knees, a scraped ass, and coming down not in the field where we planned, but in a grocery store parking lot in the middle of a busy Saturday afternoon that led to newspaper prominence, a fine, and overnight jail time.

The problem is she's my best friend and I felt obligated to support her in her quest for the perfect mate, this time, via an Eye Gazing party.

We were coming off a light, me driving, when Erin said, "I think it sounds romantic."

"With a room full of people doing the same thing? I don't find that romantic so much as creepy. Which celebrity started this trend?"

"I'm just trying to find happiness, Jana."

"I don't think you're all that unhappy. You just think you're supposed to have a man to make you happy. What's that old saying? A woman needs a man like a fish needs a motorcycle."

"Bicycle," Erin said.

"Well, if a fish doesn't need a bicycle, I'm going to bet they don't need a motorcycle either. Thing is, you'll find someone, and if you don't, well, we can play cards at your house all day when we're old. You got to stop obsessing about having a relationship. I mean, you got all the tools. You're smart and pretty, have a good job and all your own teeth, so eventually someone who has all their parts working and isn't too scary to look at is going to end up with you."

"Gee, thanks."

"Hey, I'm in the same boat here. My last date spent the whole night at dinner talking about his Lego collection. Let me say this without meaning to hurt your feelings, Erin. You're too desperate, and guys can smell desperation the way animals smell fear. They either feed on it until there's nothing left of you, or it makes them nervous and they run."

"You may have a point," she said as I hit the main highway and honked at a truck that tried to switch lanes with me in it. "Yet, I feel like I'm running out of options. Jordon, girl I work with, she went to one of the events once, met a guy there she's been with ever since. They've even started to dress alike."

Obviously mine and Erin's idea of what's adorable in a relationship is quite different.

"We turn around now, chicken out," she said, "and I end up with a house full of cats and a passion for macramé, you will be to blame."

"I'm more than willing to carry that burden."

"Well it's too late, because we're here."

We certainly were. It was a long rambling piece of property right in the middle of town. There were hedges around it high enough you'd have to have a ladder to see over the top, and there was only a gap between them to serve as an opening to a driveway. I wheeled through the gap and along the driveway that wound through a number of tall and well-groomed trees, parked behind a car in a row with a lot of other cars, all of them so expensive and cool they made my ride look like a hay wagon.

All along the walk were little signs with orange hearts painted through them, and above the hearts were a pair of sleepy, blue eyes and at the corner of each sign was a black arrow pointing up the walk.

"This is either the place," I said, "or an elaborate scam to murder us and sell us for body parts."

"You're always negative," Erin said.

"Experience has been a harsh teacher."

At the door, Erin knocked, and we were greeted by a small, pretty, dark-skinned woman decked out in traditional East India garb; flowing, bright-colored fabric that always made me think of Tandoori chicken and saffron rice. The woman at the door looked the part, but she moved as if she missed her high heels. But thank goodness she kept her chewing gum. I wouldn't want to have done without all that loud smacking.

Erin showed her a prepaid receipt, and I showed mine, thinking this was two hundred dollars that I might as well have just wiped my ass on.

The place was decorated with photos of exotic spots in India, a few from China. There were shelves containing knick-knacks, including a small statue of an elephant with a stick of incense sticking out of its uplifted trunk. The incense smelled like damp earth perfumed lightly with burning silk. Love paid well.

The woman took our coats, put them away in a hall closet and silently led us down a long hall to a doorway draped with a beaded curtain. When we reached that point, she stopped, said in an accent that had a lot more Texas in it than India, "Go on in, the swami awaits. Watch that step down, though, it's a booger. I've busted my butt there twice today."

She went away and we took caution of our asses and made the step. The room was huge, but no bigger than Grand Central Station. There was a series of small card tables all about, a chair on either side of each. There were people everywhere. The men were on one side of the room, the women the other. They were about as diverse as a jury pool, and I was relieved to see there was no one here I knew, though, come to think of it, had there been, they might have been as embarrassed as I was.

At the far end of the room, almost far enough away a pair of binoculars would have been helpful, was another beaded curtain, and out of it came a man who looked like a badly drawn cartoon character. Mid-sixties, short and thin, white socks with orange stripes and sandals, a ponytail of gray, frizzy hair. He carried a staff, as if he might later in the afternoon have to do a bit of mountain climbing in search of his goat herd.

I said, "Is he really wearing a cape?"

"I believe he is," Erin said. I think even she was thinking she might want to go back to her horoscopes and numerology.

"At least he didn't come in behind a puff of smoke," I said.

Our swami moved to the center of the room and lifted his staff like Moses about to strike the rock and bring forth water, and said, "I am Swami Saul, and tonight, you will bathe in the sweet essence of each other's souls."

I thought, oh shit. But I must admit he had a very nice voice, deep and resonant, just the sort of thing to lull you to sleep when counting sheep fails.

Gently lowering the cane he smiled and showed us he had some really nice teeth. "The eyes are the windows to the soul. Humans have known this for centuries. Sometimes we forget the obvious. We don't always allow them to do the speaking. We look away. We look down. We don't even make eye contact when we talk. How many men in here really look at women when you speak with them? I mean their eyes, not their bodies. I'm not denying that can also be a treat for the eyes, but think about it men. How many of you fail to actually concentrate on the eyes, and the soul of the woman?"

There was a bit of a shuffling, and one of the men, an average looking guy with a comb over said, "I'm guilty of that."

"No need to comment," said our swami. "It was a rhetorical question."

"Oh," said the man with the comb over, and he made a seemingly practiced step that placed him behind one of the other men.

"Today's society is too fast paced," said the swami. "Too reliant upon instant gratification. I promise you, after tonight, you will have truly touched each other's souls, and though I cannot make an absolute promise you will match one another with your internal essence, you are more likely to do so than through traditional dating, and therefore have a real opportunity to meet your proper soul mate. Is that what you would like? Is that why you're here?"

No one said anything.

"That question is not rhetorical," he said.

There were a few murmurs and some words of agreement, but there was still that sensation of being a bunch of cattle trying to decide if we were about to enter a feedlot or a slaughterhouse.

"Erin," I said. "Later, when we're out of here, remind me to beat you to death with my purse."

"Sshhhhh, Jana. Be quiet."

I thought, oh hell, now she's into it.

"Here is how it works," said Swami Saul. "You are not allowed to speak. You sit across from your partner, and you first gaze into the left eye, then move slowly to the right. This is not a staring contest, so do what feels natural."

Nervous laughter from the group.

Swami Saul held up his hand for silence, got it faster than a snake strikes a mouse.

"You must do this as I say, not as you want to do it, if you hope to have the results you desire. It is a far better method than just choosing your mate by appearance."

"He says," I said.

"Shush, Jana," Erin said.

"Your left eye is your receiver, and your right the activator," Swami Saul said. "You do this for a full two minutes. We will tell you when time is up, then you move to the next table and the next person into whose eyes you will gaze. So on and so on until finished with all the tables. When that is done, you will make a note of the number of the person with whom you felt the greatest sensation, and you will then have the opportunity to return to them for conversation. If that works, well, the rest will be up to Mother Nature. But remember, the eyes. The windows to the soul. That is where Mother Nature best reveals herself."

"That makes sense," Erin said.

"Mother Nature is also responsible for what goes on in the bathroom," I said. "And I think this operation has a similar smell about it."

"You're always such an old stick in the mud," Erin said.

We were individually guided to tables by Swami Saul, who I thought had a bit of a heavy hand on my elbow. I was placed in a chair in front of a guy who had had garlic for his last meal, and seemed proud of it. The problem was not only the strong aroma, it was the fact my eyes were hazing over with garlic fumes. He was nice looking enough, though, and I tried to smile and be nice and look him in the eyes without blinking, which made me feel a little bit like a lizard.

I was gazing like all hell when Swami Saul came by and touched me on the shoulder. "Blondie, blondie," he said. "Relax. Breathe. Let the experience unfold. You are not trying to melt him with heat vision."

I thought, oh yes I am.

"You act as if you're facing the sun head on... oh, sir. Let me offer you a mint. I can smell your lunch from here."

Swami Saul had less tact than I did.

The man was mortified, and I felt sorry for him, but I was glad when he took the mints Swami Saul offered him. By now my time was over, and I moved on to let the next in line deal with his garlic-and-breath-mint aroma.

By the time I was trying to look into my fourth partner's soul, only to find that I was not sinking down into his essence, but was instead bouncing off his retinas, I was starting to slip looks at my watch. I had been there about fifteen hard minutes. Only an hour and forty five minutes to go.

As we were changing chairs again, Swami Saul was gliding by. I said, "I don't think I'm doing this right. Can you give me some pointers?"

"Believe," he said. "Let faith carry you."

"That's it?"

"Okay. Here's a tip. You're making crazy eyes at everyone. Relax. Think only of his eyes. Only of his eyes. The left, then the right. Each eye has its own soul-felt story."

I tried to focus on Swami Saul's instructions. Focus on one eye, not both, and blink on occasion so as not to appear psychotic. The mousy guy in front of me, both in attitude and appearance, made a jerky head bob, and I couldn't tell if he was seizing, having a chill, or giving me some kind of signal. Turned out he was nodding off a bit, and it was all I could do not to break out laughing. We kept moving around the tables, and behind me I heard Swami Saul offering calm reassurance in his melodious voice, which reminded me of the narration you hear on crime programs where they're describing some horrible murder with the same calmness you might use to describe calm weather.

Glancing at Erin, who was seated to my left, I saw she was deep in gaze with her current partner who was a good enough looking guy that her attention was understandable. He'd done nothing for me in the soul department, but I could see why she would find him attractive. I know that's shallow, but hey, I was at an eye-gazing party, which is the definition of shallow, as well as stupid. Okay, there were a few times when I thought I felt something here and there, though in the end it was more likely a headache from eye strain due to my having astigmatism.

It really didn't take all that much time to go around the tables at two minutes apiece, but it felt to me like it was about the equivalent of the first Ice Age.

"Attention, attention," Swami Saul announced to the room. "If everyone would break gaze and return to your place along the wall, and this time, please use the chairs, no need to stand. Be comfortable."

A beat passed and no one moved.

"Now," Swami Saul said.

This time everyone moved. Chairs squeaked and scraped across the floor as everyone attempted to get seated. I tried to catch Erin's eye, I'd had enough training by this point, but she was as dedicated to finding her chair as a workhorse is to finding the barn. I went over and sat beside her, was about to speak to her when Swami Saul spoke again.

"Under your chair you will find a basket containing papers, pens. Please use these materials to write the number of the person with whom you felt most connected. It is not uncommon to have several choices. Place the number given to you at the top of your notations. We will then tally the numbers, make arrangements for another sitting, this time with timed communications with the person of your choice."

I pulled the basket out from under the chair, trying to think if anyone had really made my eyes twitch and my heart beat faster, and for the life of me I was having a hard time remembering which man went with which number. I decided garlic breath hadn't been so bad, and the breath mints had helped, a little, and there was the guy in the blue button-down that had a nice air about him, unless you counted his over-abundant use of a cologne that smelled like a horse saddle. I wrote down a few numbers so as not to seem odd woman out, folded the page and tossed it into my basket.

When I looked up I was surprised to find that everyone seemed to have finished well ahead of me and were perched in their chairs like seals expecting a fish for balancing a ball on their noses. Even Erin was staring straight ahead with the same intensity.

Swami Saul collected the baskets, and his assistant, the gum chewer, came into the room and helped him. The baskets ended up on a table at the back of the room with a large dry erase board on an easel near the wall behind it. The female assistant, smacking her gum like a dog eating peanut butter, went through the baskets and arranged the numbers in separate piles. After going through the goods, she paused and looked at Swami Saul and said something to him. He went over and examined the slips of paper, carefully, then more carefully. He scratched his head hard enough his ponytail wiggled as if it might swat a fly.

I admit that at this point I was curious if anyone I had gazed at tonight had felt a connection to me. This was only a mild concern, but my ego kept me engaged enough I didn't get up with a pee-break excuse and leave Erin to fend for herself.

"Interesting," Swami Saul said. "I don't believe we've ever had it happen quite this way. We have a wide variety on the part of the men, but, except for one woman, all of the women here have chosen the same man. This is a first."

The women in our row against the wall turned and looked first left, then right, except for those on the ends of the row, of course. They just turned and looked. They all had that deep country-fried look that seemed to say, "Was you lookin' at muh man?"

I smiled, wishing to appear neutral, which I was. Even the men I had listed had about as much connection to me as a mollusk, if those things could wear button down shirts, too much cologne and had a taste for garlic. I was more than willing to forgo my pick in lieu of anyone else's interest, lest I end up with one of my soul-gazing eyes scratched out.

"As all but one woman will know, as she did not choose him, that number is lucky thirteen."

I held my breath, tracking the numbers hanging on the bottom of the seats across the way, waiting to see who this stud muffin was, the Adonis that I had somehow overlooked, and then, there he was. Number Thirteen.

I had to rub my eyes and take another look, just in case my pupils had glazed over. But nope. Number Thirteen. I could see him clearly.

"You got to be shitting me," I said without really meaning to.

"What is wrong with you?" Erin said, turning at me in what I can only describe as anger. "Jealous? You want him like everyone else."

"I do?"

"Of course you do."

"I didn't pick him," I said.

"Oh, bull," said Erin, actually good and mad now. "You came here with me and now you want him and you don't want to see me happy with him."

"Say what?" I said.

She turned away from me, her face as red and shiny as a wet tomato.

I gave him another look. He was an uninteresting fellow of indeterminate age, could have been thirty-five or fifty-five. Pudgy with his few straggly hairs arranged as if by a weed eater. The suit he was wearing was thin and too large for him. It was cuffed unevenly at the sleeves and was either blue or gray; the color seemed undecided. He had on a white, stained shirt and a wide tie with palm trees on it. I didn't really remember him, but I remembered that tie. After a few moments of trying to concentrate on his eyes I had decided I liked the tie better, and believe me, I had to split some serious hairs to make that decision.

"This is certainly a first," said Swami Saul. "A real first."

By now all the men had turned to look at Stud Muffin. The looks on their face were akin to having just been told they were about to be electrocuted for the good of mankind. I didn't blame them. I don't want to be tacky. I mean, I know, it's not about looks when it gets down to what matters. I do know that. But come on. This is the beginning, when it's *supposed* to be superficial, and being shallow is all you have. And as conceited as it may sound, Erin and I are something to look at. I know. It's egotistical sounding, but there you have it. I wasn't the kind of girl that upon chance meeting was going to give a damn about a sweet personality. Of course, I was also the kind of girl whose last boyfriend, though handsome and clever, turned out to be married and have two other girlfriends on the side and a website that had something to do with farm animals. I never had the courage to examine it in depth but one of the sections I saw before I turned off the computer was titled THE HAPPY GOAT.

"I think the women have chosen, gentlemen, sorry. Only one lady here has picked a variety of numbers, and she now has the opportunity to visit with some of you."

"Pass," I said.

"What?" said Swami Saul.

"I'm that woman, and I'm going to pass. If anyone picked me, sorry. I'm passing."

"Oh," he said. "Well, okay."

It was rude, but I really didn't want to spend a lot of time hanging out with people I didn't really want to hang out with and had only written their numbers down so as to not be such an outsider. What I wanted to do was follow all the other women over to see Number Thirteen, decide if I had missed something, or if the others would get close up and realize he wasn't really such a hot number.

The throng of giggling women beat me over there, but I was able to peek between the teeming masses and get a closer look at Thirteen. He had looked better from a distance. I went over to Swami Saul and his assistant.

"So, one man, huh? And *that* man? All the women here, except me, are attracted to him? Really?"

"Really," he said.

"What kind of racket is this?"

"Do they look displeased?" he said.

I turned and saw they did not. They were mooning all over him, pawing at him and shifting in closer and closer. He stood in the middle of them smiling and still like a pillar of salt.

"I don't get it," I said.

"Me either. And you and I and Mildred here are the only ones who don't."

"You two didn't look into his eyes. I did. There's nothing there. I don't get it."

By now my head was pounding and my eyes were watering. My astigmatism had been given a serious work out, eye-balling all those men, and I felt I needed a new set of contacts, something I'd been putting off doing for a year. Maybe with contacts Thirteen would look like an Adonis.

"Maybe all them women have brain tumors," Mildred said, smacking her gum. "I wouldn't take that little balding fucker to a dog fight if he was the defending champion."

"Now, now," Swami Saul said. "Remember, you are enlightened now."

"Oh, yeah," she said. "Sorry. I forgot."

"So what's the answer?" I said.

"I don't know," Swami Saul said, and his voice had lost that deep down-in-the well resonance. He sounded now like a regular Southern cracker. He shook his head and watched the women clamoring after the little man like he was a rock star.

Standing there, looking first at the women crowding in on the little man, then glancing back at Swami Saul, I got a real sense that he had not rigged a thing, and was as confused as I was, as Mildred was. Of course, Mildred struck me as having come into the world confused and had gone through the years without noticeable improvement.

I noticed the rest of the men had started filing out, dejected and anxious to go.

It took some doing, but I finally got Erin pried loose from the crowd, and to facilitate an end to the evening, Swami Saul had started gathering up chairs and carrying them out, and Mildred was gathering the baskets. She stored them away somewhere, came back and flipped the light switch a couple of times, blinking them in warning.

It took another fifteen minutes to pull Erin out of there, and when she left she had an address for the little man, but so did every other woman in the room, excluding me and Mildred.

Erin and I didn't talk as I drove her home. It was obvious she had yet to forgive me for my lack of agreement on her pick, and frankly, by the time we were out of there and on the highway, I had begun to feel guilty, but also a little spiteful.

"Look," I told Erin. "I don't see it. But I think I could be wrong."

"Could be?"

"Well, you don't know if something works until it works, do you?"

"Oh, it'll work. He told me so."

"He told you that?"

"With his eyes," she said, "with his eyes."

***

When Erin was dropped off and I was nearly home, I realized I had forgotten my coat. I wheeled the car around and headed back, hoping Swami Saul or Mildred would still be there.

By the time I arrived it was dark inside and the door was locked, though I kept trying it, tugging like a fool until my arms hurt.

Of course the right thing to do was to go home and find out who owned the place, see if I could get them to let me in tomorrow, because I was pretty sure Swami Saul, who traveled across the country with his little circus act, had rented it for a night, and had decamped for parts unknown with his cape, Mildred, and a small crate of chewing gum.

It was a good coat and I wasn't ready to give it up. I went around back and tugged on a door there with the same lack of results. I looked around then, felt the place was tucked in tight by hedges and it wouldn't hurt anything if I went around and found a window open. In and out, and no one but me and my coat would be the wiser.

Circling the house I tried the windows. They were firmly locked. I considered knocking out a glass, undoing the latch, and pushing one up. I liked the coat that much. This was an idea I was floating, when the last window I checked moved up with a surprising mouse-like squeak.

I hiked my dress and stepped through the opening without breaking the heel off my shoe, then edged around in the dark.

My hip found a piece of furniture that hurt bad enough I made a sound like a small dog barking. I waited until the pain subsided and my eyes were accustomed to the dark. There was the desk I had run into, a few chairs folded and leaning against the wall, and a bit of light on the far end shining through a door. The source of the light was from streetlights beyond the hedges. The light was up front of the house where Mildred had stored my coat, and now, I realized, Erin's.

Able to navigate now, I made my way to the foyer where we first met Mildred. All the knick-knacks that had been on the wall were gone. All that was left of them was a kind of dry stink of the incense. The closet where Mildred had hung our coats was empty too, which didn't entirely surprise me. Somewhere tomorrow she would be wearing one of our coats, the pockets full of gum wrappers. I was fit to be tied.

I had started back toward the open window, when my foot banged into the trashcan. Nothing serious. No toes were lost. But it made me glance into the can. It was full of papers. I recognized them. They were the pages we had all filled out before the event on the Internet. They had been printed, and after serving their purpose, dumped upon Swami Saul's and Mildred's exit.

I pulled them out of the can and tucked them under my arm for no good reason outside of curiosity, went out of there through the window, and to my car. Coatless, I drove home.

***

At home I put on my pouting pajamas, which are large enough that I can jump in a full circle inside of them, sat at the table and had a bowl of cereal and four chocolate chip cookies. I moped around for about thirty minutes, picking crumbs off my front, then decided it was time for bed.

I tried to go to sleep, but lay in the dark, twisting and turning as if the mattress were made of tacks. I finally went to the kitchen and picked up the stack of papers I had taken from the trash.

I felt a little guilty, because at the bottom of each we had been asked to tell something about ourselves, our strengths and weaknesses, what we were hoping for in love, and so on, but I didn't feel so guilty that it stopped me from reading.

I found mine near the top. I glanced at it. It read: I think it's everyone else that is messing up. I'm a real catch. Anyone would be damn lucky to have me. I'm handy with a glue gun, can spell like nobody's business, and some people say I look like that movie star that everyone loves so much right now. Oh, and I got good teeth.

I always had been proud of my teeth.

I felt mildly conceited for writing such a thing, but still considered the comments accurate. I thought about calling Erin, but as it had passed the midnight mark by now and she had work in the morning, I decided not to. I had work too, but I write romance novels, which is ironic, and I was able to set my own hours. I wrote under a pen name and was just waiting for that free moment when I could write the great American novel. Susan Sontag didn't have anything on me. Except true success, of course.

I decided I'd keep thumbing through the pages, maybe even get some material for one of my books. I read all the comments at the bottom of each one. Some of them were really sad and desperate. I felt sorry for those women. Only material I was getting was for a suicide letter.

The papers had everyone's address and phone number on it, except mine, as I had given a false address and had given them my old boyfriend's phone number at work, the one with the animal website. I hoped they'd call. Asking for Jana was bound to make his wife or mistresses unhappy with him.

At the bottom of the stack I came across the forms the men had filled out, and there it was, Number Thirteen. His address was a place well out of town. I didn't know the exact spot, but I knew the area. It was pretty backwoods out there, even though it wasn't that far away. Occupation was listed as MIKE TUTINO'S JUNK YARD. Was junkyard an occupation? I guess so.

Oddly the man's name was listed as John Roe, not Tutino. The name was not too far off John Doe. Either he had an unusual last name, or he thought he was way too clever. The rest of the information about him was vague, and there was a notation that he paid for his eye gazing service with cash.

I thought in circles a while, finally took a sleeping pill and went to bed.

When I awoke the next morning I was still worried. I went to Erin's work place, a coffee house that has a kind of touchy-feely atmosphere about it and a very good Café Americano, as well as books for sale. You could drink and read and buy a book if you took the urge, though some of the books had chocolate biscotti finger prints in them, and I admit some of them were mine.

Erin wasn't there and no one knew where she was. She was supposed to have come to work. A friend of hers, another barista I knew a little, said the boss was mad at Erin and she wasn't answering her cell and she had better show up, and with a good excuse, or the best damn lie since Bigfoot.

I tried calling Erin on my cell, but got nothing. I left a message and drove over to Erin's place. It was a condo, which was essentially an apartment traveling under an assumed name. I had my own key that she had given me to feed the cats when she was out of town, and after knocking and ringing the door bell, and noticing her car wasn't in its spot, I went in.

Funny, but the minute I was inside I could feel the place was empty as a politician's head. I looked around. No Erin. I got a Diet Coke out of her refrigerator, and knowing where she hid the vanilla cookies, I had one of those. All right. I had four or five.

I ate them and drank my drink while sitting on her couch. I tried to figure where she was, and I won't kid you, I was becoming a little scared. After a bit I had a brainstorm, and went to her computer. I used it to examine her search history. And there it was MIKE TUTINO'S JUNK YARD. I assumed she already had the address from Mr. John Roe, Number Thirteen himself, but she had looked up directions. Could she have gone out there last night and got lucky? If you could call bedding down with that little dude lucky. I'd rather have a root canal performed by a drunk chimpanzee.

I searched on the computer a little more and saw the junkyard was no longer in operation, and that struck me as an odd thing unto itself, an abandoned junkyard for a home. I probed around some more but didn't find anything spectacular.

I went home and tried to write, but all I could think about was Erin, and the rerun marathon of *Friends*. I figured that was just the thing to keep me from thinking silly thoughts.

It wasn't. I watched about five minutes of an episode and began to channel surf, when I hit a local channel airing a news alert about a missing woman. Then another. And another. I was about to surf on when I thought I recognized one of the photos as a woman at the eye-gazing party, but I could have been mistaken. I hadn't really paid that much attention to everyone, being more interested in myself, which some might say is a failing. But, it could have been her.

Calling the police was a consideration, but since what I had going for me was that we had all been at the same place last night, and it was an eye-gazing party, it was hard to believe at this stage I would be taken seriously. Frankly, I was a little embarrassed about asking them to go out and harass a junk yard owner who might have acquired a harem of eye-gazing groupies due to inexplicable optical powers, and that I was immune to his loving gaze because of astigmatism. This was a thought that had started to move about in my brain quite a lot, that I was immune due to a natural malfunction. I wasn't sure how true it was, but I had started to embrace it, started to think maybe Thirteen was something a little different, and for his particular talents nothing could have been more perfectly made for him than such an event.

I mulled around all day, and just before dark I couldn't take it anymore, decided I'd drive out to the junkyard, just for a look. No big deal.

At least that's what I told myself.

***

The junkyard was way out in the boonies off the main highway, down a narrow road crowded by pines. As I came to a hilltop—the moon up now and bright as a baby's eye—I could see it. It lay in a low spot, and the junk cars spread wide and far. Fresh moonlight winked off the corroded corpses of all manner of automobiles and the aluminum fence that surrounded it. Back of all those cars was an old house that looked like it needed a sign that said HAUNTS WANTED.

I coasted down the hill until I came to a metal, barred gate that made a gap in the aluminum fence. The gate was about twelve feet wide and six feet high with a padlock no smaller than a beer truck.

I sat there in my car in front of the gate, decided to back up and turn around, and for a moment I was heading safely back to my house, feeling silly and knowing for sure Erin was probably home now, that she would have some logical explanation, like an alien kidnapping.

I activated the phone on the car dash and called Erin's number, got her answering machine again. I didn't leave a message. I got to the top of the hill, turned around and went back down, but this time not all the way to the gate. I was dedicated to the mission now.

I parked on a wide spot off the road under a big elm, got out and took a deep breath. It seemed I had begun a new career in trespassing, and possible breaking and entering. I hoped I'd find Erin, or the only thing I was going to get was prison time and a close relationship with a tattooed lady with muscles and a name like Molly Sue who liked it twice on Sundays.

I walked slowly, staying close to the side of the road where the tree shadows were thick, glad I had worn comfortable tennis shoes and a warm sweatshirt parka and loose Mom jeans. I pulled up the hood on the parka, and for a moment felt like a ninja.

I went along the fence toward the gate, but found a gap in the aluminum wall, decided that would be the way to go. I pulled the aluminum apart, slipped through without snagging anything, then crept along between rows of cars that looked like giant metal doodlebugs. The cars were really old, and if there had been any activity in this junkyard it was probably about the middle of last century. Grass had grown up between the rows of cars and died, turned the color of rust; it crunched under my feet like broken glass.

Sister, I thought to myself, what the hell are you doing?

No dogs with teeth like daggers came out to get me. No alarms went off and no lights flashed on. There wasn't the loud report of a rifle shot, so I soldiered on.

The cars were like a maze, and at one point I wound myself into the metal labyrinth and came out near the front fence again. I climbed up on the hood of one of the cars and got my bearings, studying my situation carefully. I did everything but break out a sexton and chart the positions of the stars.

Finally, with it all firmly in mind, I tried again, and this time, after more trudging, I broke loose into a straight row that lead directly toward the house.

***

Standing at the foot of the porch steps with only the moon and a dinky keychain flashlight as my guide, which would have come in real handy earlier had I remembered before now, I crept up along the side of the railing, careful of my footing. I had intended only to peek through the windows, where I was sure I would see Erin laughing and sitting on the couch, drinking a soda and having a hell of a time with Thirteen, but before I could, I heard something.

There was a clang, and when I looked a possum was hustling away from a pile of old hubcaps it had upset amongst the death camp of vehicles, and that brought my attention to the side of the house, and there, its nose poking out from behind the side was Erin's car. I was certain of it. I went over for a closer look and saw the miniature dream catcher she had made the summer before last, hanging from the rearview mirror. That served as a final confirmation.

Glancing around I saw there were a number of cars I had seen that night at the Eye Gazing event. I took some deep breaths to try and calm myself. I could call the police, but it would take them too long. Erin could be in serious trouble right now and I couldn't afford to wait on the cops to get off their asses and mosey down to this side of the tracks, and the truth was, the cars were here, but that didn't guarantee there was a problem. Maybe Thirteen's appeal had led to an orgy of epic proportions and no one was harmed. I decided I should at least check out the situation a little before throwing myself into a panic.

I fumbled through my pockets, searching for anything I could use as a weapon. I had an old paper clip, a pencil stub, and the keys already in hand, and that was it. Maybe if I found a rubber band somewhere MacGyver would appear and help a lady out.

Looking through the windows proved useless because upon closer inspection, I realized they had been blacked out with paint. I was left with no other option. It was time to go in.

I pushed at the front door, but to no avail. It groaned a bit, but it didn't budge. I backed my way down the rickety old steps and shone my light around the base of the house. Near the far left end, behind the overgrown and twisted up hedges, I spotted a broken window near the ground that looked just big enough for me to crawl through, if I sucked in tight and thought about celery while I shimmied. I pulled back the limb of a bush, gently kicked out the remaining fragments of glass, and in a feet-first motion, I slid inside the basement with one swift, effortless move.

Despite the off-putting appearance of the outside, the inside looked pretty normal save large amounts of a superfine, sparkly dust covering every surface. It looked as though nothing had been moved or cleaned in years, and ironically, could use a woman's touch. Unless it's my touch. All that would get you was a pile of dirty laundry in the corner and enough drain-hair to create a rope doll.

With every step, I left my tiptoe footprints in the shiny dust like a mouse tracking over a snow-covered hill. After several more minutes of searching, I started to feel the churn of my gut lessen. I was pretty sure I was alone in the house. Still, I opened the basement door that lead upstairs and connected into the kitchen with the stealth of a hired assassin, just to be sure. I bobbed my light around and once again found nothing but that dust. It was all over the house and where there were cracks and gaps in the old rotten roof, the moonlight shimmered on the dust and made it glow like glitter.

I coasted out of the kitchen and into a large room with bulks of cloth-covered furniture, backed myself against the wall and leaned there into the shadows. I let the weight of my thumb come off the button of the light, causing it to go black, letting my eyes adjust to the darkness.

I was really nervous now, and since I had not found Erin, or anyone in the house, but had found her car and recognized the cars of some of the other women from the eye-gazing party, I assumed I had enough material to take to the police. I could leave my suspicions about Thirteen's magic eye and my astigmatism out of the explanation when I spoke to them, and would probably be the better off for it.

It would certainly be smarter than wandering around a dark house and having the squeaking floor give way and drop me into the basement faster than green grass through a duck's ass, to lie in a heap of lumber, broken bones, and if I knew my luck, my Mom jeans hanging on a snag above me.

It was then that one of the pieces of furniture that I had taken for an ottoman stood up with a sound like cracking walnuts and a dislocation of sparkly dust that drifted across the room and fastened itself into my nostrils tighter than in-laws at Christmas.

The dust, however, was my least concern, it was the fact that the ottoman was not an ottoman but a moving wad of clothes and flesh that, though I couldn't see it clearly, I felt certain was Thirteen. How he had been bundled up like that on the floor, I have no idea, nor did I have the inclination to ask him, but I can assure you, the sight of him coming into human shape that way was enough to make my legs go weak.

I wondered if I had been seen, or if the shadows concealed me, but that was all decided for me when the dust in my nostrils decided to exit by way of a loud sneeze. It was like a starter's pistol being fired, and here came Thirteen, shuffling through the dust, coming right at me. Track had never been my sport, but right then I wished it had, because I broke and ran. Behind me I heard the floorboards squeal and the pitter-patter of feet, and then Thirteen had me.

***

His hand came down on my shoulder, and I'm ashamed to admit it, but I let out a scream that would have embarrassed a five-year-old girl with its ear-splitting intensity. I was yanked back and it caused me to wheel about on my heels, and I was looking right into the shadowy face of the little man.

I clicked on the key ring light in my hands, lifted it quickly for a look. I can't explain it. It was just a reflex. Thirteen's eyes were still flat and uninteresting, but then something moved in them, and I actually heard a crackling as if a fuse had shorted, and for a moment it seemed as if his eyes had slipped together and become one. I blinked, and then he looked the same, bald and doughy with ugly gray eyes.

We held our spots.

I swear I smiled and once more, the light went off and I dropped it, along with the key ring, to my side, said, "Have you seen, Erin?"

Really. I did. He didn't respond, just leaned forward giving me the hairy eyeball, and then I got it; he was waiting on me to swoon. He couldn't figure why his evil-eye wasn't working, why the hoodoo didn't do whatever it was supposed to do, and that's when I brought my keys up again, and raked him across the face, cutting his flesh in the way a knife cuts paper. I shoved him, raced past, and into the big room.

Glancing over my shoulder, I was horrified to see he was pursuing me, but on all fours, moving fast and light as a windblown leaf. Now I was in a hallway, and there was moonlight creeping in through a rent in the roof, and I had a pretty good view of everything, and one of those things was my reflection in a huge mirror with a small table next to it supporting a pitcher of some sort. I grabbed the pitcher, wheeled, and struck Thirteen on the forehead, causing him to stumble back and fall. It was a short-lived victory. He rose to his feet, came at me with his doughy arms spread wide and making a noise like a cat with its tail caught in a door.

I turned, took hold of the table, saw in the mirror that his image was contrary to what I had been looking at. Now he was little more than a skeleton topped by a bulbous head centered by one big eye, but when I turned he looked just the same, a stumpy, balding man in an ill-fitting suit, his mouth open wide and his arms outstretched, ready to nab me.

By now adrenaline was running through me like a pack of cheetahs. I swung the table as he lunged. It was a good shot, resulting in the table coming apart in my hands, but I had caught him upside the head and his head moved farther to the side than I thought a head could move. He did a little backwards hop, dropped to the floor, lay there shaking his head like he was collecting his brain cells one by one. On the floor the shards of the mirror winked fragments of my reflection. It was not a happy face.

I darted down the hallway, came to a stairway, hurried up it silently as I could, pranced along until I saw a hall closet with sliding doors. In my great wisdom as one of the world's worst hide-and-go-seek players, I carefully opened one of the two wide doors, slipped inside, and snicked the closet shut, plunging myself into total darkness.

***

It was a choice a two year old might make, but until you've been chased by an unknown creature, a supernatural being, an alien from the planet Zippie, or whatever Thirteen was, don't judge me.

I lifted my keychain light near my face, not yet having released my grip since attacking Thirteen, clicked it on and flashed it around. There were clothes on a rack, and I pushed in amongst them. At my feet were piles of shoes, and I must admit I spotted one really nice pair of high heels that I thought I might take with me when I finally decided to depart my hiding place, jump through a second story window and hope my legs didn't get driven up through my ass. Most likely I would be found with the high heels clutched tight in my teeth. They were that cute.

The cuteness factor faded and I made a little noise in my throat when I realized that the clothes hanging in the closet looked familiar, or some of them did. They were outfits the women at the Eye Gazing party had been wearing—okay, I'm shallow, I take note of these things—and one of those outfits belonged to Erin. There was something odd about the clothes. They were all pinned there by ancient clothes pins, but drooping inside of them was what at first looked like deflated sex dolls (I've seen them in photos) but was in fact the skins of human beings. One of those skins belonged to Erin. I couldn't control myself. I reached out and touched it, but... it was not what I first thought. It was her, but all of what should have been inside of her had been sucked out, leaving the droopy remains, like a condom without its master in action.

Describing how I felt at that moment could best be summed up in one word, ill. That's when I heard the squeaking steps of Thirteen on the stairs, then the shuffling sound of feet sliding down the hallway. I pushed back behind the hanging clothes and skins, feeling weak and woozy. I clicked off the light and held my breath.

After what had to have been a world-record time for breath holding, I heard the steps make their way back to the entrance in the hall, and heard the squeak of the stair steps again.

Flooded with relief, I cautiously let out my breath. At that moment there was a rushing sound in the hallway and the doors slammed open, and there I was, glancing through the skins and clothes, looking Thirteen dead in the eyes once more.

There was no question in my mind he saw me. I did my squeal again, ducked down, grabbed the high heel shoe, and came out from under the hanging rod, right at the dumpy little man. I was thinking about what I had seen downstairs in the mirror, his true image as a bony creature with a big head and a single gooey eye in its center. That's where I struck. I was on target. It was as if his forehead were made of liquid. The heel of the shoe plunged into his skull and went deep. There was a shriek and a movement from Thirteen that defied gravity as he sprang up and backwards like a grasshopper, slammed into the wall and fell rolling along the hallway, the heel still in his forehead. No sooner did he hit the floor than his body shifted and squirmed and took on a variety of shapes, one of which included a paisley-covered ottoman (nothing I would buy) and finally the shape I had seen in the mirror.

I pushed against the wall, trying to slip along it toward the stairs, taking advantage of his blindness. He staggered upright on his bony legs, weakly clawed at the shoe in what was left of his eye, jerked it loose, began waving his arms about, slamming into the wall, feeling for me. He stumbled into the open closet, knocked the clothes rack down, scattered the clothes and deflated bodies all over the hallway. When I got to the edge of the stairs I turned to look back. He lifted his blind head and sniffed the air, then shot toward me. I wished then I had not had the vanity to wear the perfume I was wearing, but I bought it in Paris, and had made a pact with myself that I would wear it once a week, even if I was merely shopping at Target.

He had smelled me, and now he was springing in my general direction on all fours, and before I could say, "Oh shit," he was on me. But, smooth as a matador, I stepped aside and he went past me scratching the air and tumbling down the stairs with a sound like someone breaking a handful of chopsticks over their knee. He hit just about every step on his way down, finally tumbled to the base of the stairs and came apart in pieces.

The pieces writhed and withered, then turned into piles of blackened soot. No sooner was that done than the house was full of an impossible wind that sucked up the sparkly dust that coated the house, whirled it in a little tornado and started up the stairs. Quite clearly, even in the dim light, I could see the faces and shapes of women in that dust. I saw Erin, whipping around and around, her long hair flying like straw.

The black soot piles that had been Thirteen did not move, no matter that the wind went right over them with its dusty passengers. As the dust twirl neared the top of the stairs I stepped back, watched it hit the upper hallway with a howling sound and smash into the closet.

I followed and watched the dust dive into the mouths of the deflated women lying on the floor of the closet. It filled up their bodies and they filled up their clothes. They tumbled out of that closet and lay in the hallway blinking their eyes, unaware of what had just happened.

"What the hell?" one of them said, and then I saw Erin, rising to her feet from the pile of women, looking blankly around, gathering thoughts slowly, her hair in a knotted clump around her head and shoulders.

I laughed out loud at their confusion, laughed too because I was alive and not an empty skin dangling on a clothes rack by a set of grandma's old clothespins. I began to weep a little with delight, mixing laughter and tears. I grabbed Erin and hugged her tight.

"What happened?" she said. "Where are we?"

"You were eye gazed by a monster of some kind and all your essence was sucked out and turned to sparkly dust for no reason I can figure and you were a skin hanging in a closet inside your clothes and I rescued you by killing the monster with a shoe to the eye, causing the dust to crawl down your throat and fill you up again."

"Oh," Erin said. "Wait. What?"

"I think this is going to take some time," I said, watching as the women scrounged through the closet looking for their proper shoes, knowing that one would be hobbling her way downstairs, "but I prefer we talk about it somewhere else."

As we descended the stairs, the others following, chattering amongst themselves, I saw the black piles of soot, all that remained of Thirteen, had turned gooey and were sinking unceremoniously into the pores of the wood like ink into soft paper.

The Case of the Bleeding Wall

by Joe R. Lansdale and Kasey Lansdale

After an odd personal experience, I started reading about what I called weird stuff, and the person I found that claimed to actually investigate and experience weird stuff, was Dana Roberts. I had a friend that belonged to this club she spoke at now and then. It used to be one of those all male clubs, all cigar smoke and testosterone, but in recent years they had let the times catch up, and women were invited to attend. Still, you had to know someone, and I did, and the one I knew I once dated. It hadn't worked out, but we were still friends. I had a coffee with him now and then so we could tell each other the disasters that were our lives, at least as far as romantic involvement went.

Actually, I wasn't doing poorly except in the relationship department. I had a little money, some from a recent inheritance, so I wasn't hurting, but not exactly feeling like I was living, and it wasn't the kind of inheritance that was going to see me comfortably into my old age, though it might brighten my cupboards with canned beans for the next few years.

There had been this whole weird as hell incident that had led me to Dana, but that's another story. Like Dana, I wrote it down. I figured since she made money from sharing her true adventures, well, two could play at that game. Except I didn't sell my story. No one cared. And no one believed it. Why would they? It was seriously weird. Again, off the subject.

This friend I used to date, Tom, knew about my weird story from a recent conversation. He thought it was bullshit. That maybe I had been drinking and hallucinated the whole thing, which I hadn't. It wasn't that he didn't believe in strange things, he just didn't believe me. He did however, believe some lady who frequently spoke at this club he belonged to, and somehow he found her more convincing than me, and invited me to attend with him. I think he figured I was in need of something interesting, and my story was an attempt to liven up my life. I don't know, I thought I sounded pretty convincing since it really happened. Of course, the lady speaker was Dana Roberts.

Dana was a favorite speaker at the club, and she came frequently to tell of her adventures, which I would call weird, but she called them supernormal. She saw them as things we were yet to understand, that were true.

Her view was, once lightning was thought to be supernatural, thunderbolts from the gods, or some such, but now we understood and had scientific reasons for why it happened, how it existed. Me, I don't really care. It boils back down to what I said before. It's weird stuff. Once you find out the world as you see it is a lie, you start to think and see things differently. You can't go back to where you were before. Stuff is out there, and I wanted to know more about it, so I went to the club to hear her speak.

Dana Roberts arrived that wind-whipped night in October, and I, like the others, sat poised on the edge of my seat, waiting. Dana took her time, eased her long black pea coat from her shoulders and folded it neatly over a stray chair in the corner of the room. She scooped up the bottle of red wine that had been set out for her, and though there was no shortage of gentlemen willing to pour her a drink, she declined. To the outside world, she appeared uninterested, and unaware of the male attention she was receiving, but I could tell she was very much aware, and even used it to her advantage. I know because I do it too. Hey, here's the facts. I'm not bad looking and neither is Dana. You use what you got.

Dana, though in her thirties, same as me, had a cotton white forelock that mixed in with her warm blonde locks. I found it oddly attractive, but it was clear that some in the room were in a hushed debate over if it was real, or an artistic sweep by her hairdresser.

We waited as she theatrically prepared herself to tell us her most recent adventure. It was all a little too stagy, I thought, but the frequent club goers were used to it. I was someone who not long ago would have stood with my arms crossed in the corner, mocking the sheep that made up the crowd, thinking they were such idiots to believe this crazy business. Now I had had my own crazy business, so I decided I could put up with a bit of unnecessary theatrics to hear her talk about hers.

The people at the club were nearly all true believers. They may not have started out that way, but Tom said over time they all came to accept Dana's stories as true. They also felt special. She always told her adventures at the club before writing them up and selling them to magazines and websites, and later collecting them in books. She was what you might call a spook hunter, though not all of her adventures involved spooks. The non-believers were mostly new members to the club. Tom said the non-believers pretty soon became believers, as far as he could tell.

So there we were, waiting on Dana. She sipped the wine, placed the glass on the end table as carefully as if it contained nitroglycerin, glanced at the roaring fire in the fireplace, pushed her shoes off, and curled her legs under her. Despite the contorted position, her dark blue pantsuit remained slick and perfect. Unable to handle the anticipation, a gentleman in the crowd shouted out to her, "Please tell us." I found this amusing. Dana smiled, took another sip, looked contemplative for a moment, and then she began.

***

Well, it was a hell of a tale, and I admit I had goose bumps once she was finished. Dana took time afterwards to sign books, a few autographs on paper napkins. She allowed the men to drool over her for awhile, and then just as she started to leave, I caught her gently by the elbow, said, "I know people do this all the time. But I had a very odd experience. I'd like to tell you about it."

"And I'd love to hear it, but I have a car waiting on me, and a time schedule," she said.

It was obvious she had dodged this kind of thing before, the fan trying to grab her ear to tell her about the time their long departed Aunt Mildred came back as a ghost and pulled the storyteller's leg while sleeping, causing her to awake and see Aunt Mildred smiling false ghost teeth at the foot of the bed.

For some reason though, as I walked outside with her, she paused at the car that was waiting for her and said, "You know what, ride with me. I can have my driver bring you back. We'll drive about a bit."

That's how we met, and how I told her my story, which is not the one I'm writing about now. That night Dana heard me out, brought me back to my car at the club. She offered to look over my story for possible inclusion in a book she was editing of other people's true supernormal experiences. I was to write it up and send it to her. I think she wanted to vet it a bit, if that was possible, as well as see if I could put two sentences together without tying them in a knot. Of course, since it was already written up, I was able to send it to her right away. I hovered near the mailbox for a couple of weeks, before giving it up and going on about my business, such as it was, assuming she had in a moment of politeness listened to me and asked for me to send my story.

But six months later she sent for me.

When her car arrived and delivered me to Dana's doorstep, or at least the hotel where she was staying, I took the envelope the driver had for me, and opened it. Her room number was inside. I took the elevator up, and had no sooner knocked, than the door opened and I was ushered in.

I had just sat down at the table in the seat she suggested, when there was a knock on the door, and Dana let room service in. The waiter, who looked like he loved nothing more than pushing food around on a rolling table, smiled and unloaded the covered trays onto the hotel room table. Dana signed the tab, and he went away looking happy, which I assumed was because Dana had written in a sizable tip.

Snapping a napkin in the air, Dana sat at the table and lifted the lid off one of the trays.

"I took the liberty of ordering us a light supper. I hope you like fruit and walnut salad," she said.

"No problem," I said, though, frankly, I preferred to eat the rabbit than eat the lettuce the rabbit ate.

"I seem to be without assistants," she said, picking at a piece of sliced kiwi fruit with her fork.

"Excuse me?"

"My assistants. They are on vacation. I have a few people I turn to in times like this, but they are all busy. So, I thought of you."

"How nice to be last."

"Oh, now," she said. "I didn't mean it as a put down, like you were the last person I thought of. I didn't say that."

"But I was, wasn't I?"

"True. Don't be offended."

"How about I learn more about it, and then decide if I'm offended?"

"Would you like a free trip to Italy?"

"I no longer feel offended."

"We haven't made the trip yet. I thought about the story you told me, the article you sent me. I believe it happened to you. I have some ideas about it as an article, a bit of a touch up here and there, nothing to change the truth, just the prose, we could share a by-line, but this isn't the time for that. We have a flight to catch within a couple of hours. Private jet."

"I've got the clothes on my back, and that's it."

"I judged your size, a little larger than me, and I believe you wear bigger shoes, but there's a case packed for you in the closet. Nothing dressy, but nice and functional. Sensible shoes. I also prepared a small carry-on bag with a Kindle in it. I took the liberty of downloading a few of my books."

"I can't pay for that stuff, Dana."

"It's on me. I'm ungodly rich."

"The books you write?"

"Mostly the practice. I get paid for ridding places of unwanted presences, and that pays a lot more than the books. Though the books do pay, and there is the forthcoming film. I'll be playing myself."

"I play myself everyday," I said.

She didn't laugh, and I tried not to dwell on her assessment of me being "a little larger than her," though she was correct. She plucked a raisin from her plate and chewed on it, followed it with a walnut. I picked at my salad and said nothing. I could be as silent as she could, and just as delicate, though it took more of an effort. The silent part being especially tough. I'm a born talker. When I was little my mother used to call me Chatty Kathy. And considering my name is Jana, that was confusing when I started school.

Dana waited so long to start talking, when she did, it startled me. She also had a slightly formal way of speaking, not exactly professorial, but friendly-proper. She leaned back and made a steeple with her fingers under her chin.

"You see, Raina—"

"Jana."

"Of course. There was a call waiting for me when I arrived at the office. I had just finished a long, well paid inquiry in Georgia. A young couple had moved into a house with a haunted reputation and complained of hearing noises at night. Normally

I send my assistants on such trivial matters, as nine times out of ten they prove to be of common and explainable origin. That way my business still gets paid, and I don't have to deal with it. I've paid my dues as a common 'spook' hunter and mostly restrict my efforts to more interesting and legitimate phenomenon.

"I've said before that I don't actually believe in the supernatural, but I do believe in what I call the supernormal. Meaning unexplained events that are considered supernatural because we have yet to learn their causes. This particular request sounded somewhat weak, but the couple was well off enough to want to waste money. I explained to them that it was most likely nothing outside normal understanding. I chose to work the case myself for the simple reason I had been writing non-stop on a book of my cases for my publisher, and had gone two months over the deadline, and found myself toward the end of the book working nearly night and day. I had had neither rest nor romance, nor even a good time at a county fair to distract me. This seemed like a possible distraction."

I almost laughed when she said that. It seemed out of character to think she might attend a county fair on purpose. Me, I probably would have attended and ridden a goat around the arena.

"I was there exactly one day, proving their unexplained voices were nothing more than bees in the wall. They had slipped in through an attic window and down a ventilation shaft, and had somehow gotten into the insulation. Their buzzing was intensified by the heating and cooling ducts. I got my fee, and so did a resident beekeeper that relieved them of the bees.

"It was with a fresh, fat check, and an intense feeling of disappointment, that I returned home to a personal message from an old flame in Italy. That is how I have come to ask you to go with me."

"Are we double dating?"

"You think of yourself as humorous, don't you Hanna?"

"Jana."

"Of course."

"I do. Yes."

"I see. Well, no. Not a double date. But I need someone to assist me. Are you up for that? You have to do as I ask, but there will be nothing unseemly. No weird costumes, orgies or unseemly episodes with animals."

"Well, hell," I said. "Why go?"

"More humor. I see."

"Hey, I get a chance to learn from you about, what is it, the supernormal, and get a trip to Italy with a suitcase full of clothes, sensible shoes, and an electronic reader, what's not to like?"

"I should add that sometimes my work is dangerous."

"I eat danger for breakfast."

"You do, huh?"

"Not really. Humor again. My one adventure scared the pee-diddly hell out of me."

"Are you prepared to put yourself in jeopardy again, if the need should arise? I don't need a weak sister on the payroll."

Actually, I wasn't sure I was prepared for danger, or even a rough night at the ballet, but I thought I could make that judgment when the time came. I said, "So I get paid?"

"You do. I can only offer the trip and five thousand dollars this time, but if you work out, well, I could put you on payroll with my other assistants. You may keep the clothes and shoes and reader if you like."

As I said, my inheritance wasn't going to last forever, and I didn't have any hot prospects, other than a freelance job keeping up with medical records and shaking the butter cookie crumbs out of my computer keyboard, so I thought, what the hell?

"I'm in," I said, "assuming this trip comes with pizza and maybe a tall, dark Italian."

"For me it may be both," Dana said. "For you, pizza for sure."

***

Eighteen hours later, jet-lagged with no sleep and a serious case of intestinal turbulence from plane food, I found myself climbing out of a taxi with Dana onto a cobblestone street corner in Rome. Dana was wearing some nice and expensive high heels, and I had on comfy tennis shoes. She walked without so much as a wobble while I trailed behind, visibly tired and rubber-legged, and hot in the afternoon sun. We had to take a very narrow alley to her flat.

Of course, she would own a flat in Rome. She probably had one in Paris, Istanbul, and perhaps one in the black hole of Calcutta, if there still was such a thing. Chasing spooks had been a very profitable profession for her.

In that moment I was worn out and looking for a bed, though upon arrival at her less than humble abode, the sheer luxury of her flat gave me a small shot of adrenaline and a kick in the ass from jealousy and envy.

"Damn," I said. "Give me a ghost to wrestle."

"It is nice, isn't it?"

"I'll say."

"I don't pay my assistants as well as I pay myself, by the way."

Considering I had been promised five thousand dollars, had free clothes, and a trip to Italy, I was thinking she paid well enough. Then again, so far no ghost had tried to eat me or maim me or challenge me to a game of checkers, or whatever it is they do.

"We'll get a good night's sleep first, then tomorrow we talk to the client, also my former lover, and just so you know, I may still have designs on him, so try not to look stunning or toss your hair too much."

"Duly noted."

I had my own room, and it was nice and comfortable. Even though it was still light outside, I was knackered. I stripped down to my underwear and crawled into bed. The bed was a cloud. I lay awake for a little while, thinking about how just hours before I had been home thinking I might ought to make out a shopping list, and now here I was in Rome with the world's most famous spook hunter, and my stomach was growling over kiwi fruit and a fistful of nuts and a few scraps of lettuce. I really hoped breakfast would be a little more exciting than the salad and two bites of rubber chicken on the plane. Dead pig and scrambled eggs would be nice.

***

Next morning Dana awoke me by pulling open the door and saying, "Rise and shine. We are at it."

I didn't even look at her. I rolled over and didn't shine, but after a second appearance at the door, and a repetition of "We are at it," I rolled out of bed still consumed by jet lag. I felt as if I had been on a month long drunk. I had slept in my underwear, but found a pair of blue pajamas hanging over the back of a chair, and that led me to believe I was to wear them. There was also a pair of fuzzy blue house shoes.

I slipped pajamas and shoes on, and slid into the main room shuffling my feet, too tired to lift them. When I reached the kitchen, there was Dana, dressed in nice, tight fitting jeans and a gloriously bright green top, her hair brushed and lustrous. She had on a pair of knee-high boots that flared at the top like the old pirate boots. She had on perfectly applied makeup and a smile enviable by Hollywood. She was leaning against the sink, sticking her tits out. Sitting at the table was a man so gorgeous that all he needed to top him off was a big pile of vanilla ice cream scooped onto his head. I felt like a turd that had rolled down hill into a sophisticated party thrown by the Queen of England.

"Oh, hi," I said.

"This is Carlo," Dana said.

This vision of a man smiled. Dark eyes, dark hair, dark skin. No wonder Dana wanted to protect a possibility that they might get back together. If they ever had children they would be without sweat or intestinal by-products. Together they looked like a magazine ad for all that was glorious in the universe, and possibly a few alternate universes as well.

"I'm sorry," I said. "I didn't spruce up."

"That's quite all right," Carlo said in perfect English, though there was certainly some Italian accent to it. "You look good in blue."

"Carlo and I were just discussing his problem," Dana said. "I suppose we can begin at the beginning."

"Dana," Carlo said, "you are always so impatient with your assistants. I don't know how you keep them."

"Money," Dana said. "Adventure. Lots of travel. A certain amount of personality dominance."

I think she was kidding, though to be honest, I believe Dana and I had a kind of thing with each other. A quiet competition, at least from her view. I didn't know what there was to be competitive about. Looking at her, looking around, I think she won the contest before we got started.

"So, I assume you are the client?" I asked.

Carlo nodded.

"I have a house outside of Rome. Some of it is old, some of it is new. It is a unique house. But I can't live there. I built it for my fiancé at one point in time, but that fell through. The house is part of the reason we are no longer together."

He paused there as if there was a part to the story that was too troublesome to tell. It was a little awkward, and as there was coffee going in a very nice coffee pot, I used it as a comfortable distraction. I pulled a cup from the cabinet and was delighted to see at least it was cheap. It was the first cheap item I had come across. It was big and heavy enough to use as a weapon. I filled it with coffee, left it black. I needed a jolt without any barriers of cream or sugar.

"I've told Dana about it some," Carlo said, "but all I can say is my fiancé felt it was... uncomfortable. That someone, or something, was in the house."

"Was there someone or something?" I asked.

Carlo shrugged. "Hard to say. There certainly were signs. It's a large house, two stories, lots of glass. Very modern. Not what one would normally think of as a haunted house. There are a few older structures that have been incorporated into it, but it hardly seems like a house that would attract ghosts and ghoulies. It is only ten years old now. I haven't lived there since the night Cincia left. I offered to live with her elsewhere, but for whatever reason, she decided the house and I were somehow connected. I suppose she knew I had spent a lot of money to build it, and that I had a lot of myself invested in it. After the event, others have rented it from me, and no one has stayed longer than a month. Usually far less time. I have left it vacant for several months now. There has been some vandalism. Minimal. Dana and I, we have been friends for a long time, so I thought, why not see if there is something... How should I say it? Unnatural about the house."

"What is it you think might be unnatural?" I said.

"He'll fill you in on that when we get there," Dana said. "Maybe you'd like to at least change shoes, and we'll go."

"Great. I get to wear my pajamas."

Carlo laughed.

Dana did not.

"Is there breakfast?" I asked.

"Eaten already," Dana said.

"Dana is always in such a rush," Carlo said. "The house has been vacant this long, so a few minutes more will not matter. You should eat."

So I ate a granola bar and drank my coffee. I dressed in the Mom jeans Dana had bought for me, as well as some highly unattractive high top tennis shoes, and a pullover top that I presumed was designed by circus clowns. With Carlo driving us in a very nice convertible, we set out for the house.

***

It was a long drive and well out of Rome, and the weather was bright and clear. The countryside in places was beautiful, at least what I saw of it through my wind-whipped hair. When we arrived my hair had become something of a Gordian knot, while Dana, who had been wise enough to wear a shirt-matching scarf, was well turned out. When she took it off, her hair looked the same as it had when I first saw her that morning.

Once out of the moving convertible it quickly became hot as a goat's ass in a pepper patch, and I was immediately longing for air-conditioning, though neither Carlo nor Dana appeared to be affected. I on the other hand was as sweaty as a ditch digger.

Right then I hated Dana just a little. She always seemed prepared and calm and collected. I might also add she had brought a couple of bags with her, one I carried for her, the other Carlo carried. Dana carried nothing, and acted as if that was the nature of things.

Then again, she was the boss.

The house was set at the end of a long winding road bordered by old, large, twisting olive trees. The grass between the trees was well clipped, and there were birds a plenty, at least until we neared the house. I noted as we did, the trees became less healthy looking, more tangled, and I didn't see a single bird. I know that sounds like a haunted property cliché, but that's how it was.

The house itself was beautiful. Tall and bright with loads of glass. It covered a tremendous amount of ground. I suddenly wondered what it was Carlo did for a living, because whatever it was it paid in serious Euro. Not only was he good-looking, he was rich, as well as charming. As of late most of my dates were with men who lived with relatives, had most of their teeth, and were looking forward to the next Super Bowl and squirrel-hunting season.

The walls of the house, when they were not glass, appeared to be thick and made of adobe. The place looked well cared for, though I did spot some vandalism, spray paint markings on the outside wall, words actually. It was in Italian, so I had no idea what it said, but Dana, looking at it, read it to me.

"It reads 'Bad House,'" she said.

"It has acquired a reputation," Carlo said, "due to renters not staying here for long."

"I suppose for something like this rent is expensive," I said.

"It should be, but to have someone here to have an eye on the house, I've allowed it to let for very little. The price of a rundown cottage, I suppose. Still, no one has stayed long, and no one has been here in a while."

Inside, the windows proved to be muted against the sun, but it was still bright inside, and there was nothing haunting about it. A long, winding, white staircase with gold, metal rails wound up to the second floor. The walls were spotted throughout with unique paintings.

"With no one living here, aren't you afraid someone might steal the paintings?" I said.

"All of the vandalism is old. I haven't bothered to have it painted over. I mean, vandals could still harm the house, but I've installed some protective considerations since they first did their damage. For example, at night, when someone steps into the yard, the lights that are positioned outside, on and about the house, come on automatically. There is an alarm system. Cameras. It's less enticing for vandals to come within range. Truthfully, it's less to keep the vandals from doing damage, as it is to make sure no one enters the house at night. The house is more dangerous than any vandal. The trouble is in the Great Hall mostly, though not exclusively."

"The Great Hall," I said.

Carlo led us to a set of doors that looked as if they should have a drawbridge before them. They had great metal rings placed in each of them, and a chain was draped through them, and a padlock dangled from it. Carlo produced a key, unlocked the chain and let it rattle to the floor. He tugged on one of the doors. It opened effortlessly. He pushed it aside, and opened the other.

"If it were night," he said. "You could not get me within miles of this house, certainly this room."

Beyond the doors there was a humongous room. It was not a hall at all. You might need mules and a backpack to get to the other side. This part of the house didn't have any glass walls, though the second floor had a landing on the left that came off a staircase and there was a lot of glass up there, but unlike the other room we had been in, it was not well lit. You could see the sun coming through the glass, but it was a weak light due to the heavily tinted windows.

There was no second floor on this side of the house, just the wide, tall room with the staircase and landing on the left and the glass that subdued the light. The landing was wide and primarily for show. You could stand there and look out on the world. I could see a table and chairs in one spot, and I suppose that was where Carlo could sit on his wide landing and look out over his olive trees and mentally count his money.

On the bottom floor, where we were, there was one large window to the right, just one, and it looked out on a back yard of well-groomed trees, and a large gazebo with a solid, concrete bench in its center, in the shape and size of a coffin.

Inside the Great Hall, or room if you prefer, were statues of men and women. They were made of what I assumed was shiny gray metal. They had bulbous heads, twisted features, humped backs and long, warped legs, hooves for feet. Curious they were, pretty they were not. The paintings were what I thought of as abstract at first glance, but upon closer observation realized were of bizarre, human figures that nearly blended into their colorful backgrounds. The art here, unlike the art of the other room, was savage and unpleasing to the eye.

The hall felt gloomy, but hardly what one would describe as haunted. The most haunting thing about it was those paintings and statues. There were four normal sized doors against the wall at the far end. But the thing that caught my eye was the wall on the right side of the room. There were no paintings there. The wall looked ancient. There were figures carved deep into it. I couldn't determine what the figures represented.

Up close, I decided the stick drawings were of people, but what they were doing I couldn't tell. They all seemed to be looking toward the right side of the wall, and there was a great slash of shadow drifting at an angle from that corner. It extended like a partially torn curtain over half that section of the wall. There were grooves in the wall from top to bottom, and at the very bottom was an abutment with a groove in it. I touched it, ran my fingers over it, and though I don't want to sound overly melodramatic, touching it made me feel a little ill, as if I had handled a corpse in the dark, thinking it was a lover.

"Okay," I said, "I finally found something a little bit creepy about the house."

"The wall was already here," Carlo said. "Once the earth was higher, and when we dug down to level out for construction of the house, we found this wall. There were also some pottery shards, odd and ends, that the archeologist would have wanted, I didn't mention it to the authorities. If I did, I knew it would hold up construction while archeological teams came out and took their time, possibly years, to dig and sort through the shards. So, though it wasn't exactly legal, we didn't tell anyone. But I spared the wall. We filled it in a bit at the top and on the sides and made it part of the house. It is very sturdy. I collect art, so, unofficially, I collected this as well, as in my view it is art. Peculiar art, but art."

"It's too unsettling to call art," I said.

"The eye of the beholder, and all that," Carlo said.

Dana turned to me. "Carlo is being modest. Besides the job that has given him his wealth, he's a noted art scholar and historian."

"Ah," I said, thinking, if this shit is art, then I'm a monkey's uncle, and considering my difference in urinary equipment, that would be a feat.

"What happened to the shards and the other items?" Dana asked.

"I hate to admit it, as it's not legal, but I kept them. They are stored in a box at the back, behind those four doors. I keep that section blocked off, as the shards are delicate and I prefer not to have them handled."

He said this as if Dana and I were about to break into a run, burst through the doors at the back, and start indiscriminately fondling the pottery shards.

"You brought me all the way here, Carlo, but you don't seem eager to tell me why," Dana said.

"I suppose the whole thing does worry me a bit. Even discussing it. Come, let's go into the kitchen. I stocked up in preparation for your arrival."

I can't say how much of being in the Great Hall and feeling gloomy was due to the room itself or the power of suggestion, but the kitchen seemed cheerier than the Great Hall by a considerable degree, and in fact, I hadn't known just how depressing that room was until I stepped out of it. It was like stepping out of a cold rain and into a warm house. The kitchen had a long counter, as well as a table, and we sat before it on stools. Carlo brought out wine and snacks. Cheese. Fresh olives. Very nice bread and olive oil to dip it into. We nibbled and sipped while he talked.

"My experience with my former fiancé is not too unlike that of the renters. We spent our first night here, in anticipation of, as you say in America, tying the knot. We say that too, but it sounds different in Italian."

"I bet that's because it's a different language," I said.

Dana snapped a look at me, and Carlo laughed.

"True," he said. "But what I thought would be a grand moment in the new house was anything but that. We had walked all through it earlier in the day, but except for what I can only say was a brief feeling that more light should be established in the Great Hall, nothing seemed amiss.

"We turned in late, having spent a good time talking about the house, making plans, and then shortly after midnight I awoke with what I can only describe as a feeling of dread. There was no reason for it, but suddenly I felt as if every misery of the world had descended on me. Cincia was also awake, and she turned to me and said, 'Do you feel it?'

"I admitted I did, and then came a sound, distant at first, of something banging. It didn't take a lot of consideration to know that it was the doors in the big room, probably the ones on the far wall, the four doors that lead into the hallway at the back.

"I picked up a fire poker that went with the upstairs fireplace, and proceeded downstairs. Cincia was unwilling to stay behind, and followed closely after me. As we came down, the doors to the big room swung suddenly open. The opening of those doors was such a sound as to make us both jump and cry out, losing me a large portion of my masculine credentials, I should think. There came from the Great Hall a stink that caused us to cover our mouths and noses with our hands. It was beyond anything I have ever smelled. Extremely foul. It was all I could do to keep from heaving, and Cincia was not so fortunate. She threw up right there on the stairs, and over it, splattering vomit on the floor, which did nothing to improve the already putrid smell. She refused to take another step, no longer certain I was any sort of protection. I started down with the fire poker, though it took all of my will to do so.

"By the time I came to the bottom of the stairs I was a nervous wreck. All manner of wailing and banging was coming from inside the hall. I forced myself to stand in the doorway, watching, and eventually I found the courage to enter the room, trembling, feeling dizzy and nauseous from the stench.

"You've had the hair on your arms and the back of your neck stand up from feeling a bit fearful, or cold, but I felt it as if those hairs were needles. I reached for the light, but when I flicked the switch nothing happened. The great doors swung shut behind me, and there was a sound like a satisfied sigh. That is the best way I can describe it, for I think it was exactly that. Then the shadows moved, and within the shadows there was a violet light, and the violet light showed other shadows within the larger ones. They had the shapes of people, but there were no features, and all I could think of was they were the shades of the dead, as Homer might have said."

He paused for a moment, as if the memory itself was as powerful as the event.

"Finally there was a kind of whispering, and then a whipping sound, like something being thrashed back and forth through the air. I knew then I was in the presence of something beyond any human understanding. I was near frozen to the spot with fear. I grabbed at the door and yanked. Something seemed to be pushing against it to keep me from going out. I pulled until I thought I would collapse, and finally it came open, slightly. I squeezed through the gap and into the outside room, letting the door slam shut behind me. There was still the smell and the feeling of oppressive evil, but I no longer felt as if my life were threatened. I was miserable and sick for a moment, and then the smell and evil sensations faded, and the switch I had hit in the Great Room came on, because I saw the light shine under the doors. Even with that light, I decided I was through for the night, and would not return to the great room. Not after that extraordinary experience.

"Cincia had not even entered the room, but it was all too much for her, the sounds, the smells, my telling her my experience in the Great Hall. It was a turning point for us. It put a barrier between us I can't begin to understand, and that was the end of our relationship. Within a week we were done. Afterwards, I tried to dismiss it all as a silly thing that had not happened exactly as I remembered it. Tossed it off as being bad food and creaking timbers, backed up sewage pipes. Nothing actually satisfied me.

"It wasn't long after that that Cincia died. No apparent reason. I considered having the house torn down, the ground sown with salt like in the old days, and then covering it all in concrete. But I couldn't do it. I wanted to know what it was in the Great Hall, because something is in there, of that I have no doubt."

"Sometimes," Dana said, "disappointment can make an uncomfortable experience seem more than it actually is."

"You mean because of my loss of Cincia, I may emotionally be planting false memories?"

"Let me ask, and I ask this gently, Carlo. Were you and Cincia having any problems before that night?"

Carlo ran a hand over his face as if removing cobwebs.

"In a small way, I suppose. I think she may have been having second thoughts, but I'm sure they had more to do with the feelings she had about the house, the sensations she felt even before nightfall. She was a very sensitive person in so many ways."

"So the two of you had some doubts about your forthcoming nuptials?" Dana asked.

"I'm not proud of this, but yes. I had an affair. It was nothing. Very short, and very stupid. But it happened, and it caused strife between us. I actually struck her once. I can't tell you how ashamed I am of that, but I did. It was during a heated argument. We got past that, because she struck me as well. Hit me first. But the affair, she couldn't move past that. I don't blame her. I had this wonderful and beautiful woman, and for no reason other than opportunity and lust, I cheated on her."

Dana nodded. "Sometimes feelings like that, guilt, disappointment, they can become profound, more so than a person realizes, and then it can manifest itself in all manner of ways. Sometimes it can actually become a power within itself."

"Like a poltergeist?" Carlo said.

"Exactly."

"I have done reading on such things, Dana. But I assure you, it wasn't anything like that."

"You can't be sure," Dana said.

"You're saying I imagined it?"

"I'm saying you may have compounded something simple into something extreme."

"What of Cincia? She heard the sounds in the Great Hall as well, smelled the stench."

"It's about how you remember it, and that may not be how it was."

"I am not lying," Carlo said.

"I didn't say that," Dana said. "I'm merely trying to cover all the bases, all possibilities."

"Of course," he said. "That's why I brought you here. To cover those bases. After that night I decided to rent the house cheaply, all the while thinking at some point I'd return and live here. I don't know what I expected to happen to make that possible, but it was a thought. I closed off the Great Hall, leaving it as you saw it, and allowed only the remainder of the house to be rented. The stairs go all the way around and come down into a hall behind those four doors, but I blocked off the stairway, saying to renters I was using the upstairs landing and the hall behind the four doors for storage. I chained the Great Hall shut. Still, even though none of my renters entered the big room, the sounds at night, the stench, the rattling of the chain on the doors, banging and sighing, was too much for anyone to stay here, no matter how affordable the rent. Another reason it's hard for me to see this all as some trick of my mind. Could a lot of minds be tricked in the same way?"

"Did you tell any of the renters about what happened here?" Dana asked.

"I should have, now that I think about it. I suppose in a way I was testing to see how much of it might be suggestion. You see, that did occur to me, Dana. If they had a similar experience, but were protected by a chained door and blocked staircase, I felt they were safe from any actual harm. The worst they could suffer would be sounds and smells and discomfort."

"That does make it seem a lot more legitimate," Dana said.

"I should have thought of you immediately, Dana, but, well, I didn't want to stir something between us, there having been plenty at one time. Not until I had properly grieved anyway."

"I understand," Dana said. And I could see that a little something moved across her face. Hope perhaps?

"I'm willing to pay whatever it takes if you can rid the house of this... whatever it is, and I might even be satisfied just to know what it is."

"Sometimes one doesn't come with the other," Dana said. "I don't always know exactly what it is I've discovered. Other times I know what it is, but can do nothing about it. That seldom happens, but it does happen."

"I understand," Carlo said. "I only ask that you be safe."

"That's our plan as well," Dana said.

For the first time, I started to feel a bit uneasy. Some of it was the cheese. They eat a lot of cheese in Italy.

***

We left after that short visit and Carlo's explanation. Dana suggested that she and I would start again tomorrow morning. She left the two bags she had brought in the house, and Carlo drove us back to Dana's flat.

As we drove, Carlo said, "Is what I've told you reminiscent of any of your previous experiences, Dana?"

"I've investigated similar situations, but the problem with the supernormal is though many things seem similar, they are not always as alike as they first appear. Some apparently sinister things are frequently nothing of much consequence, and sometimes an innocuous haunting can in reality be deadly. Sometimes you are merely meeting a harmless spook, and sometimes something altogether different."

"So on a moonless night with the sky in flight, the spirit of the dark one comes through," Carlo said.

Dana glanced at him as if he had suddenly sprouted a horn.

"I have done a bit of reading," Carlo said, and smiled.

"Of course," Dana said. "What Jana and I will need to do requires thought and a bit of research. That will take the rest of the day. We can start tomorrow. Is it possible you could provide us with a car tomorrow morning?"

"I can have a man drive you out," Carlo said. "He's a good man, a very down-to-earth fellow named Vito. Vito, well, he knows the stories and doesn't believe them, and would love a crack at proving that I've let a squirrel in the attic to cause me nightmares."

"That sounds fine," Dana said. "But he will have to understand that what I say goes, and that my orders can be strict, and must not be violated. They have to be followed to the letter."

"He will do as you say," Carlo said.

***

First thing Dana did when we got back to her flat was consult a number of ancient looking books she had, and while she did that, I was sent to pick up a few items she had asked for. I wanted to dig deeper into that afternoon's exploration with Dana over a cup of coffee, but it was clear once we returned home that Dana wanted me on my way. Perhaps Carlo's dedication to his dead fiancé made him even more appealing, and she wanted to be alone not only to examine her books, but to pine over lost opportunities. It hadn't occurred to me that the lovely, wonderful Dana Roberts could be heartbroken, and even lonely. Don't get me wrong, I didn't expect to come back to her place and find her in a tub of warm water with slit wrists, or hanging by the belt of her robe from a shower rod, but I felt sorry for her nonetheless, and could sense her feelings of disappointment. Even the bright and the beautiful were often disenchanted.

Dana had given me a list of shops that carried the supplies we needed. They were often disguised as magic shops, or herbal shops, and a few were Chinese medicine shops. They sold the common things you would expect, but the ones on Dana's list also provided more esoteric items, or so she said.

My feelings of sympathy for Dana faded pretty quickly as I went from one shop to the next, searching for all of the supplies on the list she had given me. Candles made from human fat, and various other oddities, weren't exactly readily available at the Conad down the block, but the shops on her list were not always able to provide what we wanted, either. In case you're wondering, the human fat was actually purchased from liposuction operations, though I'm not sure that was a happy by-product that the hospital sold legally. But someone got their mitts on it, and it was shocking to find out there was a market for it. There was also a really nice market for pig placenta.

After being disappointed at the shops on the list, I used my cell to call for a taxi, as the jet lag was almost unbearable, and the idea of walking around aimless after failing to find the items on Dana's list was too much to bear. I suppose things had changed since Dana had frequented those shops, and in some cases, so had the proprietors. Not speaking Italian made it even more difficult for me, though most of the shop owners I met spoke some English, and when I asked about certain items in one shop, the English they used was derogatory. At least they understood me when I spoke back to them in a similar idiom.

The taxi driver was my last shot, and when he sped to the spot where I waited, I at first thought his plan was to make me into a bloody hood ornament. But he stopped in time and waved me inside. Once inside, I went into broken English.

"Magic shop." I showed him the list. "Need items on list. None have them."

He looked at me curiously. "So, you want a real magic shop?"

"You speak English?"

"Like a champ. I'm originally from Houston, and from the sound of your voice, I think you sound Texan, too."

"I started out in Texas," I said, "but I've been living out of state, as I see you are."

"I'm also Italian. Dual citizenship. My father was Italian. I'm Jake, by the way."

I reached from the backseat and shook his hand, said, "Jana. Have you heard of an author named Dana Roberts?" I asked.

"The ghost buster?"

"Close enough."

"I have all her books."

"All right, then. Can you help me out?"

I gave him a general explanation, and stressed how I was her assistant, because, I might also add, the taxi driver had a kind of scruffy charm about him. He looked classic Italian, though he had very green eyes and what I think of as American mannerisms.

He did know a place he said that sold the real deal, and that's where he took me. The shop he referred me to wasn't one you could find directly. It was on the outskirts of Rome and in the back of a furniture shop.

"No shit?" I said, as we pulled up at a large storefront with plate glass windows. Behind the windows was furniture designed for form not function.

"No shit," Jake said. "A lot of the shops on your list are the more general ones. Rumor is this one is the real thing. It sells to the serious. It's not exactly top secret, but as I said, on the down low."

There were a bunch of teenaged girls out front giggling and laughing, so I wasn't sure how serious the shop was, or for that matter how secretive it was. Then again, maybe it was the furniture that had them tickled. Some of it looked pretty silly.

Jake guessed my concern. "They also sell a variety of odds and ends that interest other crowds, and of course magic tricks for stage magicians, so it's not all serious business. I should also add that a lot of teenagers come here to play role-playing games. It's a source of income. Magic isn't exactly a thriving business."

"How do you know about all this?"

"I've brought others here. People who were serious about the real thing. And, I've read Miss Roberts' books. Then again, who hasn't?"

"Right. Can you wait?"

"I can."

I strolled inside, through the furniture shop, nearly losing an eye on the brightness of one lamp that seemed to have been a survivor from a nuclear blast, and made my way through a narrow doorway with a beaded curtain hanging over it, and into the magic shop. There were more giggling teenage girls back there, and you would have thought the way they acted the room was filled with laughing gas. They were milling around a glass display cabinet, pointing and laughing at whatever was behind the glass.

It was a big area back there, and in the far corner of the room, on the opposite side of the giggling girls, was a long rectangular table. Planted in the chairs pulled up to it was a timid looking, sweaty group of what I guessed to be fourteen- or fifteen-year-old boys. They were playing some sort of card game, wrapped up so intently in it that it likely hadn't occurred to them that their future ex-wives were across the room. Here I was, working with a world-renowned supernormal investigator, and I had to gather our supplies at the same place as these teenage nerds played board games and picked pimples and a horde of teenage girls giggled over something under glass.

For a moment, I thought maybe this had all been some elaborate prank. That I was on some hidden camera show, and this would be the great reveal, me holding a sack of freshly purchased dog testicles and candles made of human fat. However, nothing of the sort happened. Instead, as I moved to the counter at the back of the room, I was greeted by a short, balding man who spoke English with the thickest Italian accent I had ever encountered. And I'd spent a summer on the Jersey Shore.

"Can I help you to find something?"

"I hope so. Dana Roberts sent me. Do you know the name?"

This stopped him in his tracks, or would have, had he been moving. To be more precise he froze and the expression on his face changed. The whole place had gone from a bustling teenage hangout to so quiet you could have heard the proverbial pin drop in a mattress factory. The boys stopped playing cards and looked in my direction, their mouths hanging open, and the girls ceased to giggle.

"I guess I spoke a bit louder than I meant," I said.

"Anyone seriously interested in magic and the supernormal knows that name."

"She sent me on an errand for certain supplies that are, well, to put it mildly, hard to come by."

I handed him my list, heard the giggle fits from the girls near the glass case behind me start back up, and the boys had gone back to their role playing game. The old man looked up from the list, peered across it with watery eyes, leaned across the desk, and spoke to me in a soft, mint-tinted voice.

"What do you need these for?"

"To be honest, I'm not exactly sure. Miss Roberts knows what's up, not me."

"Ah. Ah."

I thought he was going to say Ah one more time, but instead he nodded. "I see. I see. This is very serious stuff. Not itching powder for rivals, love spells that don't work—nothing works on love—and little spells made of boiled bull testicles and grave dirt to help you receive a promotion at your job. This is the real thing."

"Someone boils bull testicles?"

"It's a stinky business," he said.

"You speak from experience, I take it?"

"The tough part is having the bull hold still while you boil its balls."

"You boil them while the bull's alive?"

"No. Just fucking with you. Little magic shop joke. No. The bull is killed and eaten, the balls separated and boiled later. They're also edible. They can be prepared quite nicely if you are willing to soak them in vinegar for a while, and then sauté them in olive oil. But, then you can't use them in the magic."

"I'll pass."

He shook the list at me. "This list, we are talking some potentially dangerous ingredients. Come with me. Signorina Roberts shops in our 'special' section. Or she did, when she lived here years ago."

"But you weren't on the list of shops she gave me," I said.

He laughed. "She does that to all her apprentices. It's her way of seeing how clever you are. She sent you to other magic shops, correct?"

"Yes."

"They are shit. She knows they are shit."

"So it was a lesson?"

"She must have clever people to do clever things. Also, she probably wanted you out of her apartment for awhile."

I didn't feel all that clever right then, and in fact, I felt as if I might like to give Dana a thousand paper cuts with her list. Clever, my ass.

"My name is Matteo, by the way."

"Call me Confused," I said.

We proceeded behind an inconspicuous green curtain, hung loosely by wooden hooks. This area was empty, save one, seated older women I could see in the far back corner. She looked like she might have been around about the time the last dinosaur died, and from her expression, may have assisted in the death. There were rows and rows of metal shelving, and it looked more like a convenience store than a magic shop. Matteo wandered up and down each aisle, consulting the list, making humming noises, chuckling, saying something in Italian now and then, as he tossed various items into a brown paper sack.

Across the room the old lady eyed me so hard I checked the zipper on my pants, and then made sure a titty wasn't hanging out.

Nope. I was all good.

Matteo talked as he gathered the items, telling me something about each of them. When he had all that was on the list, I paid up with the credit card Dana had given me, while I listened to the girls giggling behind me. On my way out, carrying my large bag of magic items, I passed the counter they were looking into. It was full of candles shaped like penises and vaginas, and if I was not mistaken, a very large leather dildo covered in studs with a happy face for the head.

I wasn't exactly sure why those items were there, and chose not to ask.

***

Back home with supplies in hand, I found Dana slumped over the kitchen table. A large leather valise was open on the floor beside her chair. Startled by the sound of my entrance, she shot up straight, and I could see she had been crying. She smoothed down her hair, sniffed, and stretched out her arms to indicate that she had been asleep. But I knew better.

"I got everything on the list," I said, proud that I had ventured out into a city so grandiose as Rome and survived. "And also, Matteo says hello. Oh, and let me add, I hate you."

She smiled.

"You passed the first test," she said.

"At being the sorcerer's apprentice?"

"That's right."

"What if I failed?"

"You'd finish helping me, though if I thought the situation was about to become rough, I would fly you home with your five thousand dollars and a homemade sandwich for you to eat while in coach. I might have provided a ten dollar alcohol allowance."

"Well, here it is," I said, holding the large bag of supplies. "And by the way, Matteo said you should never boil a bull's balls while it's alive. It was, I think, a serious tip."

"He loves that joke," she said. "Just set it there on the counter," and pointed to an empty space near the sink. "I am taking a break to consider our next move."

"Sad about Carlo?" I asked, as I placed the bag on the counter and leaned against it.

She looked me full in the face and smiled, but it was obviously an insincere smile.

"I suppose I had considered, briefly, that this might have been some clever ruse to be together once again, but clearly, he still mourns for Cincia. And there may be other factors."

"Other factors?"

"Nothing to concern yourself with for the moment. I don't like to work myself up about things from which I have yet to draw complete conclusions."

"Well, maybe with some closure on this whole house ordeal, there could be hope for you and Carlo yet."

"Perhaps," she said.

But I could tell she was far from convinced, and was anxious to change the subject. I helped her. I nodded at the open valise, said, "Looks like you had plenty of supplies without sending me out for more."

"Some," she said. "I like to keep items fresh. Sometimes they get old and lose their potency."

"My grandfather used to say that. He was talking about himself."

She smiled again, and this one seemed more legitimate. I glanced down at the valise again. There were little racks inside, and in the racks were tubes of what looked like dust, chopped roots, mud, maybe even blood. There was also a box of salt.

I said, "Is all that for tomorrow?"

"Depends on what we find. There's all manner of stuff here. An attraction potion—"

"Matteo said love potions don't work," I said.

"They don't. Attraction potions do. It can cause someone to be attracted to you, but being attracted doesn't mean falling in love. Just puts two people together. After that, it's up to the two involved."

"Have you ever used it?"

"No. But I have considered it."

"Carlo?"

"It was a thought, but that's all it was. We are already attracted to one another, so probably not necessary. As I was saying, that's not the same thing as falling in love. That works best when it comes from both parties. Naturally."

I found I had gotten right back to what she wanted to leave alone. I nodded at the bag. "What else is in there?"

I reached down and pulled out a glass vial full of a nasty looking concoction. "And what's this?"

"That's a dead potion."

I put it back in the valise quickly.

"It's harmless unless ingested," she said.

"What exactly is a dead potion?"

"It allows you to enter into the realm of the dead."

"And you would want to do that because..."

"If the dead come back, meaning if a corpse rises from the grave, you might want to go into the realm from which they came, where their real essence is, and find out why they have come back."

"If they come back, I already know why," I said. "They don't like being dead."

"No. They are still dead. Their bodies move, function on a simple level, but their essence, what some people call the soul, remains in the realm of the dead. With that potion, you can visit that realm, and according to the book, confront them, console them. It depends. Sometimes you can actually coax their essence back into their living body."

"I like it here," I said. "The realm of the dead doesn't sound like a hip vacation spot to me."

"It's not. If someone were to take too much of this little potion, they might not come back. They could be trapped in the realm of the dead forever."

"How much is too much?"

"The entire container is way too much. You took all that, your earthly body would die for good, and your essence wouldn't be coming back from the realm of the dead no matter how much it was coaxed. It would take up permanent residence there."

I reached down and picked up the box of salt. "So this fights evil?"

"One of the strongest defenses against the supernormal," Dana said.

That's when I saw the small automatic pistol that had been under the saltbox.

"Does that gun work on things from the other side?"

"It works well on things from this side."

"Since this is Italy, I don't suppose that's legal?"

"It was an illegal purchase. It's a Berretta. This is the country where they are made. They have strong gun laws here, which I'm for, but I had to have it once due to a case I was investigating that also involved some very human criminal types. Thank goodness I didn't have to use it. I leave it in Italy. I only carry it with me on certain cases."

"Like this one?"

"Yes. Jana, I was up late last night studying our situation, and I overdid it. I should rest a bit, and then get a good night's sleep before tomorrow. I'm going to nap for a while. We'll walk to a restaurant I know for dinner. They have incredible pasta there, and a wonderful spinach dish you should try, then we'll turn in."

"Okay," I said. "Six?"

"Eight," Dana said. "This is Italy."

I excused myself and went to my room, but not before I captured a few crackers from the cabinet. Eight o'clock was a long time to wait for dinner.

***

There was a buzzing sound that echoed throughout the apartment. It took me a moment to realize it was the door buzzer. Unlike yesterday, I was up and ready to go, but still sitting in my room, on the edge of the bed, trying to collect a thought or two and find how they could fit together in some coherent fashion.

After dinner last night, we returned and went to bed. Not early, but not late. I had trouble sleeping. All night I thought about that house. I sensed this case was shaping up to be a doozy, and that I might discover in fact, Danger was not my middle name. Run Like A Goddamn Deer might be, however.

Then again, I still had hopes it was mice. But considering how serious Dana was the day before, how quiet she was at dinner, I had begun to suspect her mood wasn't merely disappointment at not being able to rekindle her romance with Carlo. Seemed to me she had an idea what might be going on at that house, and whatever that idea was, I was fairly certain it was unpleasant.

I heard Dana moving around outside my room, hastening to attend to the door buzzer. I got up to pee in my private bathroom, and decided haunted house or no haunted house, I was going to shower and wash my hair and put on make up. I was not going to die with bad hair and without makeup. Most likely Dana had already been up and prepared herself to look beautiful, in case she needed to charm a demon.

I took about thirty minutes to get ready, but let me tell you, it was worth it. For a demon quest I looked stunning. I was wearing jean shorts and a dark blue tee shirt that fit me like a glove, and man, my hair was dynamite, and so was my makeup. The tennis shoes were nothing special.

When I came out Dana looked stunning as well, but she had only put her hair back in a ponytail and was minus makeup. She didn't need false glamour. Damn her. She was born glamorous. I required a bit more attention.

Our driver and soon-to-be companion Vito was there. He was dressed as if for a wedding, full suit and tie, crisp, white shirt beneath. He looked natural wearing it, as if it was his skin and he couldn't and wouldn't remove it. He was a jovial looking man, and it occurred to me how much he looked like Massimo, the kid who brought me pizza on delivery back home. Only Vito was older, thicker, and slightly more red-faced.

Dana gathered up her books and the items I had brought her, placed them in a canvas bag that Vito took from her without being asked. She placed the leather valise on the floor by the door, and he took it in his other hand before I could grab it up. A moment later we were down the stairs and in the car.

As we went along, I felt I should say something assistant-like (I prefer that to apprentice, by the way), so I asked if Carlo would be joining us.

"Perhaps," Vito said in very good English. "If so, it will be later in the afternoon, before nightfall. He has business this morning."

After that we cruised along for some distance in silence. Silence bothers me, which is what makes me kind of a blabbermouth. I asked Vito, "Did you know Carlo's fiancé?"

"Quite well. Her death was a sad thing for us all."

"Do you think that her death could have anything to do with Carlo's feelings about the house?" Dana said.

"Of course it does," he said. "But that isn't exactly what you're asking me, is it? You want to know if the house is all in his mind?"

"The idea has been broached," I said.

Dana, who was sitting in the front seat beside Vito, turned and glanced at me. I couldn't tell if her expression meant shut up or forge ahead.

"I have never been witness to anything strange," Vito said, "and to be honest, as you are asking, I do not believe in these matters. I think they are all tricks of the mind. But, those who have rented the house have not liked it."

"Have you been there at night?" Dana asked.

He shook his head. "No. But I'm only a driver. I work for Carlo, and I do my job."

"He led me to believe you were more than a driver," Dana said. "And you carry a gun under your coat. I can tell."

He turned slightly and gave Dana a brief smile before turning back to the wheel. "You are very observant. True. I am a bodyguard and assist him in many matters. Still, I do not believe things come back from the grave."

The car ride over was the first chance I had to actually see Rome, even if in passing. Vito, in true chauffeur fashion, pointed out as many historical sites as possible while battling the insane traffic. I clenched the seat using the strength of my butt cheeks while Vito laughed and told stories about many of the sites, pointed, looked off, and chatted as he drove, weaving in and out between cars, slamming on his brakes right before almost colliding with the back ends of several slower drivers. None of this appeared to cause him any consternation.

By the time we arrived at the house, I was a nervous wreck and the idea of spooks seemed pleasant compared to Vito's driving.

***

As it was late morning, there was nothing particularly ominous about the house. Some of my confidence faded once we were inside. Not immediately, but by the time Vito removed a key from his pocket and unlocked the padlock and pulled the chain loose from the doors of The Great Hall, and threw the doors open, I began to feel a sense of dread.

"Do you feel anything, Vito?" I said, as the three of us stood on the boundary between rooms. I wanted to see how much of what I felt was due to the power of suggestion.

"A bit of chill," Vito said. "And the room is darker due to there only being one window, and the second floor windows are naturally dark. I think that old wall gives it a creepy aura as well. But do I actually feel anything unusual, like a tickling from beyond? No."

I looked at Dana. She appeared to be totally unaware of our conversation. She was examining the room like a soldier trying to spot a sniper. The suitcases she had left from the day before, she picked up without asking me or Vito to help her. She carried them into the room, and Vito followed with the canvas bag and the leather valise, and I followed them as if I were a pull toy. Dana stopped in the center of the room and placed the bags on the floor, and Vito followed suit with the two he was carrying.

Fully inside the room the air seemed even cooler, and I had the sensation that the shadows were moving in a manner that had little to do with the light that was coming through the tinted, upper windows. Still, I practically skipped over to the light switch and flipped it on. The room eased out of darkness and into what could only be described as a muted light.

"That's it?" I said.

"I admit there is one peculiarity," Vito said. "The light here. The bulbs have been replaced many times, and it always seems somewhat dim. That, I feel, has nothing to do with spooks, but much to do with inferior wiring."

Dana had still not said a word. She opened the valise, took something small from it, got down on her knees and began drawing a large circle freehand with blue chalk, scooting along on her knees as if she had been born without feet. I had bought the chalk the day before. It was supposedly blessed by priests of many religions, and the chalk was blended with dandruff flakes from a known murderer. I kid you not. That's what I was told when I bought it and the other supplies. Matteo had explained to me each item as he bagged it, and as a faithful assistant looking forward to five thousand dollars in payment, I tried to pay attention and memorize what I was told.

"Is there anything we can do?" I asked Dana.

"For now, just stay out of my way. Your time will come."

Vito glanced at me, grinned, and lifted his eyebrows. I suppose as a driver, bodyguard, and probably house servant, a regular Alfred Pennyworth to everyone else's Bruce Wayne, he was used to rich eccentrics.

So there we stood, watching Dana crawl about on the floor making that circle, and then carefully drawing a pentagram within its center. I knew from what Matteo at the shop told me, the chalk once marked on a wood floor was not easily removed. At least not by common methods such as wiping with a rag or slopping with a mop. It required a buffer and some serious detergent as well. But Carlo's house cleaning was not my problem.

When Dana stood up, the circle was complete and the pentagram was drawn, and she had begun placing the human fat candles all around it, just inside the circle. I suppose there must have been nearly a hundred of them. They were short, compact candles, and were said to burn slowly. I remember reading in one of Dana's books, while on the plane, that the candles would burn a strange blue color if something supernormal were in the room. For now they remained unlit.

I walked over to that large single window, and looked out at the gazebo. Vito followed.

"That is a beautiful gazebo," I said.

"Until you know the bench is a tomb," Vito said.

"What?"

"That's right, a tomb."

Dana heard this, stopped her work and came over for a look.

"Tell us about it," she said.

"Why, it's Cincia's tomb," he said.

"She's buried in the backyard?" I said.

He nodded. "She had no family, and no one to claim her body that was as close as Carlo. He had the tomb built and she is buried there. I was at the service, which was simple and there was only Carlo and myself there. And, of course, the guest of honor. Cincia was such a nice and beautiful lady."

"Still," I said. "He buried her in the backyard and made a bench to sit on with her under it?"

Vito grinned. "He thinks of it as being close to her, and sees no insult in the idea. I am actually speaking, how do you say it, out of university?"

"Out of school," Dana said. "No problem. We won't mention any of this to Carlo."

"I appreciate that," he said.

We stood for a while and looked out at the gazebo. Finally, Dana said, "Vito, would you mind preparing some sort of lunch? It's about that time. I would like to consult with my assistant privately, as what we have to talk about would, I promise you, be less exciting than preparing the meal."

"What we have in the way of food is simple," he said.

"I'm sure it's fine," Dana said. "And no wine. I want a completely clear head."

When Vito left the room, Dana said, "I would like to look at the back hallway, and then go out to the gazebo."

"I find that creepy, that Cincia is inside a concrete bench seat. Don't you?"

"It's certainly odd," Dana said.

"I mean, really. 'Hey, I think I'll go outside and sit on my dead fiancé's body.'"

"As I said, it's odd, but not necessarily heavy with meaning. Then again, I find certain things less creepy and offensive than I might have some years back. I knew a man once who slept with the skull of his ex-wife for ten years."

"Eewwww."

"But, I assure you, my familiarity with the strange doesn't cause me to drop my guard. And right now, I'm holding it high."

***

Outside, we stopped at the gazebo and Dana took a look at the bench/coffin. There was writing on top of it. It wasn't English, but even a Latin class dropout like myself recognized it to be just that.

"What's it say?" I asked Dana, assuming she understood Latin.

Of course, she did.

"It says: You are briefly detained."

"Briefly?"

Dana nodded. She continued to examine the bench.

"Is there anything I should know as your assistant? I mean, about what you're doing? Should I get a running start or something?"

"You should know when to shut up."

"You mean shut up right now?"

Dana gave me a look that wasn't quite enough to make smoke come out of her ears, but I thought I heard the kettle boiling.

"Right," I said. "Shut up."

We finished there and returned to the house, taking in what was behind those four doors. All four led into a wide hallway, and most of the hallway was cluttered with storage. Among the storage were boxes of pottery shards. I leaned against one of the doors while Dana plucked up a few shards and studied them. Then she paused for a long moment and looked down into the box. She replaced the shards without saying a word. She stood in front of the box for a moment, her face pale, and then she swallowed heavily and stepped away from it. Before I could ask her what was wrong, she was through one of the doors and into the Great Room, with me hurrying along behind her.

As soon as we entered the Great Hall, I felt as if we were plowing our way through invisible muck. A feeling of depression settled on me like a vulture on road kill. I glanced about at the statues and artwork, and I liked them less now than before. The twisted metal forms were to me repulsive, and I had a cold impression that the eyes of the statues were watching us. The odd colors of the paintings were bright the way light is like when you've drunk too much.

This feeling passed as we crossed the room and exited through the double doors that stood wide open, and made our way to the kitchen, where we washed our hands at the kitchen sink and perched ourselves on stools at the counter.

I can't say exactly what change had occurred in Dana, only that she seemed to have her thoughts elsewhere. I assumed she was contemplating the house and what we were to do about it, and I had no doubt by this point that there was something that needed to be done.

Vito laid out a variety of cheeses and meats, olives and tomato slices, some thick bread. There was olive oil on the table, along with salt and pepper. We had what Vito called water with gas to drink. He poured it for us as if he was a waiter, doing so with a flair highlighted by a crude chain bracelet dangling from his wrist. It had little silver human and animal shapes hanging from it, and they tinkled together like little bells when he poured.

Vito told us some stories about this and that, silly stuff really, but I hung on every word, trying to distract my mind from what was at hand. Soon we were finished, and Dana and I returned to the Great Hall, Dana having suggested to Vito that he wait outside until it was over. Whatever that meant.

Inside the hall, the feelings of before swept out of the shadows and gave me the forlorn sensation I had felt previously. At the back of the room Dana and I went to work taping papers with protection spells written on them to the doors. She had a small fold-out stool in one of her cases, and she used it to stand on so she could completely seal the cracks of the doors with wax from the human fat candles. I melted it for her on a metal plate she had brought for just that purpose. She scooped up bits of the wax with a small trowel to do the work. It was slow and tedious work and took some time. When that was finished she used the blue chalk again to draw a line with it across the path of all four doorways.

She removed all manner of esoteric things from the bags, including a large bottle filled with goat blood. This she used on the ancient wall with the grooves in it, and as she did, the blood hissed gently and was quickly absorbed into the wall.

"That's what I was afraid of," Dana said.

"Is it okay for both of us to know what we're afraid of?"

"Let's enter the circle and talk," she said. "But first, I need to place some serious charms against evil right here."

I was all for serious charms against evil. The process involved strange colored powders and silver flakes being strewn against the wall, me melting wax for Dana to jam in the grooves at the top and bottom of the wall, then a new line of fat-ass candles were placed on the floor in front of it. So far, none of the candles in the room had been lit. I was beginning to long for them to be ignited if for no other reason than we had spent a long time placing those protection spells, and the day had slipped away from us. It was growing gray outside. Nightfall was not far off.

All that was left was for me to make a thick line of salt between the candles and the wax in the groove at the bottom of the wall, and in the process I managed to spill enough salt to slide and slip in, busting my ass on the floor. I got up quickly, almost at a bounce, and we were ready to enter the circle. I took that to be a safe place, though since I could step in and out at will, I wasn't sure how that worked. But, if it would protect me from night crawlers, I wanted to be there, so I gathered up our goods, packed them away, and was inside of that sacred circle made of Dana's special chalk before Dana was. She entered the circle and sat down on the floor with her legs crossed. I sat the same way beside her.

"It's a sacrifice wall," she said.

"That sounds unhappy," I said.

"You can go if you like, Jana."

"Nope. I'm here. I've had a good lunch and I have the phone number of a very attractive cab driver, so no, I'm sticking this out so I can feel victorious later on my nice date. I'm not going anywhere unless you do, but I would like to persuade you, beg if you like, to do just that. Unlike you, I'm afraid."

"Oh, so am I."

"You are?"

She nodded.

"Damn, that's not what I wanted to hear," I said.

"If you didn't feel fear doing this sort of thing, you would be an absolute idiot, and you would lack the necessary caution it takes to survive. And now that I have some idea what we're up against, what's really going on, I'm feeling more than a bit of my normal consternation."

"Consternation is a kind way of saying you feel like you're going to shit yourself, right?"

"Let's say it means I'm fully aware now that we are up against something powerful and dreadful, and that Carlo is as much the cause of it as that ancient wall. I suspected that early on, but I feel now, sadly, that I've confirmed it."

You could have knocked me over with a tossed rabbit turd.

"Carlo?" I said.

"Yes, Carlo. Knowing that, I'm tempted to walk. I trusted Carlo. But he has gone a distance from which you can't return. That sounds melodramatic, I'm sure, but that's exactly what he's done. Vito is in on it too. Would you mind shutting the great doors?"

"Before I do," I said, "might I suggest we shut them behind us and we hit the road together."

"It's a long way back to central Rome on foot," she said.

"And longer yet if we don't get started."

"I have to finish this. If I don't, Carlo will get someone else, and what will be let loose shouldn't be free in this frame of existence. He might actually find someone who is on his side and will do it knowingly. He knew I wouldn't do what he wanted done purposely, and that's why he didn't tell me the truth."

"Now that really sounds bad."

"The ancient wall, it's not designed to keep something out, it's designed to let something in."

***

I closed the doors on the Great Hall, and by the time I did, Dana was behind me with her valise. She used the same sort of spells on that door as she had on the ones at the back, then she draped a chain and lock through the doors and locked it from the inside.

"What about the doors across the way?"

"The spells won't keep humans out, but I'm out of chains. This one is made of silver, and so is the lock. Maybe it will work to keep both the supernormal and our lying friends from coming into the room, should they choose to do that. I loaded up heavy at the rear of the room with protection spells. Again, I did that to try and keep *it* out. If Vito or Carlo want in, they'll get in. At some point they may want to enter."

As if on cue, early night descended and dimmed the big window that faced the gazebo, and the windows on the second floor of the Great Hall darkened slightly as well. Blue shadows swam across the room and filled the corners of it in a way that seemed to me to be unnatural. But at this point for me everything seemed unnatural, so I wasn't a true judge.

"Let's light the candles," Dana said. "We have plenty of time to do that. In fact, my guess is we have until darkness is complete and deep. You do know this is a moonless night, right?"

"I didn't," I said.

"It is. That's why Carlo arranged for this to happen tonight. It's part of the invocation."

I didn't ask Dana what it was she was expecting to happen. Not right then. I grabbed up a lighter from one of the bags, and with Dana armed with one as well, we lit the candles one by one. The smoke from the candles was foul.

When we finished, we stepped back inside the circle, went around it and lit the candles there last, careful not to disrupt the chalk. Dana said the slightest breach in the circle, though that chalk's imprint was sturdy, and whatever was coming through the wall would be able to get to us. The pentagram had been drawn with a stronger, waxier piece of chalk, made from who-knows-what, and it tenaciously stuck to the floor as if it were part of the wood itself. Still, we were careful about smudging it.

With the candles lit, we made an inner circle, dripping ingredients from a couple of bags, Dana with one, me with the other. According to Dana, the material in the bags was a mixture of charcoal from burned animal bones, grave dirt from the grave of a suicide, and a thin line of salt from the saltbox, for seasoning perhaps. All done, Dana took from one of her cases two small folding stools with canvas bottoms, and we sat down on those. She also produced from a case two plastic water guns.

"They contain Holy Water. Please do not play with them. The water is blessed by a priest."

"And what if It, as you called it, isn't religious?"

"Has nothing to do with it. Actually, I'm an atheist. But there are all manner of dimensions and dimensional alleys out there, things that exist right alongside of us and would love to get in. That's science we don't understand, but probably will some day.

Some of the things in those dimensions can be called up by what we think of as spells, or certain mathematical equations, but it still has much to do with the power of belief systems, any belief system. What are behind the walls of our world are other worlds, and some of them are pretty distasteful."

"But don't I have to believe? I'm not a Christian, Buddhist or Muslim. Any religion you name, I'm not it."

Dana shook her head. "The water in that gun is water to you and me, but not to who put it there, and not to what we will encounter tonight."

"The It?"

"Exactly."

"But Carlo and Vito? Really? You're sure?"

"When I saw the markings on the tomb inside the gazebo, I knew what was up. Those markings are from the ancient tome, *The Book of Doches*, which I've mentioned before, the latter word in the title being a dimensional region beyond earthly understanding."

"Sounds like my home town," I said.

"Carlo, being a historian, a collector of ancient items, he knows that this wall was built to let a dark spirit in from one of those dimensional alleyways. A spirit that can raise the dead and wreak havoc on the living. The only thing he may not know, or maybe it doesn't concern him, as he's so focused on another plan, is it's a tied spell. Once the dead rise, and It comes through that wall, neither dead nor demon will want to return to where they came from. For It, humans are a nice snack, and our world is its smorgasbord."

"And we are first on the menu."

"Correct. We are part of a necessary sacrifice before it's totally free."

"So how do we stop this thing?"

"I think we have our best chance if it comes through. That wall is an offering wall. Blood from victims was poured on those designs. They create a kind of pattern not only of art, but of mathematical construction. The right spells and the thing from beyond enters our world, bringing some rather nasty companions with it, not that it isn't nasty enough on its own."

"But we haven't said any spells to bring it through," I said.

"Carlo has. I can sense it. The blood I dripped on the wall, it wouldn't have been absorbed like that if it hadn't recently tasted blood. Something has been sacrificed to and against the wall to awaken its appetite, rituals have been performed. 'So on a moonless night with the sky in flight, the spirit of the dark one comes through.'"

"Carlo said that the other day, when we were in the car."

"He did. And you would have to know *The Book of Doches* to know that line and translate it from Latin. He knows Latin. And obviously, he knows that book. You don't order that one from Amazon. It's rare. There are a handful of originals known to exist, mostly owned by private collectors, and there are a few translations, some in Italian, some in English, one in German, I think. But there aren't many of those either. Privately done. If you read the book directly you have to have a spell to keep it from driving you mad, or you have to read it backwards reflected in a mirror. I've done that, and I know the protection spell, and have used it. The translations are merely words on paper. Oh, the information is there, but the words themselves are not going to affect you the way they might if you are reading from an original copy. Thing is, when Carlo mentioned that quote, part of a resurrection spell, it got me thinking. It all started to add up."

"He wants to bring Cincia back?"

"Yes."

"That's kind of sweet."

Dana laughed. "I don't think Cincia came here and was frightened, went home, and died of some unknown illness, or of delayed fear from having been in the house. I think Carlo was messing with dark magic, for lack of a better term, and it led to her death in some way. And now he wants to bring her back with the same dark magic. But anytime you use it the end result is always, shall we say, flawed. The spell that awakens the dead is tied to the one that lets the demon in. You don't get one without the other if you want to bring someone back from the other side. And Vito. His gun, that's to eliminate us if we should try to make a run for it, or if for some reason the spell fails."

"You can't know that," I said.

"That chain around his wrist. That's not a teenage girl's charm bracelet, it's a real charm bracelet, and those little human and animal shapes are a protection spell. Soon as I saw that, any doubts I had went away. I knew Vito's claims about not believing in things coming back from the dead was a lie. He and

Carlo are both in on this up to their necks, and my guess is Vito may know as much about art history and black magic as Carlo."

"He said he didn't believe in magic," I said.

"Lying to relax us. So we wouldn't suspect that we are in fact this evening's sacrifices, along with what has already bled on that wall. And listen, Jana, I'm not suggesting they rubbed hamburger meat into, or sacrificed a lamb or goat. Remember when we were looking in those boxes of shards?"

I remembered the way she had turned pale.

"When I scraped aside a covering of shards, I found bloody clothes beneath. A child's clothes."

"Oh hell."

"That's the main reason I can't leave. He has to pay, Jana, for what he's done. Did. Once I loved him, and because of that I feel tainted."

"You couldn't have known he had this inside of him," I said.

"Perhaps," she said.

"But if Carlo knows all this about the wall, the sacrifice, what does he need us for?"

"He doesn't know how to bring the demon through the wall, only how to prepare the way. I think he and Cincia were trying to do just that, failed, and she died. I think he's serious about how much he loves her, and now his mission is to bring her back, no matter who dies. But it takes a lot of sacrifice, a lot of blood to completely open the dimensional gate."

"We're the final sacrifice."

Dana nodded. "The house was built on an ancient worship spot. I know that because of the wall. I had to study my books to make sure the wall was what I thought it was, that I remembered the designs correctly. Those same designs can be found on the walls of ancient graves all over the world, some of the markings are hieroglyphics from *The Egyptian Book of The Dead*, a few Aztec designs as well. A culture unlike any we know combined a lot of knowledge from a lot of other cultures to build that wall. How those cultures crossed here in Italy, I can't say, but they did, and therefore, that wall is very powerful."

"At least it's multicultural," I said.

"Still joking?"

"It's the only weapon I have against fear. It's what keeps me from bolting. This thing behind the wall, what's it like?"

"It's always in a bad mood, according to *The Book of Doches*, which describes it as A Devourer of Light. And that doesn't mean daylight, or house lights, or a campfire. The light it's referring to is life. It's also called Cerberus, like the three-headed dog in Greek mythology. There are other names as well, but this is no time for me to give you a list."

It had grown very dark by this time, and the air was full of the stench of those candles. They guttered in a draft, but didn't go out.

"Why don't we just destroy the wall?" I said.

"Tearing it down could open the gate permanently, and perhaps not just to what we'll see tonight. It has to be closed by, for lack of a better term, magic, and to do that properly, the thing on the other side has to come through first, and then we have to send it back."

"You have to let something in to let it out?" I said.

"I'm afraid so," Dana said.

"I'm starting to feel ill."

"Well, don't feel ill inside this circle. This is our source of power and protection, and besides, I can't stand the smell of vomit."

"So, if we don't defeat the demon and we get eaten, and Cincia rises from the grave, the wedding is on."

"That's what Carlo is hoping for," Dana said. "But he's ignoring what he actually gets if she comes back. I can promise you, once she shows up, he's going to be a lot less excited to see her than he expects. He knows just enough about the supernormal to put himself and others in jeopardy, and worse yet, he's willing to kill us to bring her back. I suppose that's true love, but in Carlo's case there's nothing romantic about it.

"For Carlo and Vito, I have my gun. That's why it's in the valise. I wasn't sure of my suspicions until I came here and saw the grave, found those clothes, and realized there had been a sacrifice to prime the pump."

I realized then that she had been crying the other night because she had those suspicions. Now she seemed calm and cool, all things considered, the prime consideration being someone was coming back from the dead, and a monster was coming from another dimension for a visit, her former boyfriend had betrayed her, and his hired gun was going to shoot us if we made a break for it. In the end they would mop up, and no one would have any idea what happened to us.

"Are you any good with that gun?"

"I hate the damn things, not to mention that whole illegal part, but I can hit what I aim at if it isn't running too fast."

By this time the window on our right was nothing more than a black rectangle.

"Wouldn't it be nicer to work at demon killing by electric light? I think I would enjoy that more."

"The electric lights won't work in the presence of dark powers, Jana, I assure you. It's candlelight or nothing. I do have a flashlight. They work in supernatural situations if blessed by a priest, or some other form of religious leader. This one got a good word from a Rosicrucian."

***

As we spoke of lights, artificial lights made an appearance. They rode up high on the windows of the second floor, dipped down and were gone. A car had come over the top of the hill that led to the house, then coasted down on our side of the hill, causing the beams to disappear as it reached the building.

"Carlo has arrived," Dana said. "He always liked to make a late entrance. The rotten, lying, son-of-a-bitch."

We heard a car door slam, and a moment later we could hear someone coming through the front door into the house, and then we heard the mumbling of voices. Vito and Carlo.

"It shouldn't be long now," Dana said.

She said that as if I were looking forward to it.

As I huddled on my little canvas seat, a water gun full of Holy Water clutched in my hand, feeling like the biggest fool that had ever complained about her life being boring, the air changed. It went from cool to cold in an instant. We could see our breath frosting out of our mouths in little clouds. I glanced out at the gazebo. The window was still too dark to see through. The night out there was like chocolate pudding. And then we heard chains fasten on the double doors that led into the Great Hall, and other chains rattling on the four doors on the other side. That would be Vito and Carlo, one at each set of doors, locking us in, not knowing we had chained one side of the room ourselves already. When the chains stopped rattling, I felt a terrible sense of defeat. There was no way out even if I decided to turn tail and run.

Dana used the flashlight in the bag to look at her watch. "Get comfortable. There's nothing we can do until the thing beyond the wall makes its move, and it will need assistance to do that."

I wasn't sure exactly what she meant, but I had no urge to ask. I was really scared. I could feel myself trembling. Dana gave me a hooded sweatshirt from her bag, and there was one for herself. I pulled the sweatshirt on, hoping my trembling was due to the change in the air and not blind fear. Even wearing it, I continued to shake.

"Remember, the thing it has going for it is our own fear. Calm yourself. Breathe slowly, and stay alert. We win by not being fearful and by paying attention. Follow my lead."

She picked up her water pistol where she had placed it on the floor, and dropped it in her lap.

The smoke from the candles grew thicker than before, and then the doors at the back began to creek a bit, and rattle, and then the ones behind us rattled as well, shaking the chain on the outer side, and the one on the inside as well.

Chanting came from the other room. It was Carlo's voice. The words were like cold-footed insects crawling up my spine.

"That's how it begins," Dana said. "By now I'm sure he knows we've figured it out. There's no going back, for him or us."

The chanting went on for a while, and the air became stiff, and breathing was difficult. The smoke curled and coiled, and there were shapes in the smoke, but I couldn't identify them. They were lit by a blue light of sorts, and in the light other shadows moved, and there were darker blue shadows within those shadows. The light and the shadows draped over the statues in the room like tarps.

The statues moved.

I kid you not.

They moved. They twisted and writhed their way off their pedestals and began to move toward us as we huddled in our circle of ash and candles. The statues looked less like metal and more like thickened shadows. They scraped along the floor, their sculptured feet stiff, their metallic bodies bending and stretching. The faces of the statues moved their heads from left to right, as if curious, the eyes of the sculptures bright now, like animals looking out from the woods.

"Hold tight," Dana said. "This is merely an illusion. That's all it can do until it comes through the wall. I think it knows we are a real threat to it, so it's trying to scare us."

"Working," I said.

I noticed too that the paintings on the walls were swirling, the paint moving about until it was as if we were looking through windows to the other side of... well, I don't know what. There were shapes, and the shapes were wrong, totally wrong. They didn't remind me of anything I could identify, but they made me feel uncomfortable, as if I were looking into something no human eye was meant to see.

"Ignore all of it," Dana said.

This was easier said than done. The statues were near the circle.

Dana stood up, said, "Follow my lead."

She walked to the edge of the circle. One of the statues reached for her. When its hand reached the border of the ring of candles, it screeched, vibrated, and was gone. In a blink of an eye all the statues were back where they had originally been, and they weren't moving. They looked as they looked before.

"See. Illusion," Dana said.

"A really good one," I said.

I glanced at the paintings. They swirled with color, and then the colors reformed into the original paintings and were still again.

"That was to check our resolve," Dana said. "Probe our defenses a little before It puts itself at risk. By now it knows we mean business, so when it shows up, it will too."

"Do these things ever come through not really meaning business, you know, a little irritated, but easily dissuaded?"

"Not really."

I took a deep breath. I tried to stay alert and see what Dana did. That damn chanting from Carlo was still going on outside the doors of the Great Hall and it was nerve-wracking. I thought a real cure to all of this might be to shoot him in the head, but if it was that easy, Dana would most likely have suggested that already. There was Vito and his gun.

I detected a change in the room. Not just the cool air and the stench, but a feeling of vibrations. It was as if I had my head lying against a train track and could feel the tremor in the rail of an oncoming train. The candles were flickering wildly now, and the smoke was moving more slowly and the smoke grew thick and made crawling shadows on the floor. Outside the Great Hall, the chanting from Carlo had ceased, and as much as it had bothered me, the dead silence that came after was worse.

***

Dana turned on the blessed flashlight, placed it on top of one of her cases where it rested and sent its beam smack dab onto the ancient wall. The wall began to bulge, like a big man expanding his chest, and the images on it glowed red and grew clear. They moved. The shapes, the hieroglyphics, were angry little creatures running about. They clashed together and made new shapes, and the long dark shadow on the wall began to slide away from its corner, downward toward the floor. Then there appeared a crack in the wall, dead center. It was about a foot long, and as we watched it opened wider. We could see something poking through it, wiggling about. It was a finger. An enormous finger, gray of skin, long, thick as a hoe handle. And then other fingers followed, clutching at the crack in the wall, tugging it apart.

I had yet to see all that went with those fingers, and I already felt like a silly fool waiting there with my little water gun, a book of spells, and some candles made from a fat person's ass. It was as if I had been given a switch and kind regards and sent tiger hunting with it.

More fingers showed up, ten of them, and that was on one hand. Another hand appeared, grasping at the edge of the wall with another ten fingers. Whatever it was on the other side, it was spreading that wall as if it were made of rubber. Then a long, thick snout appeared, pig-like and hair-covered. It wriggled as it sniffed the air and pulled back, disappeared from view along with the fingers.

"It doesn't like our spells," Dana said.

"That's showing it," I said.

And then the fingers came again, and then the snout, and I saw one dark eye, and the eye roved in our direction. The eye was a sparkle in a pink, knobby head crusted with scales, and that head was pushing its way completely through the gap, and then I saw there were two other heads just like it, though I think I can safely say the one in the middle was the ugliest and probably took shit from the other two. It thrashed its heads about, the wall crumbled, and fragments of it flew in our direction, but instead of passing through our circle, they struck our invisible barrier, hissed and dissolved. The wall, like the dark magic in the room, was vulnerable to our protection spells.

"Will our spells hold it?" I said.

"Yes."

"You're certain?"

"Of course not," she said. "I'm trying to sound positive."

Now the heads and shoulders of the beast were through the gap and the gap was widening and the wall was collapsing, some of it dissolving as it fell to the floor on top of the spells Dana had laid out. And then a large foot with long claws on the tips of the toes appeared, and for a moment it seemed almost comical, but when the foot came through, followed by a leg, and then another leg, followed by the rest of it, I couldn't find any humor in the situation. White smoke rose up from the floor, from the spells Dana had prepared, but if they were slowing the thing down I couldn't tell it. It might as well have been having a trip to the sauna.

"Okay," Dana said. "Some of our spells aren't as strong as I had hoped."

***

When it moved, the claws scratched on the floor, and the knobbed and scaly heads bobbed from side to side on a long, loose neck. The body was large and misshapen, covered in patches of hair and pustules, and the pustules had little worms inside of them. I could see all of this because that goddamn thing was *huge*. Did I mention it was a big boy?

There was the intense light from the candles, because now they were burning nearly as bright as if they were electrified. Our magic was working overtime. Yet, the thing seemed to be evolving even as we watched. Shadows coiled and curled around it like pet ferrets scurrying from head to toe. A thick, reptilian tail thrashed in the air behind it, rising up high above its middle head. An eye, bigger than those in the faces of the thing, was on its tail. That eye looked at us and blinked. The air had grown harder to breathe. It seemed full of icy crystals. I began to pant.

"Get hold of yourself, Jana," Dana said. "Or so help me, I'll throw you to it."

I got hold of myself, but it took effort. I started squirting at the behemoth with my water gun.

"Too far away," Dana said. "Save it."

It seemed damn close to me. It trudged toward us, cautiously, as if expecting a pit it might fall into. Its scaly chest heaved and the pustules popped, and the little worms fell against the floor and writhed and grew instantly into a mass of little white snakes, moving quickly toward our barrier.

Outside in the hall Carlo was chanting again, and right then if I could have got hold of him, I would have beat his head in with Dana's flashlight, shoved it up his ass and set him on fire with one of the candles.

I heard a loud, grating noise, turned my head toward it. It was outside the house, and through the window there was light now, a kind of blue light that floated in a cloud over the gazebo. The stone top of the bench was sliding loose, and I could see a delicate, white hand reaching up from the interior, pushing it aside.

"Outside," I said.

"I know," Dana said, not even turning her head to look. She was concentrated on the big boy coming our way. It hit our invisible barrier in a terrific rush, garnering more speed than one would have thought those Tyrannosaurus like legs could muster, hit it with what seemed the impact of a train. There was a sizzling sound and a burst of blue waves that rose from floor to ceiling, and the waves knocked Big Boy backwards a goodly distance and onto its beastly ass. The room shook and the candlelight wavered throughout. The white snakes crawled against the line of candles that encircled us, but couldn't push past. The shadows that scurried over the beast had grown thick and showed teeth, and they leapt from their host and struck against our invisible barrier, slid down it like wet boogers on smooth glass.

I had started with the water gun again, and when a stream from it struck one of the shadows, it reacted in a way that satisfied me. The Holy Water hissed against it and it deflated and dissolved. As for Big Boy, as I had come to affectingly refer to him, he was up again, and he came closer now, more cautious this time. Big Boy circled our barrier looking for a weak point, or so I assumed. I squirted it with my water gun. Unlike the shadows, it was unaffected. Shooting Holy Water on it was like trying to piss out a forest fire.

That's when I noticed the blue light was brighter at the window, and in the light, clearly seen, was a woman standing with her hands pressed against the glass, her face close to it. I didn't need for her to have a nametag to know it was Cincia. Dark-hair hung to her shoulders, some of which was falling out of her head and drifting down her body. Her flesh was wilting and a cheekbone poked through. She was wearing a nice, blue dress. I had a feeling this wasn't her at her most attractive. She pressed and pushed harder against the window glass, cocked her head one way, then the next. When she saw us her eyes went wide, like a surprised raccoon caught in a dumpster.

"Uh, Dana."

"I see her," Dana said.

Big Boy stretched up to his full height, made a loud sound as the three heads opened their mouths and sucked at the air. The candles wavered. Some of them went out. The demon let out its breath and the room shook, leaving only darkness.

"Don't move," Dana said.

I shut my eyes and tried to find my happy place, imagined I was back with the cute cabbie and we were drinking wine, far from Big Boy and the dead lady. That really didn't work that well.

***

The aftershock of Big Boy's exhale vibrated against our protective barrier, and it was enough to come through our protection, at least a little, and it knocked me to my knees, but still within the circle. Dana must have expected it, for she was still standing, and was now bent over, fumbling for the Rosicrucian blessed flashlight. She got hold of it and pointed it directly at Big Boy's chest. It hit him like a laser beam. The monster screeched and stumbled back amidst white smoke and sizzling skin. It was a short victory, because about that time, the window glass cracked. Dana swung the light there. As she did the glass began to fall from the window. Even as the flashlight beam rested on Cincia and made her smoke like a forgotten weenie on a grill, she came through the tumbling glass, stepped into the room, crunching the great, burst window pane beneath her bare feet.

"The circle can hold one back, maybe," Dana said, whirling the light back to Big Boy, then back to Cincia. "But if both come at the same time. Not so much."

In the flashlight beam I could see that our little barrier was starting to grow thin and some of it was picked up by a cool draft and carried away. The blue chalk was looking less bright.

I don't know exactly what I was thinking, if I was thinking. Perhaps it was panic, but I grabbed Dana's leather valise and pulled it to me, reached in and took out the tube she had shown me. The one that allowed you to visit the realm of the dead. Before she realized what I was doing, I had the cap off and was swallowing half of it.

"No," I heard Dana say, and then there was a sensation like my very insides were being jerked out through my mouth, and I was snapped out into the universe amidst swirling constellations and bands of cosmic colors, and I thought: Oooh, pretty. Then I was moving along a dark corridor, and then out of the corridor I came as a puff of smoke, and the smoke that was me formed my body, and there I was, standing at the broken window, right in front of Cincia. But she looked different there, young and beautiful, a living dream. She studied me calmly, as if recognizing an old friend whose name she couldn't place. Time moved slowly, like a fly struggling in a jar of molasses.

"You are where you belong," I said. "You can't come back."

This bit of reasoning had about as much effect as trying to turn over a tractor with attitude. She merely twisted her head to one side, and I mean twisted. A head wasn't supposed to do that. It made me wonder what she was seeing, what I looked like in this realm. Sure, there was the window, and there was Cincia right in front of me, but around us was only darkness and silence. We were not actually in the house. We were in a splice in space and time.

It was the realm of the dead, I knew that much, but that didn't mean I understood it. I could see other shapes moving around in the shadows, faint white shapes that reminded me of the Greek myths about the underworld, but I couldn't let my attention waver. What was it Carlo had called them? Shades? I concentrated hard on Cincia who stood in front of me with her head turned to one side, bathed in a blue glow. And then she came for me.

***

My self-defense lessons kicked in, and I grabbed her by the neck and tried to knee her in her lady parts, but she was moving too fast, and I was knocked back. But there was this: she was solid and so was I. We were not mere shadows or human-formed smoke, even in her realm we were flesh and blood, and in that realm her dead spirit was more alive than her animated corpse in my dimension.

She jumped at me again, and this time her impact drove me to the floor, causing me to realize I needed a few more lessons from my self-defense trainer. Her mouth hovered above me, opening slowly, and out of it came a light blue mist. The mist drifted down on my face. It was damp. I felt sleepy, the kind of sleepiness you know is going to take you way down into the dark and you aren't going to come back up. And down in that dark will be considerable unpleasantness. I could sense this as clearly as if it were explained to me, that if I went out, I was going to remain in that realm, due either to the mist or having swallowed too much of the potion. I fought against it, tried to fire up my adrenaline. She was on top of me still, her cold hands at my throat, and her mouth was lowering down closer and closer and the mist was thick and rolling over my face, moist and scratching, like being licked by a cat tongue.

I tried to bring my right leg around and over her head to push her off of me, having become flexible through yoga classes, and when I did, I hooked my ankle at her neck and pushed back with my leg and moved her away from me. Something sprinkled down off my shoe, something I had brought with me from the real world. The sprinkles fell on my face and into my mouth and I tasted it. Salt. There was salt on the bottom of my shoe, and I could see it there in the blue light, little white dots stuck into the treads of my tennis shoe. Normally, I would be appalled at having just tasted shoe salt, but at the moment, I had bigger problems.

I rolled my hips and brought my foot around square against Cincia's face, and when I did there was a sizzling sound like bacon in a pan, and I knew the salt was doing its thing. I pushed it toward her mouth, giving the dead bitch a taste of my salty shoe sole, and when I did she let out a howl like a pack of wolves, and then there I lay on the floor in the house, outside the protective circle, Cincia above me, her lips smacking over the salt as she tried to spit it out.

But it was too late. She had tasted what I have heard Dana call in later days the spice of the living, the bane of the dead. She came off of me very fast and did a series of back steps, collapsed on her back, one leg kicking like a sleeping dog, then she rolled onto her stomach in a fish-flop move, rose up on her palms and the balls of her feet, gave me a look that made me feel like I was taking a nude bath in the arctic sea, and then she scuttled backwards on all fours, out through the broken window, her beauty falling away like autumn leaves, flesh flaking off her face as she became as before, thin and boney. Her eyes fell back in her head and she continued to scramble backwards to the stone coffin, losing so much flesh that within instants she came to look like a knobby grasshopper being yanked backwards on a string.

She flexed and leaped effortlessly backwards and into the interior of her stone coffin, and then her hand came out of the coffin on an arm that was now too long, and blink-an-eye-quick, she grabbed at the stone lid and pulled it shut over her. The blue light that had encompassed her all this time went out. The sky turned black as the bottom of the ocean again.

When I felt pressure on my ankle, I knew Big Boy had me.

***

I was about to give up, curl into the fetal position, and hope like hell to be swallowed whole, when I heard Dana say, "You moron. Back inside the circle. Goddamn you, Jana."

It was she who was holding my ankle.

By this time I was on my feet, and knew I was in my world, such as it was. I glanced toward the great window, and it was back together, as if never broken. Cincia was no longer in sight, of course, but someone had turned on a light out there, and I could see Carlo next to the stone coffin-bench, and I could hear his loud bellows of grief. In spite of what I had seen, what I knew he had done, at least for a passing moment I felt sorry for him. He had gone outside to join Cincia, to be united with his one true love, even as she tried to come inside the house to find him. But my trip to the netherworld had stopped their reunion. My feelings of sympathy for him passed quickly when I thought about the bloody child's clothes in a box under some pottery shards.

Even as Dana hustled me into our protective circle, I looked toward the back of the room, and one of the doors stood open, Vito came through it with his drawn pistol. He had entered the room for whatever reason, maybe thinking it was all over, and there was Big Boy, along with his white snakes and swirling shadows. Vito's entrance also revealed a hall light, framing Vito nicely. This distracted Big Boy away from us, and now his attention was concentrated on Vito, who at that moment most likely wished he were back in the kitchen munching cheese and cracking open a bottle of wine. More likely, he wished he were back at home doing just that, and would have even settled for being on the toilet battling a case of diarrhea.

Perhaps it was Vito's job to remove our back door protection spells so that Big Boy might roam free, doing whatever three headed monsters do. But Vito had arrived early, before Big Boy had devoured the planned sacrifice, us, of course, and at that moment any meal would do.

Big Boy almost skipped toward Vito, his tail waving wildly. I thought of Fred Flintstone's pet dinosaur. Vito lifted his gun, fired a couple times, but he might as well have been blowing peas at it through a straw. It grabbed him and lifted him up, held him close to its three heads. Three mouths snapped and blood splashed out of Vito in dark gushes and a shady mist, and then the thing tore him apart as easily as if he had been nothing more than damp newspaper. The devouring of Vito took about as long as it takes a hungry dog to eat its dinner. As his blood splattered on the floor, the white snakes writhed into a pile, and you could hear them from across the room, sucking the blood off the floor like little vacuums. As Vito was eaten by Big Boy, the ferret-like shadows twisted in and out of Vito's tooth riddled body, making snacks of his essence, or so I assumed, for there was a blue mist rising out of Vito's body and the shadows absorbed it like water into a sponge. The little charms that had been on his bracelet trickled to the floor with a tinkling sound; in the close presence of Big Boy, his charms had been for shit.

With the appetizer bolted down, Big Boy turned his attention back to us, raced across the room, seemingly having forgotten our little circle of power, and when he struck it, he was thrown back as before. At the same time Dana was shining her Rosicrucian blessed flashlight on him and I was squirting at him with my reacquired water gun. At this point, even though Big Boy had been knocked back, our barrier hadn't been as successful as the first time, and in fact he had only been thrown back a yard or so by it. I felt so close to our three-headed friend, that if Big Boy had a shirt pocket, I could have climbed up and into it.

So there I was, shooting at the beast with my little water gun, the candles all over the room bright again for some reason, and Big Boy shook violently and howled, turned and moved back toward the wall, followed by his entourage of white snakes and ill-tempered shadows.

"I don't get it," I said.

"The back from the dead spell and his entrance into our world are tied. Carlo did that. He used a spell from *The Book of Doches*. It allows the thing to come through, but at the same time Carlo was to get his wish, for Cincia to come back. But you stopped her. After our beast had his sacrifice, a Vito snack, he didn't have the power to stay. Without Cincia, without the tying of the two spells, the completion of both, the creature has to go back."

Dana said this even as Big Boy stepped backwards through the gap in the wall and the gap closed up. Then the center of the wall pulsed, and pretty soon the entire wall throbbed, and the part that was ancient collapsed into itself and was sucked away, followed by a shattering sound like the busting of a Mexican piñata. Then there was only the hole in the wall and the night seeping in.

"Damn," I said.

That's when we heard the shot.

***

With the spell collapsed and the wall gone, having been hurtled into Big Boy's dimension, it no longer served as a portal. We went to the gap and cautiously peeked through, Dana waving the flashlight about.

It was as I assumed. We made our way to the gazebo. Carlo was draped over the stone bench, Cincia's coffin. The gun he shot himself with had dropped from his hand and lay at the base of the bench. He had a small hole right between his eyes and scorch marks from the blast around it. Suicide.

"Here's a final rub," Dana said, looking down at Carlo with tears in her eyes. "He won't even join her in some kind of afterlife. Where she is he can't go."

***

Not much to tell after that. We found the keys to Carlo's car in his pants pocket and left him where he lay. Dana had not had to use her gun, but Vito had used his, and Carlo had used his own. There was nothing left of Vito, not even a drop of blood. The snakes and shadows had sucked it up before making their exit with Big Boy.

As for our magic spells and the like, we left the floors marked and the bits of this and that we had used for our protection. It wouldn't matter. We wiped the place as well as we could, hoping to remove our fingerprints. We did that in the room and in the kitchen, anything we might have touched. We used Carlo's car to drive back into Rome, wiped it down where we had touched it, something we had done to Vito's car before we left, and then, sharing the toting of the bags, we walked for a couple of hours back to Dana's apartment.

We stayed in Rome for several days. Dana read the Italian papers daily, reading them aloud to me in Italian, as if I might understand them. I said nothing. I knew she knew I didn't understand. When she stopped reading them she explained to me what they said. It was simple. There had been a suicide and some sort of black mass ritual at Carlo's house outside of Rome, and the clothes of a missing child had been found. It was suspected Carlo shot and killed himself due to his loss of a loved one, coupled with his cruel deeds. Another theory was a missing man named Vito Perali had left his car there and was missing, so maybe he had shot Carlo at close range and gone on the lam. No real answers, just theories. There was of course no mention of dimensional demons or two brave demon hunters armed with water guns and a blessed flashlight.

"If those spells hadn't been tied together," Dana said. "I don't know if we could have stopped that thing. The circle was broken in a couple of spots where it had been hit by the demon. It was only a matter of time. I ought to scold you for chancing to take that elixir, but I can't. That's what saved us Jana. You. If you want, consider yourself a permanent member of the team. I'd love to have you on board."

"I want that," I said. "But if you supply clothes again, next time no Mom jeans."

Dana smiled at me, that smile that lights up a room and makes men melt inside their clothes and women wish they were her.

"From now on with the salary you're going to make," Dana said, "you can buy whatever you choose for yourself."

***

For obvious reasons this won't be like Dana's previous adventures. It won't appear in one of her books, nor will anyone read this anytime soon. We don't want to go to jail. I merely wrote it down for my own satisfaction, a kind of catharsis, and it's worked quite well. It will go into a vault at my bank tomorrow, and in my will I will indicate that it is not to be opened until fifty years after my death.

By then it won't matter anyway. It probably wouldn't be believed, but I will admit to a certain gratification as I finish these words. I think Dana and I may have saved the world.

Or at least a small part of it.

And we did it with nice hair, and in my case, carefully applied makeup.

The Case of the Ragman's Anguish

by Joe R. Lansdale and Kasey Lansdale

This was one of our stranger cases, one of our most deadly, but it started out simply and without fanfare, like an ice cream social before the ants arrive.

I drove us from the Houston airport to Mainland, Texas in a ragged rental, and Dana didn't enjoy the ride. She had money, and frankly, she was spoiled because of it. All those bestsellers and fees for supernormal research had fattened her bank account like a Christmas pig.

She was used to traveling in class. I had a bit of money, but not so much I wanted to waste it. I got us a rent-a-wreck. I could have charged it to her, but I was trying to show my independence, even if she was my employer. She could take care of the hotel and meals, and while she was at it, she could replace my laptop the airlines shattered, but I picked and paid for the car.

As for wasting money, don't get me wrong. I like a nice hotel and a nice car as much as anyone else, but too much luxury is wasteful, and frankly, too ostentatious for my soul.

It fits Dana's soul just right, like the proverbial glove, as long as you can make that glove out of silk and silver trimming with goose down lining. The more I thought about that, driving from the airport to Mainland, I decided I'd put the rent-a-wreck on her bill too. Hell, how much independence can you declare?

So, there we were, riding, Dana not talking. She was dressed like she was going on a date, and I was wearing sweats and a tee-shirt with a frog on it, tennis shoes, and to cap it off, I was toting about a slight case of constipation. Look, I know it's not lady-like, but I get away from home, I back up a little.

But, there we were, riding along, Dana glancing around at the car, and at me, with a look that indicated she'd like to set the car on fire with me in it.

I thought I might discuss the case with her, if it turned out to be one, but she wasn't biting. I tried talking about a previous case, one that she wrote up as "The Case of The Whispering Sister," but even appealing to her vanity didn't pull anything out of her besides grunts, and yes and no, and watch where you're going, and how old is this car anyway?

I tried to stop off for a snack, but Dana wasn't interested, and since we had plenty of gas, I couldn't use that as a ruse. We drove on, and about two and a half hours out of the airport we arrived in Mainland, Texas, bordered by trees, crossing bridges full of trickling water. It wasn't anything like people think of Texas as being, at least not this part. East Texas is wooded and wet and humid as a hot towel wrapped around your head.

I ought to know. I was from East Texas.

***

We checked into the hotel and the mayor had left a note for us at the front desk with directions. We had a bit of a fresh-up, which means I shucked the sweats and the frog shirt for a presentable dress, and then I drove us over to his office. It was in one of those old courthouses you hate to see disappearing in small towns across the U.S., but this one was well kept and large and made of pink marble, and there were lots of cars out front. The sun bounced off the marble and made me squint a little as we got out of the car. I could see the clock tower read twelve, though it was well past two-thirty.

Inside, it was as cool as a meat locker. Texans air-condition with a vengeance, as if they are trying to cool the bowels of hell. We found the mayor's office, and waited in the foyer briefly near a desk about the size of a small yacht, with the captain of that craft being an attractive blonde woman with a hair-do that was popular about the time Sputnik hurtled around the earth, and mounded high enough to have touched it in orbit. She talked to us sweetly for a few moments about things no one really cared about, and then the door at the back opened and The Honorable James Hightower came out.

He was a pink-faced guy with a head of black hair that looked as if it had been trained with a whip and an entire bottle of mousse. Not a single hair was out of place. It almost looked like a plastic cap. His smile was big and gave the impression of having too many teeth. He was dressed in a black and white sports jacket, white shirt, black tie and blue jeans, along with black-as-doom cowboy boots with a bumpy surface. He was nice-looking in an overly coiffured, used car salesman kind of way.

He waved us into his office, and once inside he shook our hands vigorously and offered us chairs. They were like clouds to sit on. The lady with the big do came in with a rolling table on which sat a coffee pot, cups, and cookies and an assortment of doughnuts.

Dana passed on refreshments, but I had coffee with sugar and milk, as well as several cookies, managing to sprinkle a number of itchy crumbs down the front of my dress. And I should add that it was with grim determination that I turned down a doughnut, though I thought about it for a couple days thereafter.

As I sat there slurping as quietly as possible, chewing on cookies, Dana gave me a sideways glance. She believed you should always avoid unplanned meals, while I on the other hand looked forward to any possible chance to eat, though it caused me to spend a lot of time in the gym, and at that moment was probably not aiding my problems of digestion.

After a few pleasantries, the mayor waited until Big Hair rolled the table out and closed the door before speaking. The smile on his face seemed to collapse inside of him, as he said, "I'm desperate. I really need help."

"Then let's get right to it," Dana said. "Explain."

"I've had suspicions that I'm dealing with something supernatural, or at least unnatural."

"We call it the supernormal," Dana said. "Meaning it isn't supernatural, it is just not yet explained."

"Whatever it is, I couldn't tell anyone in authority, the police chief for instance, or I'd be out of my job as a mayor, and would end up working hard to get the job of dog catcher."

"We aren't judgmental," Dana said. "Weird is our business."

I thought, well, sometimes *I* am judgmental. You know, there's that whole wearing wool hats and snow boots in the summer as some kind of fashion statement. I hate on that, and what the hell is up with those ball caps with the bill slanted to the side?

"It's always sighted first at the top of Old Car Hill."

"What is?"

"That's the problem. It's uncertain what it is, but it isn't human. Has the general shape of a human, but it moves like something else. It's dark and faceless, appears to be wrapped in rags. I know every town has those kinds of stories, but I've seen this thing, and it's deadly."

"In what way?" I asked.

"After it appears, a death occurs."

"An omen, then?" Dana said.

"That's your business, not mine," said the mayor, "but I think it has evil intent. It has been seen a couple of times up on the hill and each death occurs shortly thereafter, and in two cases it was seen near, or actually in a victim's car."

"According to witnesses?" Dana said.

"That's correct."

"Eyewitness sightings are among the most unreliable," Dana said.

"I know. But I have seen it, and just the other night. I was driving by and the moon was beginning to be bright, and I saw it, clear as could be. I saw it come out of one of the cars up there, catch on the air like a kite, and sail high up. It made a kind of screeching sound. I could hear it with the windows rolled up. You can bet I drove away pretty fast. During the night, I awoke thinking it was at the upstairs window. I could hear it tapping on the glass. I thought, my God, how could it get up here, and then I thought, easy-peasy. The damn thing can fly. I got my gun and went to the window, and there was nothing there. I thought I saw a quick shadow race across the yard, and then there was not even that. I worked everything over in my mind to explain it and came up with very little.

"I'd seen on the news not too long ago about a girl from this area," he pointed in my direction, "that had teamed up with the world's finest investigator on this sort of thing, and I thought maybe having someone who was local on the case would be helpful. And I want to say this with the deepest respect," and then he glanced at Dana. "She sounds like us, and you don't."

I knew exactly what he meant. Small-town people prefer to deal with their own, especially when it comes to things that are only rumor, and might make them look foolish.

"Most people are hard pressed to believe things like this are caused by powers beyond our realm, but you seem to have jumped right into it without so much as a blinking," I said.

"As I said, I saw it."

"Yeah," I said, "but most folks explain it to themselves in another way. A trick of the light. A misconception. Something wrongly identified, but you jumped into the supernormal with both feet."

The Mayor nodded.

"When I was growing up, we had a mammy. I know that's an outdated term these days, some might even claim racist, but that was the term. A black lady who was what would now be called a live in nanny, or some such. She pretty much raised me, and she believed in hoodoos and charms, ghosts and so on. My family dismissed such things. My mammy, June May, she was old school. Once she said she found out that a bad spell had been put on our family, and she protected us with a reverse spell."

"Did it work?" I asked.

He smiled. "I have no idea. I never knew what the threat was, and since nothing happened, well, there may have been nothing, or it may have been the spell kept us from harm. Hell, she may have been yarning me, but my whole life I've been a lot more open to those kinds of beliefs than others. I saw a ghost once, as a child. In an old house, and I never said a word. You are, in fact, the first I've told. But it made me believe that what we think we know may not be how things actually are."

"Out of curiosity," I said, "what kind of spell was supposedly cast on your family?"

"To be honest, I'm not certain. Business rivals or some such had gone to a spell maker, and June May, she protected us. That was her story, anyway. She never told my parents. Knew they wouldn't believe it. But, you know, from the window that night, she watched, and I watched with her, and all I saw was a big, black dog. It came out of the woods and looked up at the window, and ran off. But no spirits, nothing out of the ordinary."

"What is out of the ordinary often looks ordinary," Dana said. "Like the black dog. That may have in fact been your family's enemy personified. Black dogs are often the form evil spells take. Hell hounds."

"I hadn't thought of that," he said. "But why didn't it try again?"

Dana shrugged.

"They may have, but the spell your mammy cast may have been strong, and sometimes an evil spell, even a protection spell, can only be cast once, and then it's over. If they were soundly defeated, they may not have had the dark forces available to them to launch it again. But as to your problem at hand. The deaths. How many, and how long has it been going on?"

"Few months, every time the moon is up it might show. Maybe there are times it shows and no one sees it, I don't know how it works. I just know when someone sees it, soon someone will die. I need outside reinforcements for this kind of deal, and that's you two. One victim, Mrs. Standfield, got caught in the car when it was on fire, burned to death. The witness could see her shape in the flames, screaming at first, then consumed. No one could help her. It was too hot, and she was too far gone. Three others were killed under odd circumstances. One just drove his car off into the river, drowned like a rat. The other two, well, one ran up under a semi-truck and lost her head. And the other drove straight into a brick wall at high speed. Cops said he must have hit the gas instead of the brake. Possible, I guess."

Dana thought a moment, then spoke.

"We'll need a list of those who have died in car accidents, and more details on how they died, and where. It could just be coincidence. People die in car wrecks quite a bit."

"At least two of them were accidents where witnesses claim the car had someone else in it, and after the wreck, no one else. One of the witnesses described the passenger as a mass of rags, all wound up like a colorful mummy."

"Colorful?" I said.

"That's what they said. The rags were bright, multi-colored. That's what one witness told the police, and I admit he had been drinking. Down on the river, night fishing, coming up to his truck parked at the end of the bridge. He said when Mrs. Standfield's car hit the bridge, the driver was thrown against the glass and the car was knocked to hell, turned over, and somehow it caught on fire. You know, like a movie car explosion. It happens, but not too often, and this was one of those not too often times. Suspicious, I think. He saw the woman burning like a hot dog too long on the grill. Said where the window glass was cracked, this thing crawled through it, and then sort of gathered itself. Those are his words. Gathered itself. Then it took off running, darted right past him, then leaped right off the bridge. But he didn't hear nothing hit the water. Instead, what he thought might be a great bird rose up from below and sailed up into the moonlight. Police decided something like that, a guy drinking all day and fishing, seeing the accident in the night, he might have seen pink elephants in Christmas socks walking on the bridge railing just as easily as running rags and a flying shadow."

I could see that Dana was already considering alternatives. She had seen a lot, so she could evaluate possibilities quicker than most. Certainly quicker than me.

"Ok," she said. "Interesting."

"I'll get you the list of the victims, and the two witnesses, including the fisherman, and the people who died," the mayor said. He cleared his throat. "The fisherman is a relative, by the way."

"Why didn't you mention that right off?" I said.

"Witness is my brother-in-law. Peculiar fella. Doesn't quite fit in, you know. I wanted to tell the story first without adding that connection. Danton is known as the town drunk. When he was younger he used to sniff airplane model glue, so, you can see the hesitation I have. But what he says he saw, it corresponds with what I saw, what the other witness saw."

"All right," Dana said. "We'll get started. But one thing I want you to do, and I don't mean contemplate on it, I want you to do what I ask."

"What's that?" the mayor said.

"I'm going to give you something shortly, before the evening, before the sun goes down, and I want you to put it on the sill of your upstairs window, and I want you to put it at all the doors, and you have to explain to anyone that lives in the house—"

"Just me and my wife."

"Fine, she has to know not to break the line."

"Line of what?"

"Goofer dust protection," Dana said. "It's usually for bad spells, but it can be reversed with the addition of certain things, and it can become a protection spell."

"If you say so," he said. "My wife will be fine with it. She's much of the mind I am. Meaning she believes me and her brother. A little dust isn't going to bother her."

"As long as you put it out before nightfall, and don't break the line once it's put down."

The mayor considered for only a moment.

"Are you saying my life's in danger?"

"Seeing it on the hill is one thing," Dana said. "Many do. But it came to your house. It may have picked you, for whatever reason."

"I'll do what you ask. One thing you should know, the fellow that owns the junkyard, place of so many sightings. He doesn't use it anymore. I think he hangs onto it out of nostalgia and maybe a bit of spite. Expensive houses have grown up all around it. Hell, you can see the clock tower and two subdivisions from there. He won't sell that land and he won't relinquish it or let loose of those old junk cars. It's quite the eyesore, and right in the middle of town."

I noted an old black and white photograph in a frame with tarnished gold edging. It hung slightly crooked on the wall behind him. A row of men and a couple of women, the men in suits and fedoras, the women dressed in the style of the era, stood in front of what appeared to be the very building we were inside of. You could see bits of scaffolding and construction debris behind them. One man, blurry, stood in the background holding a toolbox.

"That this place?" I asked.

"Sure is. They were building it in that photo. That's my father out front."

"Who's that?" Dana asked.

"Which one?"

"That guy, in the background, with the toolbox."

Mr. Mayor picked up his glasses from the edge of the desk and peered at the photo.

"Well I reckon I don't know. Never noticed him before to be honest. Not sure how you did, practically blends into the background. You know, I think that man might have had something to do with the clock tower. You know, kept it working, maintenance. Seems like I was told that once. Odd that he's so out of focus."

Dana nodded.

"I think that's all we need for now. Could you have your secretary send the info to our hotel, or have it sent over?"

He grinned. "My secretary, Cindy, is my wife. Nepotism can be a lovely thing."

"Good," Dana said. "We'll most likely start with your brother-in-law. I'll be by later with that spell I mentioned. Before it's solid dark. Before the moon rises."

"Very well," he said. "And when you meet my brother-in-law, I don't want you to think he validates all of the old Southern town clichés. He's who he is on his own, and I should point out he and my wife were originally from Michigan."

Outside the office, we spoke briefly to Cindy. She mentioned she would send over everything we needed to the hotel. We thanked her, and left.

As we walked to the car, Dana said, "That photo, the man with the tool box."

"Yeah," I said.

"When that photo was taken someone accidently caught sight of a specter, for that's what he is."

"I thought he was just out of focus."

"In more ways than you might think, but I haven't deduced what he has to do with all this, if anything. Specters often show up in photographs, and no one can explain them. It may merely be a harmless ghost."

"Or an actual person, not a ghost."

"I would agree that is possible, but before we left, I glanced at the photo. He was no longer in it. That's why the mayor hadn't noticed before. That kind of thing, that's a warning, and probably to the mayor."

"That's some stuff right there," I said.

"My guess is he comes and he goes, a common result of a creature from beyond being photographed. Our very discussion may have made him materialize. Specters like that are often tied to past events. It may be near impossible to discover the original source of the problem."

"Maybe not," I said.

She looked at me quizzically.

I smiled, didn't say anything. I thought, Dana, even you who are wise and experienced don't understand a place like this. I grew up around here. The past here isn't forgotten. It gathers dust, but it's always there, and whispers of the past never stay quiet for too long.

***

Back at the hotel, Dana and I sat at the small round dining table perched in the corner of the room. Normally, we each would have had our own room, thank God for small favors, but unfortunately, the town had only one hotel, and it was Azalea Season. Now that may not seem like something that would sell out a hotel and every home rental in the area, but it does just that. Little old blue-hairs came from miles around to walk these trails. It wasn't just some garden, it was *the* garden, and it opened this Friday.

I'd come once as a kid, and though I didn't remember it, I remembered the stories of that epic family road trip. Only about an hour away from my hometown, we'd stopped every ten minutes for me to puke and my brother to pee. Needless to say, my parents weren't in a hurry to bring us back. Visited the town now and again after that, but never again for the gardens.

Dana's concern was that with all the people in town, our specter, if in fact that's what it was, might have too many choice victims to choose from, though she leaned in the direction of this being a designed haunting. Meaning the victims were picked purposely for some connection they had to the haunting. It was like the spooks had a union and there were certain things they could do and could not do. Sometimes those odd supernormal "rules" worked in our favor.

We looked at the materials the Mayor's office sent over to us, and tried to suss out the connection between the deaths.

We decided to set aside the information about the former owner of the yard, with intention to seek him out tomorrow, and thumbed through page after page of obituaries and articles.

"Whatcha thinking?" I asked.

Dana was slow to answer. "It seems the sightings and the deaths are happening closer and closer to one another," she said.

"How long before the next one?" I asked.

Dana didn't respond and I left it at that. I already knew that was the most I was going to get from her until she felt she knew enough to have a worthwhile opinion, though the lack of answers did little to ease my concerns. We had a cup of coffee we made in the room and headed out, stopping at a feed store to buy a few things first.

***

The mayor's brother-in-law, the fisherman, was our first interview.

Unlike the mayor, or for that matter, his sister, Cindy, Danton kept it simple. He lived near the river and owned a truck that had been nice about the time Henry Ford pushed the first one off the assembly line. His domicile was a mobile home that looked to have been rescued from a fire, because one side of it was blackened, and it was propped ridiculously high up on wobbly looking concrete blocks. On the side nearest the river, the blocks had sunk, which led me to think that going from one end of the home to the other was a mite precarious.

"He really ought to get that jacked up," I said.

"Maybe that's how he gets his exercise," Dana said.

"Oh, my God. You made a joke."

"Did I?"

"Yeah, you did. It wasn't very good, but you're trying. You're not nearly as stiff as people think."

"Gee, thanks, Jana."

"Welcome."

We were looking at the trailer through the windshield, when the trailer door opened, and a stout man swung out of it, using one hand, like an ape, and landed on the ground. This was impressive, as it was quite a drop and there were no stairs. I wondered how he would get back inside. He was dressed as if had stolen the clothes off a clothesline at random. More interesting was that he had a shotgun in his hand. Yep, quite a feat, swing out with one hand and hang onto a shotgun with the other.

He walked immediately toward the car.

"Look friendly," I said.

Dana opened the car door and got out slowly. I got out with equal casualness on the other side and leaned on the open door.

He eyed us carefully as he walked over.

"What the hell you want? You selling religion?"

"No," Dana said. "We are allies of the mayor, your brother-in-law. He employed our business to investigate a series of peculiarities that have plagued your town of recent."

The man that I assumed was Danton, looked at Dana like she had just given him a Latin phrase to puzzle over. Dana can be a little stiff anytime, but when she's getting down to it, fears she might be shot, or eaten by something from beyond, she develops a severe case of the tight ass.

"She means the mayor thinks some hoodoo shit might be going down, and we're here to figure it out," I said.

"Oh, okay. I was told to expect two broads, but I thought ya'll'd look different."

"How's that?" I said.

"More like bank clerks, not fashion models."

I delighted in that.

"Well," he said pointing at Dana, "her anyways. You look like you're nice, though."

I was now less delighted. He noted that.

"I mean, you look fine. I had a girlfriend you remind me of, except she had a bad eye and limped a little. But she looked good enough when she worked at Hooters. People didn't notice her eye so much, and she wore a pirate patch sometimes. She claimed it got her extra tips. I can't say for sure. I thought it was the titties. She moved off... well, come on in."

"Do we get up there by helicopter?" I asked.

"Oh hell no. Nothing to it, but you're going to have to hike up your dresses a little, I'll drop the rope. Being up like that makes it less likely I'll get robbed, a crook has to work for it. Also, lots of floods out here. Water gets high I don't ruin the carpet or end up with fish in the commode."

He sauntered back to his trailer. The door was still open. He tossed the shotgun inside, and grabbing the doorway with both hands, lifted himself up and worked his way in. A moment later a rope ladder was lowered.

Dana looked at me.

"Really," she said, but pulled her purse from the car and slung it over her shoulder.

We hiked our dresses a bit, as suggested, and took turns up the ladder. Dana went first and he helped her in, but when I got to the top of the ladder, Danton left me to my own devices. He was sticking his shotgun in a closet.

The place was as odd as you might think, being up high without a porch, and having one side that was sinking. There were nails in the floor next to the legs of the couch, and they had been twisted to catch the legs and not let them slide. The couch looked as if something had died on it, but that turned out to be a dog. The dog looked like a giant, black mop, and it got up reluctantly when Danton asked it to. The carpet he was worried about need not have been a threat. It was worn thin as a tortilla and had the texture of a bad haircut. You could feel it through your shoes. Fact was, it was artificial turf that had been painted red with what I thought might be spray paint. There was a faint aroma of that. No wonder Danton seemed a little too happy for his circumstances; he was always sniffing the fumes.

"Sit down. Make yourself at home."

We sat on the couch, having to prop ourselves in such a way as not to slide down it. Danton sat comfortably in a large, nailed down, stuffed chair across the way.

I thought: Well, if this is our witness, guy like this probably heard birds singing in the sink and went on vacations with Bigfoot. The times they could have.

"Alright now, ask away," Danton said, not breaking eye contact with Dana.

"You're the brother of Cindy, the mayor's wife, correct?"

"I am indeed."

"Alright. Tell us what happened that day at the bridge."

That's Dana. She likes to get right to it. Me, I would have asked about the dog, the originality of the carpet, tried to buddy up a bit, but not her. She made very little time for small talk. But Danton didn't seem to mind.

"Want a beer?"

"No thanks," Dana said. "We're fine."

"I'm having one, then." Danton got up and went to his fridge, which was leaning against the wall like a drunk. He moved with the rolling rhythm of a sailor. I got the impression that the trailer shifted from time to time, and that was how he had gained his sea legs. He got a beer out of the fridge, and when he did, I heard bottles sliding across a shelf inside; the precarious nature of the trailer made stacking items problematic, I assumed.

Danton came back to his chair, sat down, twisted off the top, and tossed it onto his highly cherished carpet along with a handful of caps that were already nesting. The decor was very much early drunk or late wino, and I didn't think Danton had to worry all that much about theft. Flood maybe, but theft, not so much.

"Well," Danton said, first taking a swig of beer that partly ended up on his chin, then leaning in close like he was about to reveal the secret of the universe. "It's like I told the police. I'd been fishing, and partaking in some adult beverages, as is my right to do as an American on their day off, when I saw a car hit the bridge."

"Where is this bridge?" I asked.

"That big one over yonder." Danton pointed. Surprisingly, that didn't make anything more clear, considering there was a mobile home wall between us and the suggested bridge.

"This one?" Dana asked, opening her purse, pulling out a newspaper clipping Cindy had sent us.

"That would be the one. Anywhoo, I saw the wreck, which happens sometimes, especially 'round holidays and weekends. It's a sharp curve, if someone's driving too fast it can be their ass. But what made this particular wreck memorable was what was in the car, and I seen it clear in the moonlight as if it had been bright as mid-day. Something, like a wad of colored rags, looked like Mugsy over there if he wasn't a dog and was colored up like a pack of freezer pops."

His description reminded me of an old joke. A man sees a new Ford, and says, "Hey, I got a car just like that, except mine's a Chevrolet."

"I'm not saying it was Mugsy," he said, as if I we might be thinking Mugsy was a criminal mastermind, "just that it was hard to describe, looked like a wad of blankets or some such, kind of fuzzy. Always seemed to be changing and shifting. Looked right at me just before it jumped off the bridge, and there was no face. That's what I told the police. But they thought I was just drunk and seeing things. Hell, maybe I was. But it was so real. I saw it turn thin as a sheet of paper, crawl through that broken glass and take off running, then sort of jump and disappear. Flew off, like a big ole bird. I know that sounds crazy."

"It does," I said.

Dana cut her eyes in my direction. I grinned. Sometimes my thoughts leap right from my head to my mouth, tripping over my tongue and teeth as they go.

Dana smiled her million-watt smile. "In fact, you might say, crazy is our business."

And here I was thinking weird was our business.

"Do you want to hear about that time I saw the goat man down in the River Bottoms?" Danton said.

"I think we have all we need," Dana said. "Except for help leaving."

Danton set his beer on the floor with what I thought was obvious reluctance, and shuffled over to the doorway, grasped the frame as we had seen him do before, and lunged his way outside.

We stood in the doorway, looking down on Danton.

"I can catch you if you want to jump," he said.

"The ladder is fine," Dana said.

Much to Dana and Danton's surprise, I pushed in front of her, gripped the edge with ease, and rather gracefully exited out the way Danton had done. I was pretty proud of myself. I'd have to call Mom and tell her the gymnastic classes had paid off.

Dana used the ladder and came down it with petite preciseness. At least until she was near the end and her shoe got caught up and she fell backwards. Thank God I was there to break her fall. She fell on top of me and knocked me to the ground hard enough to fill my mouth with river sod.

"Sorry," she said, as Danton helped her up. I, on the other hand, had to help myself up. Danton was trying to brush dirt off of Dana's ass, and she was trying not to let him.

"Don't worry about me guys, I'm fine," I said.

"What I figured," Danton said.

Me and Dana made our way back to the car, leaving Danton with his mobile home, Mugsy, and a bottle of beer. Once he was inside and out of sight, I said, "I hate you."

"Hey, it was me that had her ass brushed."

"Okay. Maybe I did come out a little better than you."

***

We rode over to the river and got out and looked at the bridge. We could see where the car had hit the railing, and with considerable impact. There were ruts where the tires had dug their way into the mud just off the highway, and there was a bit of blacking on the ground where the car had burned.

We looked on the other side of the bridge, where Danton said he came up and saw the rag thing, right before it fluttered off the bridge and took to the sky.

"I don't know," I said. "This guy sees goat-men and lives in a slanting trailer on sinking blocks. Somehow, I'm surprised it wasn't the goat-man he saw jump off the bridge and fly away."

"Maybe," Dana said. "But there's another witness to another wreck. Let's look her up and hear her story."

***

Jonquil Blume—really, that was her name—proved a different kettle of fish altogether. She lived in a nice house in a wooded section of town where it looked like dog shit would spray itself with room freshener before entering the neighborhood. The great hill with the junkyard was visible though, standing high up at the edge of the subdivision like a blight.

Jonquil was a sober and smart-looking woman, answering the door in faded jeans that fit as if sewn to the contours of her body. She wore an expensive, shimmering silver top, and it was all set off by rather nice, but sensible shoes with open toes. Her gray-streaked, brown hair fell to her shoulders and she wore a light coat of makeup.

We told her who we were, and of course, she was expecting us. The mayor had laid the groundwork for us.

"First off," she said, almost the instant we were invited inside, "come with me."

She went into the kitchen, to the sink, and looked out the window that was over it.

"Look up there," she said, and moved aside so that we could.

We looked. There was a split in the trees. There were no houses in the wide split, and in the distance there was the red clay hill with its rusty cars, which from that distance, looked like the shed skins of locusts. There was a great oak at the top of the hill. It might have been hundreds of years old. Lower down the hill we could see a chain link fence that I assumed went around the hill and the cars inside.

"You see that car at the top?" she said.

We nodded.

"That's where I first saw it. One sighting there, one at the wreck. Let's sit in the living room."

In the living room we took our seats. The floors were hardwood and there was a cowhide throw rug with a coffee table on it. The couch didn't lean like the one in Danton's trailer, and the floor was missing the beer caps. The chairs were so comfortable I thought I might ask to rent one.

"That junkyard is an eyesore," she said. "I have taken photographs of it, and I've watched it with binoculars. Kids get in there to fool around, you know what I mean."

I agreed that I did, a little too quickly.

"I don't like it. Someone could get hurt up there, all kinds of foolishness going on. This is a nice area of town, and that darn junkyard brings the property value down. No one actually operates it anymore, but the owner won't get rid of it. Sentimental value, I've heard. Hard to believe anyone can feel sentimental about that mess. Anyway, I was watching it by night, trying to see who was sneaking up there. In time, I noticed kids quit coming. I didn't know why, and I kept checking. I know that sounds like a busy body, but I'm just trying to keep records of what's going on, get some nighttime photos and maybe some license numbers of cars parked outside the fence, something to make the city force the owner to at least clean up that place. Anyway, kids quit going up there, and one night I think I saw why."

Jonquil paused and considered, as if pulling memories from the back of her brain. "There's something up there," she said. "The same something responsible for Mrs. Johnson's death."

"I'd like to know what you saw, but can I ask how well you knew Mrs. Johnson?" Dana said.

"Well enough," she said. "We are... we were, cousins."

I thought it was an odd question, but Dana seldom asked a question unless she thought it important, and frequently she might already know the answer.

"But you were saying," Dana said, "you saw something on the hill."

Jonquil nodded. "I did. I thought at first it was a trick of the light, that I might be imagining it, but something came out of the car's back passenger window, something that seemed to float a little, drift to the ground and walk, and then it blew down to the fence as light as a newspaper caught up in a windstorm. Blew *through* the fence."

"Through the fence?" I said.

"Like it was smoke," Jonquil said. "Gathered itself on the other side, blasted on down the hill. I thought for a moment it might end up here, but when I dropped the binoculars from shock, picked them up again, it was gone."

"When you say well enough, what's that mean, exactly?"

"I'd see her at gatherings and such. Didn't know her in a close kind of way. Only enough to tell you she was as mean as a snake. Joke was she was so scary she had to sneak up on a glass of water. Ethel Grace, never called her by it, wasn't nothing graceful about her. I remember that night because the moon was about to be full, and it was bright on the hill. That night I figured I would have full view of that thing up there, but then I ended up going into town for something or another, and when I was coming home, at the intersection up the street, I saw Mrs. Johnson stop at the four-way stop sign as I was pulling up at the other. I was crossways with her, not facing her exactly, and I saw that thing from the hill. It came down the street like a tumbleweed blowing, but I don't think there was any wind. As Mrs. Johnson pulled away from the stop sign, this thing, this ball of rags—that's how it appeared close up—splashed over the windshield like paint. Mrs. Johnson lost control of the car, swerved and hit the light pole. Impact threw her through the glass. She smacked that pole so hard it darn near split her in two. It was horrible to see, her all over the place and blood everywhere, shimmering like oil in the moonlight. And that rag thing, when she fell to the ground, it was on her. Like it was taking something from her, and then it was up and away, took to the air like a buzzard. Hell, a condor. And, goodbye cuz. You think I'm crazy, don't you?"

"No," said Dana. "Not at all. We believe you. In fact, it's a familiar story."

"It flew toward the junkyard. I told the police what happened, and they gave me a drunk test. I wasn't drunk. They wanted me to see a doctor, a head doctor. They thought witnessing the wreck had traumatized me. Later, the mayor came over and asked me about it, because he got word from the police what had happened. He believed me. Though he told me not to spread that around. Say, you two are the experts, so what is it, some kind of revenant?"

"I'm the expert," Dana said. "This is my assistant. And as for it being a revenant... possibly."

"Never believed in that kind of stuff before, but now... I'm not so sure... Oh, hell, yeah I am. I saw it, and I believe it. I *am* sure. It was some kind of booger bear, what the old folks used to call a haint."

***

On the way to see the owner of the junkyard, Tom Craw, Dana had me tell her where there was a cemetery, the older the better. There was one I knew of just outside of town and up in the backwoods. We used to go there as teenagers, park the car and go into the cemetery, turn off our flashlights and sit. Pretty soon you could see eyes all around, animals, coyotes mostly. It was creepy as hell. And then when the eyes came closer we would turn on our flashlights. There was a sudden clamoring, a smashing of brush, and then whatever had been there was gone.

I often wondered what would happen if we didn't turn on the lights. Probably nothing, but it was a ghoulish thought full of trembling delight.

We stopped at the road that led to the cemetery, what we used to call the old graveyard. The woods had grown tighter along the trail and a car couldn't go up it now. We got out and opened the trunk, took out a couple of large bags and a shovel, items we had purchased at the feed store. Dana had bought them without explanation, and I didn't want to give her the thrill of me being curious, so I hadn't asked her why. Now the reason was about to present itself.

We walked along the trail toward the cemetery. When we reached it, we could see a lot of the old stones had tumbled down, pushed up by the roots of trees. It was even more desolate than when I was a kid. I wondered if anyone still came here. There were certainly no signs of visitation that I could see.

"Find the oldest grave you can," Dana said.

Many of the stones had been there so long they were illegible. But I knew what I was looking for. Back in the late eighteen hundreds a man had gone off his nut and axed his wife and children to death. He had been lynched by neighbors and buried here. There used to be a simple stone that said: Murderer. Dead. Dead. Dead.

In short time, I found it. The stone had toppled, but when I brushed it off, the nice little sentiment on the stone was still readable. I called Dana over and gave her the backstory.

"Good," she said, "not only is it old, but it's the grave of a terrible person."

"Is that good?"

"Yes, my trusty assistant, it is good. At least for what I'm making."

Dana had me fill the bag with dirt from the grave. The soil was mixed with rotting leaves and pine needles, and it gave a strong smell when I dug into it. It made my nose hairs twitch.

While I dug, Dana watched the birds, and looked about.

"Wish we had another shovel," I said.

"I don't know who would use it," she said.

***

Tom Craw lived on the other side away from the hill, in an old folk's home. We were given directions to where we might find him. The recreation room. Tom wasn't enjoying a lot of recreation, though. He was sitting in a wheelchair looking out at a school playground in the distance; there were no kids on it. A slight breeze was blowing through the trees that dotted the playground. Tom had a head as bald as a river rock, and his skin appeared to have been freeze-dried then beat with a club. His eyes were narrow slits. He was sunk down inside his clothes, as if he had been dressed in a bigger man's outfit. He wore house shoes. An equally old woman, but better dressed, was near him, but she was standing, and when she saw us, she shuffled off, found a chair near the far wall, sat and watched us with bird-like eyes.

As we came up on him, he turned, looked at me.

"Who are you?"

I told him who we were.

"You fall in a ditch?"

I was covered in dirt and grime from digging, so it was a reasonable question. At least I had brushed my knees off, so there were only scrapes on them now, but no dirt. Digging in a dress is not recommended.

He looked at Dana. "Well, angel, you look fresh as a daisy."

"You bet she does," I said, "but you try digging dirt out of a graveyard, and tell me how fresh you'll be. I swallowed a bug. Good-sized one. She just watched."

Dana gave me a look.

So did Tom.

"What kind of bug?" he asked.

"A bug-bug. I don't know."

"That's not important," Dana said.

"True," I said. "It may be digested by now."

Dana gave me a harder look this time.

"Sorry," I said.

"Who are you two? What do you want? And you, how come you ate a bug?"

"It wasn't on purpose," I said.

"Mr. Craw," Dana said, turning on the charm. "We're investigators."

"The law?"

"No," Dana said, and she explained.

Once again, the fact that we were ghost and ghoul chasers didn't faze him a bit. A lot of people in this town knew something wasn't right, and were willing to suspicion the origins of that wrongness as not of this world. That was a change from a lot of past investigations.

"This is about the junkyard, ain't it?"

"Can you tell us about it?" Dana said.

"You assume I have something to tell," he said.

"Yes," Dana said, "I do."

"I'll tell you girls the same thing I done told the mayor. That property has been in my family for generations, and I ain't ready to part with it."

Dana studied him a long while. She folded her arms at her chest and said, "You know what's going on up there, don't you? You know how dangerous that thing can be."

"I don't know what you're talking about, ma'am."

"I think you do. I think that not only do you know what people have been seeing around town, this rag creature, if you will, but I think you know why it's there."

Mr. Craw pursed his lips but still said nothing.

"You're covering up or protecting something at that junkyard, aren't you?"

This got his attention. Mr. Craw jerked his head to one side, and like a dinosaur might eye its prey, snorted at Dana then said, "You're messing with some juju you don't know nothing about, little girl."

"Little girl," Dana said, but before she could list off her credentials, Tom called out.

"Nurse, take me to my room, and see that these ladies find their way out."

The nurse didn't seem to mind being bossed around by Tom Craw, and I was fairly certain this was neither the first nor last time. The portly nurse came from behind the desk in the corner of the room and placed her foot on the wheelchair pedal, unlocked the brake and began pushing him down the empty white-walled hallway. Tom Craw yelled back, "And you, sassy, take a shower, you stink like rotten meat."

That seemed uncalled for if you asked me. Though true.

"Well you sure hit a nerve," I said.

"I thought I might. He knows what's going on up there and I think I do too. At least the gist of things."

***

We went back to the hotel and changed into our investigating outfits, meaning black stretchy pants for me, a loose, black top and black tennis shoes, and a black windbreaker. Dana wore nice black leggings and a dark designer top, a black windbreaker, and very nice tennis shoes. She looked like a fashionable ninja. I looked like someone leaving gym class.

Dana sat in the corner of the room, sifting through the graveyard dirt and pulling open salt and pepper packets that lived within the plastic wrapping supplied by the hotel for all your cream, sugar, salt and pepper needs. There was also a plastic fork in each package. And we must not forget the nice little folded napkin.

"I need to get this goofer dust mixture finished and to the mayor before nightfall, and then we need to get started. I can tell by the way of things, we may not have that much time, and I've got a feeling that Jonquil Blume, being a descendant, doesn't either."

"How can I help?" I asked.

Dana opened a second packet and dumped the little bits of salt and pepper in it, and then she poured some odds and ends she had bought at the feed store into it.

"You can take this," she let out a puff of air as she picked up the large plastic sack of dirt next to her chair, "and put it in the trunk of the car. We're going to want this handy. The second bag, once I finish with it, we'll drop off with the mayor, and then head up to the yard, look around for ourselves."

Now usually, I was all gung-ho about such a thing. I liked the rush and the danger, and I likened myself to Indiana Jones—brave, but an everyman, or everywoman in this case—but this ghoulie had me pretty freaked. It's hard to hear burned alive, decapitated and the like, and not feel a little bit nervous. And being protected by dirt is a little less than reassuring as well.

***

It was early evening and the sun still hung overhead. The air had cooled off, as much as it will in East Texas, and we drove on to the mayor's with the windows down, and a trunk full of goofer dust, as one does.

The first time Dana had said it, I could have sworn she said goober dust. I was expecting something peanutty and delicious. To say I was disappointed when I found out it was dirt with all the fixings, and cemetery dirt no less, would be an understatement.

"Remember, don't break the seal, no matter what," Dana said as we entered the courthouse. We were going into the mayor's office, me carrying a bag of goofer dust.

Dana either didn't notice or didn't care that such a thing was quite heavy, when she'd decided to take the stairs. Feeling as if a heart attack was near, I plopped the bag down on the mayor's desk without breaking it open and sending dust everywhere. We had called ahead and he had met us there, and Dana explained what he was to do with it.

"Remember what I told you. Use this the way I explained when you get home. But don't break the seal on the bag until you're in your house. Understood?"

"Understood," the mayor said.

He looked us over. "You look like cat burglars," he said.

"Haint burglars," I said.

The mayor decided not to extend the conversation, and we didn't encourage it either. We were on a mission.

As we went down the stairs, I said, "If we're protecting the mayor, how about his brother-in-law?"

"I believe this is about direct bloodline, descendants."

"In what way?"

"I don't know all the answers yet, Jana, but once upon a time, some people did someone wrong, and now there's a spectral retribution for past sins on their descendants, and for the original sinners who remain."

"You know that for a fact?"

"No. But at this point, I'm a pretty good guesser when it comes to these sort of things."

I was still trying to reclaim my breath as we went down and climbed back into our jalopy. The AC blasted directly onto my face. I felt like a pup going for a joyride, its head out the window, but there was nothing joyous about it. It was almost dark, and a feeling of foreboding had descended upon us, and on this sleepy town.

***

We tried to get there and be done before daylight faded, but it was growing dark when we arrived. Dana had taught me early on what I think is obvious. Most bad things hide in the light, and come out in the dark. But considering our ragman friend was waiting less and less time between appearances and attacks, we had to soldier on instead of waiting until morning.

I stood holding the remaining bag of goofer dust while Dana opened the padlock on the gate. From a distance it appeared locked, but once up close, you could see that the metal loop wasn't pushed all the way in. Presumably that was how the kids were sneaking in and out at night; it had been jimmied long ago and left that way.

We went inside and closed the gate, looked around. By this time night had truly fallen, and already the moon shone bright on the yard like someone had spilled honey on the place. In spite of the moonlight, the junkyard seemed even more dreary up close. Though, calling it a junkyard was a kindness.

At the top of the hill, like a star on a Christmas tree, was the car where Jonquil said she saw the rag thing appear. A brisk wind had kicked up, and dry leaves from the oak tree were plucked off the ground and swirled around the rusted heap like a halo.

Dana paused, said, "Up there, the junkyard hill, that's the place to start. Speed up."

"You're right, my bad, I've just been loafing."

"Shh. Hurry up."

"Who the hell's going to hear me?" I said.

Dana turned back to me, but not before giving me the side eye. I decided not to push my luck. The clock was ticking, and it was one of the few times I had ever truly sensed Dana might be afraid. That made me afraid. Usually, when I was scared of something, I found that to be the ideal time for cracking wise, but I could tell by the way Dana moved and how she'd just glared at me, that now was not the time.

"Jonquil said she saw it come out of the car on the hill," Dana said. "That's the place to start. Bring the dust."

It wasn't like I had placed it aside, but I followed her up the hill without comment.

It was quite the twisty path to the top of the hill. We had to wind through all manner of wind-blown dirt that had blown up in piles, along with banged up wads of metal and engine parts. Everything had been sitting there a lifetime or two, covered in green and brown rust and broken glass.

I trudged on, dead leaves from the oak crackling under my feet, the bag of goofer dust slung over my back, fingers wrapped up in the plastic bag, gripping hard until I reached a ditch just below the peak of the rise. The ditch had a bit of water in it and floating on the water were leaves and a film of dirt. It was a narrow enough ditch to step over, so I did, but with less energy than Dana, who had already achieved the top of the hill. But, let me add this fact, she wasn't carrying a heavy bag of magic dirt.

On the hill we stopped to stare at the car, a rusted 1957 Chevrolet Bel Air convertible, faded, but most likely, at assembly-line birth, fire engine red. Being that close to it made the hair on the back of my neck stand up. It had a kind of energy. You could feel it as surely as if you were a magnet being drawn to metal.

I would know that make of car anywhere. Used to run with a boy from these parts named Ray Jones. He had a car just like that one, belonged to his uncle, and he would drive over to my neck of the woods and go joyriding. Driving the back roads was a solid form of entertainment growing up.

I lowered the bag of goofer dust from my shoulder, and took a deep breath.

"Pour the goofer dust around the hill, into the water in the ditch," Dana said.

"You could have told me that before I climbed up here and put the bag down."

"I didn't consider that. Still, has to be done. Hey, look, there's an easy path on this side that leads down."

"Good to know, better to know earlier. And while I'm scattering goofer dust about, what will you be doing?"

"I'll be thinking. To each our own skills, Jana."

I went down without cursing out loud, managed to make it without tumbling into the ditch, and poured the goofer dust onto the water, all the way around. It hissed white smoke when it hit the ditch water. That meant this area was poisoned with evil, something from the beyond. Either an alternate dimension, otherworldly, or just plain unexplained, was well within attendance.

When I finished, I had less than a handful of dust left. I folded up the bag in a tight wad, put it in the inside pocket of my windbreaker, and went on up the hill. The wind was picking up and turning colder, at least it was above the line of the ditch. The oak leaves rattled like maracas. As I stood on the hill, I looked toward Jonquil's house. The trees in her yard were as still as an oil painting. No wind there. I wondered if she might be watching us with her binoculars.

Back with Dana, I said, "That goofer dust smells bad, but will it hold back evil?"

"Sometimes it does."

"Sometimes?"

"That's the best assurance I can give you," she said.

Dana looked at her watch. "It's just about to be midnight. Negative powers are strong then, and this dust, I believe it will hold it, but, a strong spirit, and I think this is one, can become accustomed to it. I'll need to read the spell."

She reached into her pocket and pulled out a band with a little light on it, fastened it over her head, clicked the light on, then pulled out a small notebook. She flipped the notebook open, settled on a page, looked at her watch one more time, and began to read.

It was one long-ass boring spell. Something about two dogs and a hole in the world, or some such. Wait. Maybe it was Todags. I think that's a demon or something. Anyway, just hearing the words of the spell made me uncomfortable. I decided if I was going to be eaten or pulled inside out, or some such horror, I might as well be rested. I decided to take a seat. I walked over to the driver's side of the Chevy and got in, via a door that squeaked like a dying mouse.

Dana paused the spell. "What are you doing?"

I leaned out of the open door. "Well I was trying to get out of your way and let you chant."

"By opening the car? It could be a portal to Hell, or worse."

"Well I'm in here now and everything seems fine. Finish the spell and come sit with me."

I heard her sigh heavily, and then I closed the car door and she went back to her spell.

When the spell was spoken, she came around on the other side and got in, and I let my hands rest on the cracked steering wheel. It was slightly warmer inside the car, but now it too was beginning to chill. A foggy film covered the window glass. Something unearthly was stirring about.

Dana reached into her windbreaker pocket and brought out a little square tin with a snap-on lid. She removed the lid and pinched out something white from inside. She tossed a bit of it on me, onto the driver's side door, sprinkled herself with it, then tossed some around the dash and onto the door next to her. She sprinkled some in the backseat.

"Stinks like shit," I said.

"That's only one of the ingredients."

"It'll keep something bad from entering?"

"It should decrease outside powers. Should keep us separated from whatever it is that might enter. Even if we share the same space, we should be protected."

"Should?"

"Once again, no absolutes. It should hold for a while."

"You keep saying things like, should, and for a while. Maybe you could speak with a little more affirmation."

"I'd like the driver's seat. That affirmative enough for you?"

"But I got in first."

"And I'm the boss."

"What difference does it make?"

"It makes a difference to me," she said. "Now scoot."

I huffed and made faces as I begrudgingly climbed over her and onto the passenger side, forcing her to slide beneath me. After a bit of a struggle, we found our new places.

"Really? You couldn't just get out and walk around?" Dana said.

I didn't answer. I looked off into the distance, as though I'd seen something very interesting. It was my way of pouting. But no sooner had I done so, then Dana said, "Now, that's interesting."

She leaned forward and peered into the rearview mirror.

I slid over beside her so I could see too.

There, in the reflection of the mirror, slightly hazed, as if the glass had been smeared with Vaseline, I could see two men dressed in business suits and wearing fedoras, carrying a squirming body wrapped in brightly colored rags. One man held the head, the other held the feet. Their features were clear now, as the Vaseline-like smear had lifted. They looked mighty proud of themselves, like hunters that had just killed a deer and were packing it home.

I jerked my head around and looked behind me. Nothing but blackness and a slight fog. Back in the mirror I saw two more people show up, another man and a woman. They all gathered at the back of the car. I saw the trunk lid lift, felt and heard the weight of the body being tossed inside, followed by the slamming of the lid. The group stood looking at the trunk, then they lifted their heads toward the window at the back. From the way they looked and stood, it was obvious they couldn't see us. But still, it creeped me out.

A moment later, the door opened on the driver's side, and then closed. The car seat went down, as if in response to weight behind the steering wheel, as if someone had sat in Dana's lap. But whoever was there was no longer visible.

And then the door on my side opened, and I could feel the presence of... something, something that made my stomach turn over and the hair on my arms stand at attention. A moment later I felt a sensation as if I were inside of something, or something was inside of me, and then the passenger door closed; the back doors opened and closed, then the key lock turned and the motor hummed.

The windows on all sides rolled down. I could see the old style window crank next to me turning. The cold night air blew inside. But except for the rumbling of the car's motor, the world outside had grown silent. No cicadas sung, no crickets chirped.

I glanced at Dana. I could see her eyes were wet in the moonlight. Not tears, just that strange reaction one has when something isn't quite right, when the nostrils flare and the eyes grow wet and the throat goes tight.

I reached for the door. Dana's hand shot out and grabbed my arm. I glanced at her and she shook her head. I took a deep breath and kept my seat, then the car began to move.

***

We were no longer in a junkyard on a high hill beneath a great oak tree, we were rolling down a brick street, and to our left we could see the courthouse, new and fresh, the great clock with a light inside of it, the hands black. The streets appeared damp with starlight and the glow of the moon. I could see the hood of the car through the windshield. It was bright and new, and indeed, fire engine red.

Out we went, the car sailing along, and before long we were twisting up a red clay road that climbed a hill that was thickly wooded on either side. We turned onto a smaller road, and then the woods thinned, and we were on top of a hill that was mostly barren and blackened by what appeared to have been a fire, perhaps caused by lightning.

In spite of the trees that surrounded us, I knew we were sitting right where we had started, but it was a different time. We had traveled back into the past, the nineteen fifties, I guessed, from the way the men and the woman were dressed.

I gently picked up my purse and took out my compact, opened it, revealing the mirror. I held it out to my side and turned so that I could see into it, and when I tilted it slightly, I could see a man, seemingly sitting in my lap, overlapping it, actually. As if I wasn't there. I let out a sigh and nearly dropped the mirror.

Dana grabbed me again, this time at the wrist.

She took the mirror, looked into it. In that moment, she appeared calm and in control. Her professionalism had taken over. She handed the mirror back to me with one hand, put a finger to her lips with the other.

I took the compact, kept it open.

The doors of the car opened, and the air became less cold and dry and then the doors closed. The trunk flew up in back, causing me to jerk my head around for a look. The trunk was closed. I turned back around and held up my mirror so I could see what was back there, and in the mirror the trunk was up, and the whole group was back there. The same two men were lifting the rag-wrapped body out of the trunk. The woman pulled a shovel out of there and closed the trunk.

They moved out of view of my mirror.

I twisted in my seat, moved the mirror around until I discovered they had moved to the front of the car.

I glanced a look at Dana. She had removed her compact from her purse and was doing exactly the same thing. She was so calm-looking, she might well have been checking her makeup.

They tossed their rag-wrapped burden on the ground, and then the woman with the shovel swung it up, and brought it down swiftly on the rags. It was a hard blow, and then she passed the shovel to one of the men, and they took turns like that, striking the writhing cocoon of rags. It squirmed along the ground, trying to worm its way to freedom, but the shovel came down again and again. They struck until the rags didn't move, and the smell of iron filled my nostrils.

I felt sick to my stomach.

The man who last held the shovel began to dig, and then the shovel was passed around again, and each man and the woman took a turn. In time, a hole was dug, next to a sprig of a tree. The body was kicked into the hole by one of the men, the way you might shove a log down a hill.

They all gathered to stand at the grave and look down on it.

Lights came up the hill, and after a moment I could hear a car door slam, and a woman stepped into view. She was petite and walked with a curious stride, wore an old-fashioned pillbox hat cocked on her head at a jaunty angle. When she turned, her eyes caught in the moonlight and I realized I had seen this woman before.

She would be their ride home. This was all planned out. And now something else happened, the town hall clock boomed out twelve gongs. It was midnight, either in our world, or the one many years gone, or in some netherworld that was neither here nor there.

The woman who had just driven up joined them at the grave. They all grabbed hands and stood around the grave and began chanting. I could hear them clearly, as if I were not in the car, but standing by the grave with them.

"Ygnaiih... ygnaiih... thflth'ngha... Yog-Sothoth...

"Eh'ya'ya'yahaah... e'yayayaaaa... Yog-Sothoth..."

That's the best I can duplicate their sounds, the chant they were making, but let me tell you, the words written down, or merely spoken, cannot duplicate the way they felt that night, coming to us across some great chasm of time and space, some empty spot beyond the beginning of the universe. As they chanted I was overcome with a revulsion I can neither describe or explain.

I put the mirror down, but now, as I turned I could see them without the mirror, could see them clearly, and the sky opened up, and I swear to you, something moved up there in the cosmic dark, something that gave me the impression of great repressed power. And then the light faded, and so did those on the hill.

I forced myself to look in the mirror. The car they had come there in, probably the car that belonged to Ragman, had been moved over the grave, and now the crowd of killers were moving down the hill, and I couldn't quite turn my mirror in a way to keep up with them. But I could hear a car motor, and then there were headlights, and then the lights and the sound of the motor were gone.

A moment later, Dana and I were sitting in the car, all rusty again. It was now our night, not that night from long ago. Slowly, we got out of the car.

"They used this car as a kind of headstone," Dana said. "That chant they did, it is a holding spell for the dead. Ragman was a sacrifice. That chant, along with his death, is part of a prosperity spell for the ones who sacrificed him. They killed him for prosperity."

"Jesus," I said.

"We will need more than Jesus on our side. Something has loosened him from that grave, disturbed it, and Ragman is free to have his vengeance. The spell I cast tonight, it won't hold for long."

***

We didn't talk on our way down the hill and out of the junkyard, didn't speak on the ride back to the hotel. There was nothing to say. What had been seen could not be unseen.

Each in our pajamas, still not a word between us, Dana clicked off the light and crawled into her bed. I was already in mine, as my sleepy time routine involved less maintenance than Dana's. Even traumatized, she still managed not to miss a face cream. I laid there a long while, staring up at the ceiling in the dark.

I eventually drifted off to sleep, and awoke to the sun peeking through the blinds and the sounds of our in-room coffee maker humming. Dana was up and at 'em, and I had a sneaking suspicion she had never gone to sleep.

"We need to go back to see Mr. Craw," Dana said, "and get to the bottom of things. I have some suspicions, but we don't have time for guessing anymore. We need answers."

***

We stood at the desk in the main lobby, waiting for someone to speak to. A woman in a wheelchair sat near the front door, yelling out "Help me."

I'm not made of stone, so I left Dana standing at the desk, ringing that little silver bell, and went over to her. I leaned toward the old lady, my hands on my knees.

"What's wrong ma'am?"

"Help me," she said, over and over.

"How can I help you?"

I was looking around frantically, hoping a nurse would appear, but to no avail.

"Oh, just ignore that old bat, she's always sitting there hollering about something. Needs help all right, but not the kind you can give her."

I looked for the voice. It belonged to an old waif of a woman, all of ninety pounds soaking wet. White hair coiffed, bright red lipstick, and she was dressed in what looked like Sunday's best, though it was Tuesday. She was standing right next to me, though I hadn't heard her come up. I recognized her from our previous visit, she was the one who had been talking to Tom. She appeared to have one foot in the grave and another on a banana peel.

"What do you mean ignore her?" I asked.

"The nurse will be around soon to give her some meds. There's nothing you can do, only the medication helps."

Dana came up behind me.

"And who are you?" Dana asked the waif of a woman.

"I'm Gladys. Gladys Knight."

"Really," I said.

Both she and Dana shot me a look. I didn't say anything more about it, but I'd be lying if I didn't tell you I sang "Midnight Train to Georgia" on our drive back to the hotel later.

"You're here to see, Tom, aren't you?"

"We are," Dana said.

"You upset him last time," she said.

"Wasn't our intent," I said.

Gladys turned her head at a curious angle, and in that moment I realized she was the woman on the hill that night, the one we had seen in our compacts with the getaway car. Ancient as she was, there was something in that movement that reminded me of the younger woman she had been.

My guess was Dana was already ahead of me on that realization.

The woman in the chair continued to holler out for help, and still, no one came. I felt bad for her. All these people around and everyone ignoring you, thinking you're crazy. And even if she was, it wasn't her fault. I wanted to hurry up and get out of this place, I had seen enough darkness for a lifetime, and this joint felt like it was sucking my very soul by the minute.

"You've lived in this town a long time," Dana said.

"I've been here since the beginning," Gladys said.

The beginning of time, I thought.

"I'm a fourth generation Texan, that's almost as far back as you can go."

"So you might even remember when that old clock tower downtown was working," Dana said.

That hit the old woman like a blow.

"I do," she said. "I even remember when it stopped."

"I thought you might," Dana said. "Want to tell us about that evening?"

This took the old woman by surprise. She studied Dana's face. "You know something, don't you?"

Dana stared at her, said, "The man in rags."

That was like another blow to Gladys. She seemed as if she might go weak in the knees, but at the last minute she stiffened.

"I been waiting for this moment all these years. The chickens have come home to roost." She paused momentarily, then looked at us with that bird-like gaze. "You'll want to talk to me and Tom both."

About this time, a pear-shaped woman in clean, pressed khakis, white shoes and a baby-blue shirt appeared.

"Are you helping our guests, Gladys?" she said. "You might need to rest, dear. You don't have the energy you once had."

"Yeah, and you might need to give Mrs. Wilks her meds," Gladys said, "and while you're at it, next time you're watching

TV and one of those ads for an exercise belt comes up, you might want to put down the potato chips and order two of them."

The pear-shaped lady squinted her eyes. "Run along now, Gladys."

When she was gone I gave the pear-shaped lady my sincere smile and my cheery disposition.

"We're here to visit Mr. Tom Craw," I said.

The lady led us back to the desk, looked into her log book, battling a wisp of brown hair that continued to fall into her eyes. "It seems he isn't taking any visitors," she said. "That's by his own choice. To visit, you have to be a relative or be with a relative."

"Oh that's ok," I said. "We're really just here to spend time with Auntie Gladys. Nice for people to know they're sought after."

"Gladys seems to have already gone to her room," she said.

"Gladys can be elusive," I said. "Wandering off is a family trait."

"Do you know her room number?" the desk lady asked.

I shook my head. "I'm embarrassed to say this is our first visit here. We're from out of town, but we want to make up for lost time, don't we, sis?"

"Of course we do," Dana said. "You know how time escapes you, and then you look up and everyone's dead."

Her bluntness took me off guard, though I should know better by this point not to expect anything different.

"Yes," the lady said. "It happens just that way. Let me take you to her room, and if she's not too tired, you can continue your visit."

The woman who had been calling out for help was no longer calling. Her head was rested on her chest and she was snoring deeply.

I patted her gently on the shoulder as we walked by.

The pear-shaped lady led us past the desk and down a cold corridor to a room at the far end.

"Don't stay too long," she said. "Gladys tires easily. And she can certainly be a pill."

"Another family trait," I said, glancing at Dana.

Dana seemed impressed with my ruse about Gladys being an aunt. I could tell by the amused look on her face. Once the receptionist was out of earshot, I pointed at my head and said, "Not just a hat rack, my friend."

We knocked gently on the partially open door and went inside. Ms. Knight was sitting up in a chair next to her bed. Tom was on the opposite side, parked in his wheelchair. Both of them had a defeated look about them.

"I asked Tom to join us," Gladys said.

"We knew this time would come," Tom said.

"It's overdue actually," Gladys said. "We can't protect ourselves much longer."

I thought that was a curious statement, but I didn't say so.

"Tell us," Dana said.

Gladys began to talk.

***

"I got the cancer, and any day could be my last. I held onto my youth and my health longer than most, and it was all 'cause of what happened that night. But in the end, it hasn't been worth it. I was young. I was dumb. I made a mistake. I was supposed to be dead twenty years ago, and the dark arts, they have kept me alive and protected... from it. But even the dark arts are no match for the big C."

"There's no excuse for what we and the others did," Tom said. "Greed. A desire to live a long life. But living long under a cloud like we have, knowing what we did, and why? Makes no sense now."

Dana and I sat on the bed next to Gladys, as she spoke.

"There was a young man, he worked in the clock tower, cleaning the gears and keeping everything running. He was touched in the head, as folks used to say. These days, he'd probably be labeled autistic or such, but we didn't know then what we know now. Still, he saved his money and bought a car, a very nice, red Chevy."

Gladys caught her breath, as if her soul were trying to escape her.

Instinctively, I reached out and grabbed Gladys's hand. I knew she had done a horrible thing, and there was no forgiving it, but I felt for her all the same.

"It wasn't supposed to be anything more than a prank, really. We were all sitting around one night, drinking beer, making jokes, when Paul brought out a book he'd taken from his father's place. Was all about black magic and witchcraft and raising the dead and such. It was all just fun and games, but then he started getting serious, talking about that we could have a long life and wealth if someone was sacrificed and certain rituals were upheld. We found out later his family had been part of a cult, but we didn't know it at the time, just figured they were eccentric, like most rich people. Next thing you know there's talk about the Old Ones and sacrifices, and we're loaded up in a car and heading out in caravan to the clock tower."

Tom piped up, relieving Gladys for a moment. "We were thinking with our narcissism of youth. We wanted success, and money, and we got it, but at a cost. Oh we age all right, you can see that for yourselves, but we will live until we're little more than shells with thoughts in our heads. We're falling apart, quite literally. You see this?" Tom reached under the blanket across his knees, pulled out a leather bag tied off with ragged twine. "This has been protecting us for a while now. We both have one. We are constantly making new rituals from that old book of Paul's to protect ourselves. We've learned a lot about the craft, but we can't keep it away much longer. It's getting stronger and stronger. All our old comrades are dead, either killed by the man in rags, or by old age. Paul, who started all of this, he was one of the lucky ones. He died at home in his sleep. Can you believe that? In his sleep, peaceful like. But then it got loose. Sometimes I wonder if Paul really was so lucky."

I didn't usually consider dying to be lucky, but under these circumstances, I imagine that had been a downright gift.

"People in this town don't know that a lot of deaths that have been thought to be old age, or some kind of accident, were neither. It was... him.

"Those of us who made the original pact, or their descendants. We not only brought this on ourselves, we've brought it on people kin to us, innocents. But it's us it wants the most. We were among those who beat that poor man to death. Grabbed him and wrapped him in this bunch of rags he had, you know, quilting material he used to clean the clock gears and the like, killed him so we would do well in the world. God, what were we thinking?"

"We weren't," Gladys said.

"Why do you think he's free now, after all this time?" I asked.

"Hard to say, kids fooling around up there, disturbing things," Tom said, "but I'm reasonably sure it's from all that fracking they've been doing. It's caused little earthquakes, and somehow it's disturbed the holding spell in the grave."

"Like goofer dust," Dana said.

"Exactly," Tom said. "Only this is from a moss we got off a witch doctor from New Orleans. He brought it back from the rain forest in South America. Looks like what I used to pull off the mower blades when it rained, but it's supposed to be powerful when mixed with this and that. We followed what he said, like a recipe for a cake."

"That moss is powerful," Dana said. "I had some once, but I used it in a complicated spell to destroy a demon."

"What was his name?" I said. I didn't want to get caught up in talking about spell recipes, demons and such. I didn't want Ragman to be forgotten for who he was.

"Jimmy Grate," Gladys said.

"Did you know him?"

"Knew his mama some, town seamstress. Everyone sort of shunned her for having a baby with all them problems, but she could sew a button with the best of them. She's the one gave him all those rags. Christ. Looking back on it now, the boy was brilliant, just strange. He had his knacks, and we chose him because of that. Saw him as a wasted life."

"Bottom line," Dana said, "someone has to go back up to the hill and put that protection spell back in place, and it needs to be the people who caused this mess in the first place."

Subtle, I thought.

"We're willing to do that," Gladys said.

Tom nodded. "We can't take back a murder, can't be redeemed for that. Can't blame just being young. But we can maybe prevent more murders. We have enough blood on our hands. I can walk a little if I have to, get some crutches and I'll make it up that hill."

"All right," Dana said. "To make this work, we have to open the door to the other side, at least temporarily, to give your victim all of the power that can be had. You two are the last of those who actually performed the ritual, and that makes you powerful components of an opening spell. We have to end this before the Old Ones come completely through. They don't merely grant certain things to humans, they have their own designs. They can do that sort of thing, but what they want is to break through and feast on this world, suck the very energy from it, take the life-force from everyone and everything, and add it to their own. That's what Ragman, Jimmy, is all about. He's merely a component to a bigger spell. When he does what he does, that negates the spell you used to borrow from the Old One's power. The Old Ones plan to reverse that, and come through to this dimension, and trust me, if they do, it won't be pretty. But, we might able to stop them if you don't flinch."

"We won't," Gladys said. "We've done enough damage."

"Give me those bags of protection," Dana said. "You have to, at least temporarily, be at its mercy."

***

It was as if the night knew. At the peak of the hill shadows rolled over the car and the oak, all the way down to the lower part of the junkyard, like an oil spill.

We got up there an hour until midnight, which was when Dana said our opportunity to set things right was at its strongest. The witching hour, or as Dana explained, the dimensional gates were more willing to open then, and though things from beyond could be at their strongest, it was also the best time to destroy them, or at least quell their powers. From what I understood you were more likely to stop the Old Ones, not destroy them.

Parking the car outside the fence, I got Tom's wheelchair out of the trunk and the crutches that we'd nabbed from the home. It was a spare wheelchair, one of those that had a cloth back and folded in half so it could be carried easily. Dana took that.

I helped Tom out of the car, he took the crutches, handed me a folded piece of paper, said, "Read it when this is done," and moved laboriously through the gate that Dana had flung wide open.

Gladys was moving fairly easily, just with that distinctive shuffle she had. You would have thought she was thirty-five the way she maneuvered.

It took a long time, but we got up that hill. Me using that shovel like a cane to drag myself upward, and Tom, working his way step-by-step. Tom was breathing hard, and for a moment I thought he might collapse and die on us. Dana seemed unconcerned. I knew why. She lacked sympathy for them, and maybe I should have felt that way, but didn't.

Tom had to be helped by both Dana and myself to cross the ditch, but we managed it, and then I was able to help Gladys, who had finally grown winded. The wind picked up and the rain started. We didn't have anything to protect us from it, except the car, and at the moment, that wasn't a valid choice.

Finally, we stood atop the hill near the rusty Chevy. I looked at my watch.

The time glowed in the dark.

Seven minutes until midnight.

***

Dana set down the wheelchair, Tom wobbled over to the wheelchair on his crutches. Dana could have brought it closer to him, but she didn't. He managed himself into the chair, his breath coming hard.

"I'm surprised the car is still in the same place," Tom said.

"It's not the car we're worried about," Dana said, "It's what's beneath it."

I squatted down to take a peek underneath the car to find the earth had not only been disturbed from shifting, but that the ground looked like a possum had wallowed around enough to make a pit. Or something bigger than a possum.

Dana looked over at me and I could see the urgency in her eyes. I knew we were tight on time, and we needed to get to the bottom of things. Literally.

"I'll put the car in neutral," Dana said, "and you push."

"Oh sure, you hop in and get cozy and I'll just use my Hulk strength to mosey the car along."

"Just do it," Dana said.

"Alright children, step out of the way. Mama has spoken," I said.

Gladys stood next to Tom in his chair. They were only a few feet away from me.

Dana rushed past me and climbed inside the Chevy. No sooner had she gotten in and closed the door, she made her way back out.

"Never mind," she said. "It's already set."

"Is that your way of telling me to start pushing?"

Dana just looked at me.

I slammed the shovel blade into the dirt behind the trunk of the car, and rigged it into a pry bar for leverage. Dana stood a few feet away from the car, and just a touch further from Gladys and Tom. She was over there incanting, if there was such a thing. She had put on a headband with a light on it, and had pulled a little pocket book out, and was flipping pages and reading furiously out loud.

"I'm ready when you are," I said.

With the car in neutral, shovel poised, I waited for the signal. Dana kept reading, but she lifted her left hand as though we were at a racetrack, and I waited for the drop. When it came, I put the full weight of my body into that shovel. My feet slid on the damp red clay but I could feel the car start to wobble.

I let out a karate yell like I'd heard Chuck Norris do on *Walker Texas Ranger* (summers at Grandma's house had not been a waste), and in that moment, the car shot forward like a slingshot and I, as was becoming a trend, went ass down on the earth. I laid there, looking up at the sky, questioning my life choices as the once beautiful Chevy convertible careened down the hill. It made a clattering noise, a loud bang, then silence. Between my exceptional display of otherworldly strength, and mostly Dana's invocation, we had dislodged the vehicle and exposed the grave below.

Dana ceased chanting, pulled a small flashlight from somewhere, and in addition to her head-lamp, shone it on the grave. It was full of squirming worms, and I do mean squirming. Rags that should have rotted were moving as the worms moved, and then the clay began to shift, like water was boiling up from inside. The rain was really coming down now, mixing with the worms, the rags, and the boiling clay, twisting up so tight it was getting harder to tell one from the other.

"Uh, spell's not working," I said.

"Not quite midnight, little less than a minute yet, and we have to let it loose before we can stop it," Dana said.

This somehow seemed like inconsistent reasoning. All I could do was say, "Should we run?"

But Dana wasn't paying attention. She had gone to holding up her spell book, chanting, and it was a chilling sound. It was as if she had reached into some primal part of her brain to find the sound that went with the words, and maybe that's exactly what she had done. Her voice was cold and metallic, and the words sounded like nonsense, and then the words, for no reason I could determine, began to echo. The sky cracked, I swear, and the rain ceased, and at first what looked like the moon showed itself through the crack in the sky. I realized it was an eye, golden, and looking out from that dark and empty and soundless world of deep space, something deeper than space. In that moment I felt insignificant, less than a speck in the universe. A speck of a speck of a speck, a trillion times removed.

And then the eye blinked. The grave rumbled, and something covered in those dirty, yet oddly colorful rags, stirred, and then, dripping clay and worms, it began to climb out of the grave.

I was so deeply sad for what had happened to that poor young man, but at the same time I was frightened and repulsed by what he had become, through no design of his own. It was Tom and Gladys who were responsible. They had made this thing, and now it rose up out of the grave, as if standing, and then as if being lifted up on strings like a puppet. And above us, the great eye opened again and it was golden and strange; an unfeeling thing that looked out from the depths of the cosmos. Looking at it, I somehow knew that this thing from beyond, this Old One, was the source of so many bad dreams and false promises. The devil, god, mythological monsters. It was all those things, a monstrosity behind a thin wall of protection, and that wall had been breached.

Before, only Ragman had been set free, but this night, we were tempting fate to destroy him. Dana had opened up a Pandora's box that I was uncertain we could close before Ragman was destroyed. We might not be able to snap that crack in the Wall of Forever Dark shut in time.

The swirl of rags, dirt and worms had now emerged fully from below and taken shape. It twisted and swayed from the earth until it resembled a man. Resembled, being used loosely. As the rags shifted in the wind, worms dripped off like water from a wet dog. None of it seemed to phase Dana. There she was, chanting away, cool as a cucumber as I watched the oblong split in the sky behind her spread open even wider, like velvet curtains before a show. I felt hypnotized as Ragman, floating in the air like a kite, struggled to make its way forward, fighting the protective wall Dana was holding in place. This battle went on for several minutes, until suddenly Dana was a lot less cool, and I could tell she was growing tired.

Ragman hit the invisible wall time and again, causing the air in front of us, Dana's force field, to shimmer. The split in the sky grew longer and wider, until part of it touched the ground.

Gladys and Tom were only a few feet away as the hazy light from the netherworld shone through the sky and Ragman rammed the invisible wall. Dana's demeanor had softened, and with each word she slumped more and more; she was losing her strength. Gladys noticed this too. I saw the expression on Gladys' face change, and I knew, but it was too late to stop her.

Gladys shoved Dana to the ground, sending the little book of spells and the bag of protection flying. In that instant, Ragman reached through the weakened force field and grabbed Gladys like a kid crumpling up a paper ball. Bones crunched and muscles popped and just like that, she was gone, and the rag man was looking for his next victim.

Dana was out cold and I was armed with nothing but a shovel and the remaining dust in my pocket. I took that shovel and started swinging like Casey at the bat. Ragman lunged in my direction and I made contact, smooth and solid against the side of what I assumed to be its head, and there was a popping sound, like someone had poked a big balloon with something sharp, but the blow didn't even slow it down.

Ragman slung his hand out and caught me on the jaw, slinging me backward and onto the ground next to where Dana lay. He half-shuffled, half-glided his way over to me, moving quickly. I pulled the goofer dust from inside my pocket, clawed at it with my other hand, ripped the bag open, flung it onto Ragman. He smoked like a stopped up chimney for a moment, and then he shook his head, and where there should have been a mouth, the rags twisted into a kind of smile. Ragman had grown too strong for the goofer dust to bother him anymore. He stood over me, swaying, then bending easily at the waist, bringing his face, such as it was, close to mine. I could smell the stench of mildew and death on the rags, and just as I was sure he was going to kill me dead, I heard a noise.

It was Tom. He was standing near the opening of the slit, his back toward it, propped up on his crutches, yelling for the rag man to come and get him. I didn't want to see Tom hurt, even if he deserved it, but I wasn't exactly in love with the idea of being eaten, or torn to ribbons by Ragman, either.

"It's me you want, Jimmy," he said. "And you can have me."

As Ragman turned his head to see Tom, a flash of what looked like lightning shot out from the center of that mucus filled eyeball and struck the ground next to him, plowing up dirt and drifting up smoke.

Ragman left me lying there, wheeled in that horrid boneless way he had, and lunged toward Tom. In that moment, Tom dropped his crutches and fell backwards. A calm came over Tom's face. He looked at peace, and I swear I even saw a faint smile cross his thin lips.

Ragman reached towards him, trying to grab him, but it was too late. Tom had fallen back into the abyss and Ragman had stumbled into the darkness alongside him just as the stroke of midnight sounded out from the clock tower that hadn't chimed since the fifties; it sounded like the slamming of a great door, followed by a slurping noise, like a giant trying to suck the world up through a straw.

And then I felt weak. The juice had ran out of me. I fell back down on the wet clay, and when I opened my eyes the morning sun was coming up beyond the hill, rising behind the clock tower. Birds were singing, and Dana was leaning against the back of the Chevy.

Somehow, she managed to look as if she had merely encountered a light wind, where I, in contrast, felt as if I had been rolled in a pen with the hogs.

***

We sat there, at the hotel, drinking coffee and gathering ourselves into the morning. We talked about coffee and creamer like nothing had happened, but me, I felt a heaviness in my chest that I couldn't quite explain, not to mention a throbbing in my jaw that would likely result in a purple welt. All's well that ends well, and they deserved what they got, but I couldn't help but feel the weight of Jimmy the Ragman, Gladys and Tom.

Jimmy hadn't even had a chance. He was one of life's innocents and was thrown into a circumstance beyond his control. Tom, Gladys, well, they weren't evil, but they weren't good, and them sacrificing themselves had been the first good thing they'd ever done for Jimmy. They were the last ingredients in the closing spell. I knew then why Dana wanted them there, why she had confiscated their protections. I wasn't sure how I felt about that. But I knew this, Gladys and Tom had known that too, and they had gone along with it willingly.

We showered and dressed and went over to the mayor's house to tell him he could come out from behind his protection of goofer dust.

Dana explained to him in detail what had occurred, told him about Tom and Gladys.

"You'll have to find some way to explain their disappearance," Dana said.

The mayor nodded. "I'll come up with something. So it's really over?"

"I think so," Dana said. "Before we left the junkyard I put Gladys and Tom's protection spells in Jimmy's grave. I doubt they're needed, now that the living murderers have been disposed of. That should close the gate until the next fool tries to open it."

"Holy Smackers," he said.

That's East Texas for you. He might also have said Holy Cow.

"Tell you what, whoever said women were the weaker sex didn't know what they were talking about," the mayor said. "I know this—I couldn't have done it. It would have been too much terror for me."

"Terror is our business," Dana said.

I took the paper Tom had given me at the junkyard out of my pocket and slid it across the desk toward the mayor. I had read it earlier.

"This is a document that grants the junkyard to you. I suggest you turn the whole thing into a cemetery, and that you put a heavy stone over Jimmy's grave. He's not in it, but I think it's a good idea. It never hurts to make sure those spell bags stay there."

"Very well," he said. He looked at Dana. "Your check will be in the mail."

We thanked him, and as we left I searched within that golden-framed photo where we had seen the Ragman flickering only days before. There was no sign of him, and I took that to mean that maybe Jimmy really was, finally at rest.

***

On the way to the airport Dana said, "You good?"

"I don't know if I am. You seem fine, though."

"You mean do I feel regrets?"

"I suppose."

"Just for what happened to Jimmy. Gladys and Tom deserved what they got. Just too many years too late."

"I suppose," I said.

I put my foot on the gas and urged the rental onward along Highway 59.

Black clouds darkened the horizon.

JOE R. LANSDALE, with more than forty books to his credit, is the Champion Mojo Storyteller. He's been called "an immense talent" by Booklist; "a born storyteller" by Robert Bloch; and The New York Times Book Review declared he has "a folklorist's eye for telling detail and a front-porch raconteur's sense of pace." Lansdale has won numerous awards, including sixteen Bram Stoker Awards, the Grand Master Award from the World Horror Convention, a British Fantasy Award, the American Mystery Award, the Horror Critics Award, the Grinzane Cavour Prize for Literature, the "Shot in the Dark" International Crime Writer's Award, the Golden Lion Award, the Booklist Editor's Award, the Critic's Choice Award, and a New York Times Notable Book Award. His series of novels *Hap and Leonard* was adapted into the hit SundanceTV series in 2016 and is currently in its third season. He resides in Nacogdoches, Texas, with his wife, Karen, writer and editor. For more information, visit **www.joerlansdale.com**.

KASEY LANSDALE, first published at the tender age of eight by Random House, is the author of several short stories and novellas, including stories from Harper Collins and Titan Books, as well as the editor of assorted anthology collections, including Subterranean Press' *Impossible Monsters*. She is best known as a Singer/Songwriter. Most recently, you can hear Lansdale as the narrator of various works, including Stan Lee's *Reflections*, George R.R. Martin's *Aces Abroad*, and George A. Romero's latest installment, *Nights of the Living Dead*, among others. Her forthcoming anthology, *Night Terrors*, is set to release Spring of 2019. For more information, visit **www.kaseylansdale.com**.

Connect with Joe R. Lansdale on:

Facebook: www.facebook.com/joelansdale
Twitter: @joelansdale

Connect with Kasey Lansdale on:

Facebook: www.facebook.com/kaseylansdalefans
Twitter: @kaseylansdale
Instagram: www.instagram.com/kaseylansdale